Bounded Rationality The Encounter

Bounded Rationality The Encounter

Humanity's Death Wish Comes Close to Fulfilment

KENNETH MOORE

To order additional copies of this book, contact:
Xlibris
NZ TFN: 0800 008 756 (Toll Free inside the NZ)
NZ Local: 9-801 1905 (+64 9801 1905 from outside New Zealand)
www.Xlibris.co.nz
Orders@Xlibris.co.nz
843390

CONTENTS

This book is sequential to the first book:
Bounded Rationality – The Encryption.

For my family, immediate and distant.
Specifically my dear Trisha.

CHAPTER 18

The Encounters

The four people in the room were waiting. No new movement had happened; 20 minutes had already passed. Rahman Hussain was seething and irritable as he had been put on edge following his disputes with Emma Wilson and, to a lesser extent, with Andy Nelson. He could not appreciate the importance of patience in a situation over which he had absolutely no control whatsoever. In his opinion, 20 minutes was too long—far too long.

'What's taking it so long?' he growled in Arabic, and the wall duly translated much to his surprise.

ANALYSE SITUATION

PROBLEM POTENTIAL

DATA INSUFFICIENT TO FORMALISE

'Ah, they're putting it off! That shows they're not prepared to show themselves!' Hussain was feeling smug. 'I always knew it was the interfering Americans behind this show!'

Andy ignored him and said to the wall, 'Is there any more data we can supply?'

PROBLEM NEGATIVE IF HANDLED CORRECTLY

'Do you want more clarification with us?'

CLARIFICATION REQUIRED

'Okay, how can we help you? What's the issue?'

ISSUE WITH GRAVITY

'The issue is something to do with gravity?'

CORRECT

'Are you saying your gravity differs from ours?'

CORRECT

'How much difference?'

MULTIPLY 2.8

'You mean the gravity on the planet where you came from is 2.8 times stronger than my planet Earth?' Andy enquired. 'Your planet must be much bigger than our Earth?'

CORRECT

'Wow. Are you asking us if we can withstand that level of gravity?'

CAN YOU SURVIVE THAT IS THE QUESTION

'I believe so. But can you survive on our Earth's gravity?'

EARTH GRAVITY NOT FEASIBLE AND FATAL

'How fatal is it?'

STROKE IN 3 EARTH MINUTES

'Oh gee, your anatomy is not designed for weak gravity, and with a much higher volume of blood pumped into your brain and organs which will result in rupturing them? Therefore you'll succumb to stroke and die from it within a few minutes of being exposed to Earth's weak gravity?'

YOUR POSTULATION CORRECT

'In your assumption, it's probably better for us to adjust to your gravity rather than you with ours?'

YOUR POSTULATION CORRECT

'I think it would be helpful if we are wearing G-suits!'

DEFINE G SUITS QUESTION

'It's another word for tight-fitting clothes. If we have them on us, it will help prevent our blood from building up in the lower areas of our body. It will stop us from experiencing blackouts. Understand?'

GORGASS UNDERSTAND YOUR POSTULATION

'Maybe it will help us stop from fainting at the sight of you!' He laughed.

GORGASS NOT UNDERSTAND YOUR POSTULATION

'Forget it, it takes humans to understand my humour!'

DEFINE HUMOUR

'Please forget it. It's meaningless to you. I'm sorry I'm wasting your time with it'.

HUMOUR NOT ENERGY-EFFICIENT

'You seem to have a major interest in energy efficiency. But the point is, will you be able to provide us with something like close-fitting clothes to counter the effect of increasing gravity?'

REQUEST TAKEN INTO CONSIDERATION

STANDBY

Another 30 minutes had elapsed. Nothing had happened. Hussain was starting to get restless again. He was about to speak his mind were it not for the sudden new movement detected on the ceiling. There were four new slits. Each slit materialised above each person where they were standing. The slits opened until they were approximately 12 inches x 2 inches wide. The four people were looking up and trying to peer into the void of blackness beyond the apertures.

Suddenly, several items dropped through the openings to the floor next to the feet of each person. Emma was the first to pick hers up and recognised it as clothing of some kind. The material had a very strange feeling to the humans' touch, soft and rubbery but extremely malleable, with a reddish metallic sheen. But the colour was different for each of the humans. Greenish for Andy, greyish for Hussain, and bluish for Gillian.

Emma looked up at the wall. 'Are we expected to wear these?'

OBLIGATE

Without hesitation, she sat down quickly and pushed her slim legs into the leggings of the clothing. The material was clearly elasticated, but it was a very loose fit, slipping over her clothing quite easily. Her action had prompted Andy to follow with his own clothing. She stood up and slid her arms into the long sleeves. She could see an opening in front of her but could not see any method of closing the strange material.

'How do I close it?' she said clearly, looking at the wall.

Suddenly, the front opening had started to apparently meld together very firmly on its own volition. She realised the clothing was infused with nanotechnology of some kind and able to mould itself to the shape of the humans. Then she could feel her whole suit, including the leggings and sleeves, starting to squeeze more until she felt she was wearing a very tight wetsuit. But she felt comfortable as it was a very porous but lightweight material, which also seemed to reduce her level of perspiration.

'Cool!' she exclaimed.

Andy was following her lead and in various stages of getting the strange suiting on. Hussain and Gillian were not making any attempt to dress in the amazing clothing.

It was still in piles on the floor by their feet.

'I'm not going to wear it!' said Hussain.

'Why not?' asked Andy.

'Lakum jamieaan ghabi wasadhij!'

The caption flashed, 'You all are fools and gullible!'

Andy sighed and muttered under his breath to himself, 'What an awkward bastard you are.' Then aloud, he said to Hussain, 'Please yourself, hope you can manage to withstand the dangers of the high level of gravity!'

Then he looked at Gillian. 'What's the problem? Why can't you wear it?'

'Don't feel comfortable to undress in front of you all. I need to keep my clothing as part of my spiritual requirement'.

'Fair enough, Gillian, but my advice is if you start to feel lightheaded, you better drop down and lie on the floor! You should be okay'.

Gillian nodded. 'Thanks, but I think I'd rather sit down'.

Hussain did nothing and said nothing.

'But will it kill us?' Gillian asked, showing considerable concern in her eyes.

'The gravity at the strength of 2.8 is like carrying nearly three people of your own weight on your shoulders. It would be rather uncomfortable, but it won't kill you!' Andy assured her.

Emma caught a glimpse as a new caption flashed.

UNIT GREY NON-COOPERATIVE UNPRODUCTIVE

'Does that bother you?' enquired Andy. He realised quickly they were referring to people's identity by the colour.

TWO OPPOSITE ANSWERS NOT ENERGY-EFFICIENT

'Forget him, no worry, he'll survive'.

UNITS GREY AND BLUE DECISION IRRELEVANT

Emma gestured with her arms open to the wall and said, 'Now what? How can we meet you?'

STANDBY

YOU RESIDE INNER CYLINDER

'Hang on, are we on the inside cylinder nearest to the axis of this spaceship?' Emma asked. 'How many internal cylinders are there in this spaceship?'

CORRECT AND FIVE CYLINDERS

'Gee, that many! Why so many?'

AID MAINTENANCE AND LONGEVITY ON TRAVEL

INNER CYLINDER BUILD UP MORE SPEED TO GAIN EXTRA GRAVITY

'Hold there!' shouted Andy, putting his hand up. 'Can you please assure me you'll remain behind the glass wall when we see you? We don't want to be exposed to being contaminated by any of your viruses!'

YOUR CONCERN IRRELEVANT

'Are you telling me you've already inoculated us all?'

CONDUCT NOT CARRIED OUT

'Why not?'

NOT ENERGY-EFFICIENT

'Did it require too much effort to go into creating vaccinations? Then it's easier to maintain the wall between us? More practical that way?'

His line of questioning was based instinctively on his years of scientific training and experience.

YOUR POSTULATION CORRECT

'Where are you at this moment?'

GORGASS RESIDE OUTER CYLINDER

Andy's eyes widened. 'Are you calling yourself Gorgass? And your outer cylinder is the fastest of all cylinders?'

AFFIRMATIVE TO BOTH QUESTIONS

'Un-fucking-believable!'

NOT UNDERSTAND YOUR MESSAGE

NEED CLARIFICATION

'Sorry. Forget it. Just a human word that can be strange. No need to be concerned about it'.

THEN WHY MENTION IT

ILLOGICAL AND NOT ENERGY-EFFICIENT

'Okay, okay. You got your point. Let's get on and proceed with the meeting!'

YOUR CYLINDER SPEED INCREASING

They could sense a small vibration on the floor and, at the same time, could hear a whining sound in the background. Slowly, they sensed the strength of gravity starting to build up. It had taken a good 10 minutes before it had reached the level of nearly three times the Earth's gravity. The captives were starting to feel the effect of it and struggled to keep upright.

'Oh, help me, not sure I can keep standing!' wailed Gillian. She was the first who gave away and crumpled to the floor, landing on her hands and knees. Then she repositioned herself into sitting on her folded legs.

Soon afterwards, Hussain, with blood draining slowly from his head, started to feel lightheaded. 'Hadha yakfi . . .,' he cried out. 'That's enough . . .' He could not finish the sentence because he had lost consciousness and fainted. He crashed down and lay flat on his back.

Only Emma and Andy remained standing. He looked at her. 'Emma!

Are you okay?'

'I'm fine! I'm finding it strange but no worry!'

She struggled to keep her hands up whilst signing. With extra effort, he shuffled his feet forward and staggered towards where Gillian was and held his hand out. 'Gillian, are you okay? You should stay down where you are'.

'I'm happy where I am'.

He ignored Hussain who was still lying on his back. His horizontal position had helped his blood start flowing back into his brain. He started babbling incoherently, but after a few moments, he opened his eyes, and he remembered where he was.

He was shocked to find his breathing was so laboured because of the artificially created gravity on his lungs. He tried to roll his body over in vain to get a better posture.

'Rahman, please listen to me! Please try to calm down! You're better off where you are! Stay lying on the floor! It will help you keep your blood flowing into your head!'

The idea of being positioned lower than other people incensed Rahman, and coupled with his fainting, this had enraged and humiliated him even more.

I have had enough of this! he thought. He was simply considering his injured pride. He started to struggle to find a better posture but only managed to roll over to his stomach and raised himself, with a great effort, onto his hands and knees before giving up and collapsing again. He looked up and cursed Andy.

'For heaven's sake, get a grip and take my advice!' Andy muttered, rolling his eyes. 'But if you won't, then just stay there where you are and suit yourself'.

He turned away and ignored Hussain, shuffling his feet back to Emma and the wall. He got hold of her hand. 'Emma, okay, are we ready for the curtain to lift?' he said, smiling.

Both looked up at the wall and waited—and waited.

'What's taking you so long?' said Emma, addressing the wall.

FIVE CYLINDERS NEED SEQUENTIAL RECONFIGURATION

GORGASS NEED TO MOVE THROUGH EACH CYLINDER

'How long?'

20 EARTH MINUTES

'That's fine, we'll wait'.

Gillian moved onto her knees, with her hands clasped in prayer. She was trying to raise her morale to help her face the totally overwhelming situation she now found herself. Nothing in her narrowly focussed religious upbringing in a Korean convent had given her any concept of the extraordinary scene she was now a living part of.

Suddenly, the gap between the ceiling and the floor widened. It was hard to know whether the ceiling itself had risen or the floor had dropped down or both at the same time. The space had become twice the size it had been. The reason behind this change became apparent to accommodate the creatures double the height of the humans.

Slowly, the cloudy opaqueness of the wall had started to fade, making it transparent like glass. The sheer size of the giant creatures started to emerge.

The Gorgass—there were three of them standing in a row. Their appearance was totally unexpected and beyond any of the earthlings' imagination. The humans were absolutely astounded and transfixed.

They were not expecting to see such hideous creatures that were so alien and so repugnant.

What amplified this revulsion was that the Gorgassic physique seemed to encompass all the worst features of poisonous insects and reptiles back on earth to become gigantic nightmares within touching distance.

The arthropods were apparently only kept apart from the earthlings by the unknown strength of a transparent barrier made of a completely unfamiliar material.

It did not help that some of the aspects of these creatures resembled a potpourri of insects of all kinds on Earth, which were aesthetically repulsive or toxic to humans. At first glance, they looked like parts of spiders, wasps, beetles, and scorpions all had merged together inclusively to form one complete giant arthropod. The three Gorgass were all identical in size and shape. Closer scrutiny showed that there were subtle colour differences of their exteriors. One was bluish purple, whilst the middle one was greenish, and the far right was reddish orange.

Andy was silent. He was the only human not to be troubled by the appearance of the Gorgass. On the contrary, he found them intriguing. No matter how similar various component parts were to the different species of arthropods on earth, the combination and scale of these creatures was totally repulsive. The scientific mind of Andy went into overdrive. He found them unreservedly scientifically interesting. He was an academic, and his lifetime immersion in that environment had conditioned him to be very objectively inquisitive. Questions flooded his mind: *What is their respiration system like? What about their reproduction? What about their digestion system and food? Lifespan?* He struggled to visualise a constructive question that he could put before them to build some sort of intellectual rapport and dialogue.

But Emma beat him to it with a simple word. She signalled with her hands and said, 'Hello'.

The bioluminescence in hundred small bulbous spots on the 'chest' of the greenish Gorgass could be seen flashing and dancing about. The integrated sensors on the glass wall detected their flickering and Emma's word, flashed the caption that could be seen in reply on the transparent wall.

GREETING ACKNOWLEDGED AND RETURNED

This development had shaken Andy from his deep thoughts and compelled him to regain his composure. He took a deep breath. 'I am glad to be able to meet you after so much time after we have been isolated for what seems to have been several Earth days!'

SITUATION UNFORTUNATE AND UNAVOIDABLE

'Apology accepted'.

GORGASS NOT APOLOGISE

'But you took us away without our agreement?'

The bulbous spots on orange Gorgass flashed.

ACTION NECESSARY

'Maybe, but you could have asked us to come over?'

NOT ENERGY-EFFICIENT

OUTCOME NOT ASSURED

'What do you mean by that? Takes longer to discuss with us to secure our consent to come over, so it's quicker to just snatch us off from Earth?'

CORRECT

'But wouldn't it be possible for you to come down and make your presence known to us on our Earth?'

NOT FEASIBLE

'Ah our gravity's too weak for your liking?'

CORRECT

'But you could create artificial and stronger gravity using your technology?'

CONCEIVABLE BUT NOT ENERGY-EFFICIENT

'You place great emphasis on energy efficiency. Is there a particular reason for this?'

LOGICAL TO USE ENERGY-EFFICIENT

'Fair enough!'

Andy smiled and realised the captions beamed on the wall were in unison and simultaneous with the twinkling and flickering lights seen on their chests.

'Don't you have any voices? Do you make communication sounds?'

NEGATIVE

'You communicate by using the luminous cells on your frontal area?'

CORRECT

'What about hearing? Can you sense the vibration that well?'

VIBRATION SENSOR EXCEEDINGLY COMPETENT

He searched for physical evidence of it on the Gorgass and found no resemblance of ear-like organs. 'I presumed you have fine sensory hair rather than ears?' he asked.

OBSERVATION INPUT CORRECT

He nodded at Emma. 'Wow, so much like our insects on Earth'.

'But aren't they rather primitive?' she replied.

'Not necessarily so, and don't forget the insects happened to be, by far, the most numerous and, one could say, successful species in the animal kingdom'.

'But how come they never become that big like the Gorgass?'

'Search me! Higher gravity would strengthen bones. The Gorgass may have eko-skeletons, that is a kind of external skeleton. They've got four legs that may make the difference, as their weight would be spread out evenly', Andy responded.

'Their atmosphere would be denser, and plant life would probably stoop more . . . or whatever it is, but I think evolution has played a big part in it. But still, I'd love to dissect and take them apart to find out the answers! For a start, how do they keep their blood pumping up throughout their anatomy to counter the effect of much greater gravity?'

DISSECTION NOT ADVISABLE

INFORMATION EXCHANGE RECOMMENDED

Andy had to bring himself back from the realms of his conjecture, as he had forgotten that the Gorgass were observing all the communications between the human cargo.

'I don't mean it literally!' He laughed. 'I mean, we can use our line of questions and answers in exchange to build up our understanding of each other. That must surely be the most important objective for both of us?'

The Gorgass chose to ignore the question and countered along a different track.

ENQUIRY UNIT BLUE KNEELING ACTION WHY EYES SHUT QUESTION

Andy looked around and spotted Gillian still kneeling and rocking slightly, muttering her prayers. She was clearly troubled by the appearance of the Gorgass.

'Gillian! Are you okay? What's the problem?' Emma asked her.

'Oh! Look at the sight of them! They are so evil-looking! They must be Satan!'

'I believe she's praying. Take no notice of her', Emma instructed Andy.

Somehow the Gorgass had followed her comment to Andy and picked up on it.

DEFINITION OF PRAYING? EXPLAIN

'She is addressing her God with the hope or wishing strongly that it will assist her in obtaining a particular outcome to a situation', Andy replied.

ENQUIRY IF PRAYING CAN ACHIEVE RESULT QUESTION

Emma saw the captions and replied, 'Not necessarily, but it will help her feel protected and guided by her God'.

ENQUIRY WHERE GOD IS AND CAN WE SEE GOD QUESTION

ON WHAT ENERGY DOES GOD FUNCTION IN QUESTION

It was Gillian who responded. 'You cannot see it, but you can feel the presence of the Creator! I know it is real!'

IS GOD A MAKE-BELIEVE THING QUESTION

'No, our Lord is real and everywhere and is all-seeing!' Gillian retorted with some vehemence.

WHEN AND ON WHAT EVIDENCE QUESTION

'Over 2,000 years ago! It said so in the Bible!'

DOES IT HAVE FUNCTIONABLE CONSCIOUSNESS QUESTION

'Of course, it does! He is fully aware of our presence!'

HOW DOES IT RETAIN CONSCIOUSNESS ON WHAT ENERGY FORMAT QUESTION

At this point, Gillian totally lost the significance of this question and looked at Andy for clarification. 'What are they talking about? Can you answer it?'

He understood it without question and especially could discern the direction it was leading. He tried to make the discussion take on a lighter tone. 'What they mean is if you can store and produce consciousness and self-awareness, then on what kind of form or matter? For example, in animals, our bundles of interlinked nerve fibre, or brains in short, are the basis from where our consciousness originates. You need some process or kind of energy to store consciousness or information'.

Gillian responded, with her face reddening with frustration as she tried to find the right words, as she was not speaking in her own native language, 'But that's in a completely different dimension! The energy of God is much higher and undetectable using our present technology! We live in a 3D dimension box and cannot detect him!'

UNIT BLUE POSTULATION UNCONVINCING

ALL ENERGY ARE TRANSFORMATIONAL

'What?' There was a puzzled look on Gillian's face.

'What they mean is there's always a process of changing one form of energy to another form of energy', Andy explained. 'All energies are interlinked'.

'Say who?' challenged Gillian.

FORCE OF PHYSICS

Gorgass appeared to interrupt and spoke in support of the logic behind Andy's comment.

'That is your opinion! There's always something that cannot be explained!'

OPINION IRRELEVANT

NON-EXPLANATORY REMAINS NON-EXPLANATORY

'Ah, there you are! You don't know everything!' Andy rejoined the heated discussion. 'Look, I get what they are referring to. What they mean is opinions are simply matters of expressed viewpoints and are not based on facts or other evidence'.

UNIT GREEN POSTULATION CORRECT

'No! It is not my opinion! The Bible is the source of evidence! Why can't you see that?' Gillian was getting wildly frustrated that her deeply rooted beliefs were being challenged and that she felt she was losing the arguments with no positive inputs from her earthling colleagues.

THERE IS ONLY ONE ANSWER

FORCE OF PHYSICS IS ONE LOGICAL ANSWER

'Of course, we can have more than one answer!'

MORE THAN ONE FACTUAL ANSWER NOT FEASIBLE

'Why not?'

DEFINITION AND MATHEMATICALLY NOT ACHIEVABLE

NOT ENERGY-EFFICIENT TO HAVE MORE THAN ONE ANSWER

There was a blank look on her face. She failed to grasp the significance of the comment.

'What are they getting at?' Gillian said. 'They are trying to poison my mind with such meaningless jargons!'

Andy raised his hands. 'I can see what they are getting at. If you can let me, I'd like to try to explain the concept of facts'.

'You're ganging up with them against me, aren't you?' she shouted and turned her back on him. She was clearly getting increasingly agitated and exasperated by the depths that the discussions were plumbing.

Andy tried to get the debate simplified. 'You are exiting our discussion because you find it too hard to actually weigh all the aspects logically or critically. I must admit that what is being presented to us is absolutely mind-blowing. Please do not be angry with yourself'.

He was appealing to her in a comforting way as it was clear to him that they were all under enormous stress to really comprehend the enormously complicated circumstances they were in. Nothing like this had ever been faced by any humans and over which they apparently had so little control or input.

'Don't tell me I am not capable of rationalising belief with facts!' she muttered. 'However, I am still listening!'

'Okay, thanks. But please do bear with me. What I am trying to say is that you cannot *prove* anything to anybody except in mathematics and logic. Proof doesn't exist outside deductive reasoning. Let's go back to the issue with opinions. Opinions are not part of you in person. Your opinions are just pieces of information you keep inside your head, that you've accumulated throughout your life'.

He took a deep breath and continued, 'They are interchangeable and can be changed at any time. However, you fused yourself to your opinions, and you managed to deceive yourself into believing that they are part of the *self or person*. The sad thing is that any attack on the opinions you hold will be interpreted by you as an attack on the self.

Naturally, you find it uncomfortable, and you will fight to defend them as you believe them to be wrong. You will continue maintaining your stance unchanged even in the light of evidence showing they are seriously flawed'.

'I'm absolutely unshaken in my beliefs so far!' she responded. 'But I am still prepared to listen!'

'Great!' said Andy. 'Then be prepared to change your mind. That's the privilege of being open-minded, isn't it? It requires a good source of humility to accept there could be some flaws in your perspective'.

She looked up at him from her position on the floor. 'I didn't expect you to be so philosophical! But still . . .' She could not find words to challenge him and trailed off into silence.

'Gillian, I can sympathise with you and can understand how difficult it is to take on board a new-fangled theory that challenges your lifetime assumption of what you've learnt is the one and only right thing', Andy continued.

'It's important not to take everything too literally until you can weigh up the pros and cons, and we all need time to digest what is such a militant assault on centuries of traditional beliefs'.

Emma interrupted the heated discussion, 'Andy, I can guess that what you are saying is you do question the value of the Bible as an ethical and spiritual guide?'

'Afraid so. There's no factual evidence of its origins apart from being written by men a few hundred years after the birth of Jesus', Andy responded. 'Think about it: The Romans, even with their amazing legacy of methodical records of history, did not mention Jesus. None. Zilch. Therefore, we can say the Bible is just nothing but a fabled fiction. For example, we know, according to biological evolution, which has been universally proven to be factual, Adam and Eve were never real people'. Andy shook his head. 'If they were just mythical people, therefore, the concept of original sin should not exist in the first place'.

Gillian's eyes widened in protest but said nothing. Andy continued, 'Then think about it: If there was never an original sin to reckon with, therefore, there is no need to contain it with salvation'.

Gillian was about to say something, but Andy threw up his hand, indicating her to keep silent as he had not finished. 'If there is no need of salvation, then there is no need for a saviour.

'There you are, we must consider, by basing on this conclusion alone, we need to discard Jesus to be nothing but just a figment of man-made imagination or a historical figure', Andy said, extending his hand towards Gillian in invitation for her reply.

'Sounds like you are an atheist?' Gillian said, spitting the words out as if there was a bitter taste in her mouth. 'You have no spiritual morality, so I wouldn't trust you at all!'

'You can label me in whatever way you want, be it atheist or humanist or freethinker, or whatever it is, I don't care'. Andy sighed. 'Though I like to classify myself as a practising biologist, but the point is the lack of ability to be a loving or moralising person as universally conveyed by so-called Christian mainstreams is not a valid argument. I do love my family, even my dog, and I do know my love is not only substantial and genuine, but also, above all, tangible'.

He realised he was getting tired. *Must be because of gravity!* he thought.

He needed to wrap up this slanging as it was becoming futile. The sooner it was, the better.

'Look, Gillian, when you make an assertion that the only translation mechanism you have in your brain are the rules of logic and critical thinking . . .' He continued, 'So I pose this challenge to you: I will believe *anything* you assert, providing you have strong empirical, verifiable evidence for those assertions'.

He pointed at the Gorgass. 'For a start, they are the tangible evidence that we can see with our eyes. If they came from another solar system, then there must be thousands of other life systems out there that we don't know anything about!'

'God has reasons for all this! He has a plan for everything!' Gillian sobbed with tears in her eyes.

Andy palm-faced and said, 'If he has already got a plan for everything, including you—'

'Exactly! Of course, he does!' interrupted Gillian.

'Then why bother to pray?' Andy said, ignoring her outburst. 'You are asking him to listen to your request for a possible change to his plan? That reflects a serious flaw in his plan! That doesn't make him an omniscient at all to start with!'

'SHUT UP!' shrieked Gillian, covering her ears with her hands. She crawled away on her hands and knees. 'I am not listening to you anymore!'

'I think you'd better leave her alone', Emma said. 'She's clearly not ready for any confrontation or coming to term with new ideas. We are all emotionally pressured by these extraordinary circumstances'.

'Of course, you have a point', Andy responded. 'I don't have any issue of her or anyone resorting to their deity as a source of consolation and comforts as long they keep it to themselves'. Andy raised his eyebrow at Emma. 'I hope I haven't offended you, have I?'

'Not at all', she replied. 'To be honest, I haven't really thought anything about religion to the extent that you obviously have. I don't pay any attention to any of the religious issues. I think I can regard myself to be more of an agnostic'.

'Agnostic? Well, you are technically still an atheist . . .' He laughed. 'But without balls!'

She joined him in his laughter, and the mood of the two earthlings lightened a little.

They turned and looked at Hussain and realised he was still sitting on the floor, with his legs crossed and a smug look on his face. Apart from being quiet, he had been completely absorbed throughout the heated debate between Andy and Gillian.

'No wonder people are starting to see how seriously flawed Christianity is!' he exclaimed. 'Hence, the reason Islam is becoming the new force, a new sense of purpose . . . and truth!'

'Oh, please shut up'. Emma cut in. She was clearly irritated. 'Let's stop it for now and get back to Gorgass and see what they want from us'.

'Agreed', said Andy. 'Let's ask them for their reasons for snatching us from Earth'.

Hussain was clearly still incensed and brooding over the idea of a female interrupting his earlier conversation. *How dare she! That is the problem with Western women, showing no respect for men!* He wanted to raise his objection, but before he could do so, he realised Emma and Andy had moved away from him, removing any opportunity to vocalise his arguments. In effect, their heated discussions had isolated him where he was squatting on the floor. He lay there fuming, thinking about his next reaction to the infidels. *They will be sorry!*

Andy looked at the Gorgass. They had remained unmoved and in silence throughout the heated debate amongst the four humans. Whether they were unimpressed or had made any judgements, it was difficult to determine. There was no inkling of change in their appearance to manifest any emotions. *It is going to be difficult to read their reactions!* he thought. *The only way forward is to discuss with them head on and openly.*

'Gorgass, please ignore our discussions, but we are only meeting one another for the first time and have not been able to decide what we must do to understand what your requirements are, following the great skills and scientific abilities you have already demonstrated so far. I hope this hasn't inconvenienced you anyway'.

GORGASS OBSERVING HUMAN UNITS FOR ADDITIONAL INFORMATION

'Well, your impression is?'

HOW ILLOGICAL IT IS TO HAVE DIFFERENT ANSWERS

'Why not?'

WHAT AN INEFFECTUAL IT IS. NOT ENERGY-EFFECTIVE

He thought to himself, *We go again with their focus on energy conservation.*

'But let's move on, and I'd like to establish an understanding of your objectives as this would be beneficial to you, we assume, as well as us?'

No response.

'First of all, how did you locate our planet, or was it just chance? I assume you have ulterior and significant reasons for abducting us? If so, can you please care to tell us? How did you decide which of us to abduct and for what purpose?'

He realised he was getting tired. He looked at Emma and asked her, 'Are you feeling tired?'

'Yep, must be the strong gravity we're putting up with'.

'Okay, I'll ask them if we can exit from it as soon as possible?'

'Good idea. But let's find out more about their reasons first, and then we'll make our request to them for us to get back to our normal gravity'.

Before they could continue, they caught a glimpse of new video images forming on the wall. At first, it was grainy and blurry but started to clear up gradually. It was a picture of space—black, infused with numerous stars.

'What are we looking at?' enquired Andy.

Slowly, the picture started to be increasingly magnified and then even more.

A small strange-looking object could be detected in a corner.

'Ah, look there! Can you see that?' Emma said, pointing at it. All eyes were locked on it.

'Sorry, I don't recognise it. Can you please clarify the image for us?' Andy interjected.

The object in question slowly enlarged until it filled in almost the whole of the wall with one gigantic picture. It seemed to be a box-shaped, presumably metallic object, with a long boom protruding out of a huge dish mounted on one surface.

Emma and Andy swung round and looked at each other and in absolute unison, yelled only one word, '*Voyager!*'

They looked back at the screen and marvelled at the quality of the image.

They could see how dusty the *Voyager* was, with a few observable dents and small punctures on some of the visible sides of the main fuselage. *Probably from multi-impacts with debris floating in space,* Andy thought.

Out of the intensely deep blue, they could see a brilliant light being focussed on it. The whole body was lit in a blinding flash, straight grid lines first in red, then orange, and then in yellow. The grid of laser beams started to move along the dish and the body vertically and then a moment later, horizontally. A moment later, a blindingly brilliant and intense flare lit the whole room with such brilliance that it forced them to use their hands to shelter their eyes.

A moment later, when the brilliance had dipped, they could see the whole body of the *Voyager* had been vaporised.

'Why did you destroy it?' Andy questioned the Gorgass. He had not taken his eyes off the screen. 'Why did you have to do it?'

ACTION OBLIGATORY

'I do not understand. What was the reason? This *Voyager* was just a data-gathering probe and on what was expected to be a peaceful exploratory scientific mission'.

IT BLOCKED PROGRESS OF GORGASS

'Was it a matter of it being at the wrong place at the wrong time? Was it in your way, and if you had continued travelling through, there would be a massive kinetic impact between *Voyager* and your spaceship?' Emma asked.

UNIT RED POSTULATION CORRECT

DESTRUCTION OF PROBE UNAVOIDABLE

AVOID POTENTIAL DAMAGE TO GORGASS SHIP

'But why can't you take an evading manoeuvre around it?' Emma continued her enquiry.

'Ah, must be something to do with being energy-efficient to destroy it rather than altering their direction around it. Was that it?' Andy mooted. 'Was it just a matter of the wrong place at the wrong time for the *Voyager*, was it?'

UNIT GREEN POSTULATION CORRECT

'Interesting, but I do wonder if the people on Earth are aware of that destructive measure taken by you? They would probably have mistaken your action as totally hostile and aggressive.

'You must also have realised that the unmanned object was not a piece of natural material and it had been fabricated. It must, again, have made you realise that it had been despatched from a nearby source in spatial terms by intelligent beings?'

SUPPOSITION CORRECT

'But still you haven't answered our question as to why you have taken us away in your drones?'

NEED CONSTRUCT COMMUNICATION AS FOUNDATION

'Why can't you establish communication through the radio?'

GORGASS HAVE NO APPARATUS FOR DETECTING THAT TYPE OF ELECTROMAGNETIC RADIATION COMMUNICATION SYSTEM

'But surely you aren't aware of our unusual radio pattern emitted by us?'

NEGATIVE AND UNABLE TO ENCRYPT YOUR COSMIC BACKGROUND EMISSIONS

'So you weren't aware of our presence until your encounter with the Voyager?'

UNIT RED POSTULATION CORRECT

'Is there a subsequently established reason for establishing contact with us?'

CORRECT

'What is it?'

GORGASS DEMAND RAW MATERIALS

Emma took a deep breath, reacting to the uncompromising direct attitude of the Gorgass. 'Just demand! No asking or putting in a request nicely?'

REQUEST IRRELEVANT

'Then it's more energy-efficient to demand than ask?' she signed. 'No room for a possible negotiation?'

NEGOTIATION IRRELEVANT

Andy put his hand on Emma's shoulder and said, 'Let's stop here'.

Emma nodded and signed, 'Okay, let's take a pause here'.

They turned back to face the impassive Gorgass still standing behind the screen, and Emma said, 'We'd like to continue communicating with you, but we are getting really tired because of this strong gravity and want to go back to our Earth gravity.

Is that feasible?'

REQUEST GRANTED

'Thanks, and we want to take a few hours break or rest before resuming our communication', Andy said. 'You can return to your usual high-gravity level place on the outer cylinder, but can we just continue using the texting on the wall as our means of primary communication mode? Can we agree on that idea?'

PROPOSAL FEASIBLE AND MOTION INITIATED

In a short time, the wall had started to resume its original appearance, frosty and opaque. The Gorgass were no longer visible. The ceiling came down to its former position. Moments later, the human occupants could feel their oppressive weight diminishing until it reached the Earth's equivalent level. This development brought a strange tingling reaction. They could feel their faces blushing as they had an influx of blood.

Hussain regained his strength and reacted quickly and scrambled and lurched upright.

Emma looked down at her tightly fitting G-suit to see if she could try to loosen it somehow. She could not see or feel any obvious opening and gave up for a short while. Moments later, she could feel it starting to lose its elasticity. *So again, it must be the nanotechnology doing the job!* she thought.

'Okay, let's rest for a while', said Andy, taking the initiative. 'We need to think things through as to how best to negotiate with them. I'm not comfortable with the progress we have made with them so far, something about their aggressive attitude I could not put my finger on. Even so, we have at least engaged in a dialogue of sorts'.

'There you are! I wouldn't trust them at all!' Hussain said, but he was obviously more subdued than hitherto. He had not had any scientific teaching or exposure to technology and was clearly out of his depth and, therefore, extremely uncomfortable.

Andy put his index finger to his lips and then made a cut-throat gesture to enforce the real need to keep their voices down. He said aloud, 'Remember, walls have ears! Ha, ha!'

However, the warning was lost on Hussain, but Gillian and Emma grasped the meaning of it and understood.

'What's the problem?' Emma mouthed without using her voice. *So why is he so cautious?*

Andy sat down and invited Emma to join him on the floor. They ignored the other two people. 'Whether we like it or not, it looks like we have been arbitrarily selected by the Gorgass to act as go-betweens to them and the Earth! Why, otherwise, would they have gone to all the extraordinary lengths at least so far as they have revealed?

We must have something on our little planet that they want. What they actually want, we have yet to find out, but given the advanced levels of their sciences they have demonstrated so far, we are going to have to keep extremely level heads and our wits about us', he whispered and signed for Emma's benefit.

Emma looked into his eyes and said nothing.

Andy sat and rocked back and forwards on the floor. *Earth's only ambassadors to Gorgass? Messengers? To do what? To say what? Will anyone believe us when or if we actually get back to Earth safely? How will we get back? Will we have to return here?*

The whole concept was frightening enough, he realised, and how imperative it was to play all the cards right.

Just play the fucking cards right!

CHAPTER 19

The Negotiation

Five hours of rest went by. But the four occupants were still tired. Lying on their backs on the hard floor had proved to be anything but relaxing for them. Andy looked at the other earthlings and could see the intense discomfort they had to put up with lying on the floor. No provision of mattress or soft linings that would have made a real difference to their sleeping composure. Suddenly, he had a brainwave, and he sprang to his feet quickly and faced the wall.

'Hey, Gorgass!' he raised his voice. 'Haven't you noticed we're having some difficulties with our sleeping! The hard floor doesn't really help us at all!'

OBSERVATION MADE BY GORGASS CONFIRM YOUR DIAGNOSIS

'Then could we request some kind of mattress or soft linings for us to sleep on?'

He threw a searching look at the wall. 'If you don't have the kind of soft materials available for us to use, then how about making the gravity weaker and with the effect of it can ease the pressure on our body? And in return aiding you with energy conservation?'

REDUCING THE STRENGTH OF GRAVITY FEASIBLE AND ACHIEVABLE

BY WHAT PERCENTAGE UNIT GREEN SEEK QUESTION

'How about reducing it to our moon's strength?' Andy's mood suddenly became buoyant. 'I would say reducing it by something like 80 or 90%?'

WILL REDUCED GRAVITY HAVE ANY EFFECT ON HUMANS HEALTH QUESTION

'None at all for a short term, say equal to a few days. What we call a day is one rotation of the earth'.

GRAVITY REDUCTION NOW ACTIONING

'Oh, many thanks!'

Within a few minutes, he could start to sense the effect of gravity becoming lighter as the cylinder where they were residing was starting to slow down. All other earthlings looked at him as they could sense their bodies becoming lighter. Andy jumped up and was amazed to feel the extra spring made to his jump, causing him to nearly bump his head on the ceiling. 'Woah!' he squealed as he reacted with childlike behaviour. 'Okay, let's hope it can make a difference to our sleeping!'

He flipped his legs outward like a true gymnast, and in super slow motion, he allowed himself to fall onto the floor, but the impact made was hugely reduced and harmless. He was smiling as he finally laid down on his back and sighed with relief in response to the much softer pressure on his buttocks and back. He flipped over sideways and was amazed to see how effortlessly he could achieve this simple movement. All other occupants joined him in his laughter at the new enthralling experience they were enjoying in the near-zero gravity. It took them quite a while to get accustomed to the effect of it before they could finally drift off into deep stress-free sleep.

Andy was the first to wake up after several hours as he usually did when he wrestled with scientific conundrums. But he had never experienced the deluge of questions to which he was currently exposed, and with absolutely no computer resources, on which he habitually relied, he felt extremely concerned.

Then Emma woke up later but decided to spend the next hour toying with her personal translator, checking and rechecking it umpteen times to make sure all was in working order. So much depended on this little tool as their singular communication device. There was still some juice left in the battery, but how long would it continue to operate without its solar receptor recharging panel being exposed to sunlight? *Hmm?* She speculated that the artificial light was probably charging it. Then her mind switched to her personal predicament as her cochlear implant battery would also need recharging, and this device was near ancient. *I wish the battery for my cochlear implant had the same type of technology as my PT,* she thought, *but I was lumbered with late 1990s technology!*

Gillian was huddled on the floor with her arms around her legs at the far corner of the room. She had floated to that spot by simply flicking her hands on the floor, and once she was positioned there, she had isolated herself and was not in a communicative mood. *I need to get out of this evil place!* she kept moaning to herself.

Like Gillian, Hussain remained passively silent and was not forthcoming towards any of the others. His face remained grim. He detested the way he had been thrown into the same room with these Western people, all totally lacking any moral standards. As he cogitated irritably, he became even angrier with himself as he realised that he had failed to follow his regular periodic prayer regime.

'Now I believe we've finally had some sleep, are we feeling refreshed?' Andy spoke up, breaking the silence. 'Pointless to keep wasting our time, so we might as well start discussions with the Gorgass now and try to find out more about what they want from us'.

'Agreed', Emma responded. 'The sooner we get a constructive response as to their intentions towards us, the better we will understand our position, or even better, get us returned to good old Earth!'

'Okay, here is the priority of what I am going to do, which is to ask them first about their reasons for visiting our Earth, and from that, we could hope to understand what their intentions are and see if we can persuade them to release us back to Earth. It does seem very unlikely at this early stage that they will want to take us to wherever they are intending to go or even to stay in proximity to Earth?'

'Sounds fair enough', Gillian commented as she joined Andy and Emma.

Emma looked at the wall and spoke whilst signing, 'Gorgass, can you please respond to us? We are ready for you'.

An indeterminate time passed before came the reply appeared on the wall.

COMMUNICATION RESUMED

At this reopened dialogue, Andy responded, 'From what I understand, it was the encounter with our space satellite called *Voyager* that prompted you to divert your journey to investigate our planet Earth?'

CORRECT

THIS SPACE TRAVELLER IS ONE OF A GROUP OF THREE TRAVELLING TOGETHER

THIS UNIT BREAKS AWAY FROM OTHER TWO

'Where are the other two spaceships?'

CONTINUING THE JOURNEY TO OTHER OBJECTIVE STAR SYSTEM

'Huh? Is this spaceship identical in design or smaller to the other two?'

IDENTICAL

'How long will it take you to catch up with the other two?'

EVERY EARTH MONTH LAPSED EQUAL 27.4 EARTH YEARS

'How long have you been orbiting Earth?'

3.2 EARTH MONTHS

'Are you planning to catch up with them, and is there a limit to the time of your stay in our solar system?'

9.6 EARTH MONTHS TARGET

'Then you are not hanging around here that long and want to join your other travellers?'

EXPLAIN HANGING

'Sorry, this means waiting'.

CORRECT

'What is the purpose of your journey to that star system?'

TO COLONISE A PLANET

'What about our Earth? Not planning to colonise it?'

NEGATIVE AND FUTILE

'Because of our weak gravity?'

UNIT GREEN POSTULATION CORRECT

'If it wasn't for our weak gravity, would you consider colonising us, and how would you proceed with it?'

PROCEED WITH TERMINATION OF ALL HUMANS

'How and with what?'

GENETICALLY-MODIFIED SYNTHETIC VIRUSES

'Spraying and contaminating us all with the virus! But don't you use other methods, such as weapons or nuclear bombs?'

NEGATIVE AND ENERGY-INEFFECTIVE

'No weapons! But didn't you use the laser beam to destroy our *Voyager*?'

SELECTIVE METHOD

'Huh? Your laser cannon is designed only for clearing up the debris in space during your travel but not against Earth?'

AFFIRMATIVE

'Cool. But what has happened to your original planet? What was the reason for your mass exodus?'

ABOUT TO BE DISINTEGRATED BY A MOON

NOT POSSIBLE TO DEFLECT

'Sorry to hear that. How many of you are in this spaceship alone?'

THREE THOUSAND

'I didn't expect that many beings! I assume there's a total of nine thousand of you when including other spaceships?'

CORRECT

'How long have you been travelling from your former planet?'

24,000 EARTH YEARS

'Wow, that long! How did you manage to keep living that long?'

'Must be in some kind of stasis sleep?' interjected Emma.

CORRECT

'What is your usual lifespan?' It was Andy who resumed his line of scientific questioning.

AVERAGE 500–600 EARTH YEARS

'Oh my, that long!'

ONLY IN OUR PHYSIQUE

'What do you mean?'

OUR MEMORY AND EXPERIENCE ARE ASSIMILATED AND SUSTAINED

'Huh, are you saying you manage to retain your wealth of experience and skills from your previous person and pass on to the next new person?'

CORRECT

'How?'

GORGASS TRANSFERRED THEIR KNOWLEDGE TO ARTIFICIAL MEMORY MECHANISM

'You managed to download and store your wealth of personal experience to a kind of computer and then upload to a new Gorgass that is to be born later? Like a form of reincarnation?'

CORRECT

'Gee, did you manage to retain your memory since you left your planet?'

CORRECT

'Is it a sense of immortality that you are maintaining?'

BORDERLINE AND SUPERFICIAL

'Almost? There's a limit to it?'

ONLY POSITIVE AWARENESS OF FORMER CONSCIOUSNESS PLUS SELECTED FRAGMENTS OF MEMORIES ARE RETAINED

'What's the problem? Your mechanism is not that perfect and unable to carry out fully the function of retaining all your memories?'

NEGATIVE. IT FUNCTIONS FLAWLESSLY

'But why cannot you retain all the memories?'

LONGEVITY AND SAMENESS INFUSED WITH BOREDOM IS COUNTERPRODUCTIVE

SENSE OF NEW LIFE AND EXPERIENCE STIMULATION IS THE PURPOSE OF LIFE

'Then why bother to retain your consciousness? What's the reason behind it?'

MINIMISING THE UNCERTAINTY OF LIFE EXPIRATION

'Like us, you are not comfortable with the idea that death is the ultimate ending to everything? Like there's no afterlife?'

ENERGY-INSUFFICIENT TO RETAIN LEVEL OF CONSCIOUSNESS REQUIRED FOR AFTERLIFE

Andy paused for a minute. He was trying to grasp their psychology and dynamics of how they viewed their lives. *Do they value life the way we do? Or are they playing like God and manipulating the life suited to their needs rather than ours?*

'Speaking about life then, were there many other diverse forms of life on your planet? By the way, what is the name of your planet?'

BILLIONS OF THEM ON HELIOS

HELIOS, A NATURAL SATELLITE ORBITING A BIGGER PLANET

'Wow! Your origins were on a moon or natural satellite called Helios rather on a planet!'

AFFIRMATIVE

'I assume you do have evolution as the major reason behind the diversity of life that exists on your Helios?'

AFFIRMATIVE AND PROBLEMATIC

'What do you mean by evolution being problematic?'

EXTREMELY HIGH RATE OF MUTATIONS EXIST WITH EVOLUTION ON HELIOS

'What caused it?'

RADIATION

'That does make sense!' Emma finally interrupted. 'Big planets, with massive gravity, do produce lots of radiation!'

Andy nodded in agreement without looking at her. He was still focusing on the wall. He was marvelling at the plethora of new scientific information.

'Then what can you do about it? Have you managed to overcome it?' he continued.

BY USE OF GENETIC ENGINEERING, GORGASS KEEP THE MUTATIONS AT BAY

He took in a deep breath in amazement. 'Then you are telling me you are indeed proficient in the use of genetic engineering! Did you use it to keep your generations of Gorgass relatively intact?'

UNIT GREEN POSTULATION CORRECT

'Are our living beings on Earth similar to yours on Helios? I mean, are yours basically consisting of carbon-based life?'

UNIT GREEN POSTULATION CORRECT

'Gee! I've always wondered about how did you know to envisage a means to anaesthetise us all on your first encounter with us on Earth? You must have inside knowledge of our biological construction, do you?'

UNIT GREEN POSTULATION NOT CORRECT

ANAESTHETISATION 98.8% EFFECTIVE

Andy narrowed his eyes in puzzlement. 'What do you mean by only 98.8% . . . ?'

FORMULA FOR ANAESTHETISATION FABRICATED ON USING CREATURE CLOSEST IN ANATOMICAL RESEMBLANCE TO HUMAN

Suddenly, the wall came alive with a video clip being displayed through it. For the next few minutes, it showed how a chimpanzee was fleeing and how it was cornered and up to the harrowing moment when the laser managed to pierce its chest, causing a spray of blood all over the adjacent plants.

'My god!' Gillian shrieked with her hands covering her eyes. 'How dreadful!

How could you do that?'

Emma exhaled sharply, with her eyes wide open, but she said nothing. There was no reaction registered by Hussain. Andy did not flinch. He was just transfixed. Suddenly, he had a leap in his thought processes. *Ah, isn't that the same chimpanzee skeleton I saw that had a hole in its breastbone?*

'Ah, I get it now, the genetic blueprints and DNA of a chimpanzee are almost identical to humans! Something around 98.8%!' Andy said. 'But why can't you just find a human to start with to achieve 100% effectiveness?'

RISK ASSOCIATED WITH HIGH NUMBER OF HUMANS GROUPED TOGETHER IN ONE PLACE UNACCEPTABLE

RISK ASSOCIATED WITH EXPOSURE OF DRONES

RISK ASSOCIATED WITH TIME LIMITATION

'Therefore, you searched out for an isolated human in a relatively unpopulated area?'

UNIT GREEN CONCLUSION CORRECT

'Then are we just unfortunate to be there? Random and coincidence?'

CORRECT

He exhaled. 'So using one chimpanzee to start with, was it just good enough for you to analyse the various requirements to develop a synthetic toxin to anaesthetise us . . . ?'

INDIVIDUAL LEVELS CALCULATED FOR THE DURATION OF THE JOURNEY IN THE DRONES

'How long was the journey?'

14.5 EARTH HOURS

'Why 14.5 hours? Can't it be one hour?'

WAKING UP INSIDE THE DRONE CARRY RISK OF SUFFOCATION THROUGH HYSTERIA

'What? Oh, I get it. The confined space might lead to hyperventilation. Was it a very small space with just enough air inside the drone?'

SUFFICIENT AND ENERGY-EFFECTIVE

'Here we go again!' He rolled his eyes. 'Okay, let's go to the critical reason for your need to visit us'.

Emma took a step forward and said, 'You mentioned that you are demanding that we supply you with raw materials, is that right?'

CORRECT

'Then why can't you just go to Earth using your technology and establish a mining or kind of refinery production facilities?'

NOT EFFICIENT

WHY CREATE FACILITIES WHEN EARTH FACILITIES ALREADY IN PLACE AND FUNCTIONING

'Ah, so it's all about being energy-efficient to use our already-established technology', Andy interjected. 'From your encounter with our *Voyager*, that led you to us, which you knew we already have the technology in place to provide and meet your requirements. Was that how you reached your conclusions?'

CORRECT AND FAST-TRACKED

'Why do you need raw materials from us?'

TO RESTOCK AND RESUSCITATE OUR DEPLETED ESSENTIAL MATERIALS

'It is quite a small number of materials you're getting from us, given the idea of such a long journey you are taking?' Andy was looking down on the floor in deep thought. 'Don't you resort to recycling the materials?'

WE DO RECYCLE SOME OF THEM

'Then what's the problem?'

ENERGY RESERVES DEPLETION THROUGH CONSTANT REPETITION OF RECYCLING

EFFICIENCY OF PROCESS REDUCES LIMITING USEFULNESS OF RECYCLING

'Then our materials will refresh your needs for another how long?'

30,000 EARTH YEARS AND SUFFICIENT FOR REMAINDER OF OUR JOURNEY

'Gee, that long! It must be absolutely imperative for you to get what you need from us to enable your journey to be continued!'

FACTUAL

'No other alternatives?'

ALTERNATIVES EXPLORED AND DISCARDED

'Any reason for that?'

NOT PRACTICAL AND ENERGY-INEFFICIENT

'You are actually pinning your very existence on us!'

CORRECT

'In return for what?'

GORGASS NOT UNDERSTAND YOUR POSTULATION

'Well, you don't get something for nothing', Andy said. 'You must bring the humans something in return. That is called an exchange in principle'.

EXCHANGE IRRELEVANT AND POINTLESS

'Then it's okay just to expect us to provide you with your need without consideration made for our well-being in the first place? Just grab things and go?'

MORE ENERGY-EFFECTIVE THAT WAY

'How come?'

HUMANS TECHNOLOGY INFERIOR AND ILLOGICAL

NOT IN POSITION TO DEMAND ANYTHING FROM US

'Thanks for your comment!' Andy exclaimed. 'But I'm afraid you're wrong there!'

UNIT GREEN CLARIFY AND JUSTIFY POSTULATION

Andy paused and took a deep breath. He needed to collect himself. *It's going to be a challenge! Just try to be like them and think their way!*

'I don't like their attitude towards us!' It was Gillian who spoke and moved further away into the corner at the far side of the room.

'Then don't cooperate with them!' hissed Hussain.

Andy held up his clenched hand. 'Hold on! Don't be too emotional! Let's try to cool it down and be rational!' he whispered.

Then as he spoke, he realised he had been gradually formulating an idea. 'Okay, Gorgass. Let me explain facts to you that will be of benefit to you'.

He pointed at Gillian and . 'You can already see how confrontational and hostile some Earth people are. That is a typical trait of human behaviour. We can react, defensively and aggressively. We will not go away quietly but rather put up masses of resistance. Instead of cooperation, you will have friction. No cooperation means no progress! You would run out of time as you would not be able to replicate the resources that we humans have already created. There you are, in your book, that is *not energy-efficient* at all!

'It pays to be cooperative with us on equal terms! If you have something that we want, we will be willing to consider your request in most favourable circumstances to our mutual interests. It's much more energy-effective than going through the path of confrontation. It would make our population aggressive and resist your threats, and this would require much wasted time and energy.

'See my point? I would suggest you take time to reconsider our suggestion that we cooperate comprehensively'.

No response. Time went by. Still no response.

'I think they are not used to trading with mutual benefits', Emma said.

'Whatever answers they come up with, I'm still not going to cooperate with them!' contributed Hussain.

Suddenly, the captions reappeared.

UNIT GREEN EXPLANATION PARTLY LOGICAL

'What problems do you expect?' Andy exhaled.

WHAT DO YOU EXPECT FROM US IN RETURN

THAT IS THE OBSTACLE

'Why not? Whatever you may have or suggest could be immensely useful to us'.

NOT IN OUR INTEREST TO PROVIDE YOU WITH OUR TECHNOLOGY OR MECHANISMS FOR YOU TO USE AGAINST GORGASS INTERESTS

'Then do provide us with something different that would benefit us mutually'.

NOT PROVIDING YOU ANYTHING CONTRARY TO OUR INTERESTS

WE CAN ACCOMPLISH THE RESULT ON YOUR BEHALF

'Well, that can be achievable!' Andy smiled. 'Only if you can achieve something that would benefit us all, then it is possible!' *We are getting there!* he thought.

WHAT DO YOU NEED FROM US

'What's your extreme in specialist skills that we don't have?'

ENLIGHTEN GORGASS YOUR REQUIREMENT

Emma turned around to face the other three occupants and said, 'Let's put our thinking caps on! What do we need from them—something they may have that we don't have, something that they can do on our behalf, which is beyond our current capabilities! We will have a massive problem in getting any demands of any description sorted out by the powers on Earth with all the current international squabbles, but there is really not much we can suggest whilst we are isolated here in space'.

Gillian walked back and joined Emma and Andy. 'If there's a possibility of some sort of technology exchange taking place, that would mean us going back to Earth?' Finally, she was looking hopeful.

Andy turned back to face the wall.

'Right, whilst we're thinking about it, perhaps it would benefit us to know exactly what you are seeking us to supply you. Can you define what specific type of raw materials?' enquired Andy. 'We would need you to quantify and specify precisely what your requirements are from us?'

WEIGHT CALCULATION CLARIFICATION REQUIRED

'You need to clarify with us the meaning of actual weight?'

CORRECT

'Well, I personally weigh 100 kilograms or around 220 pounds'.

'1,000 kilograms equals one tonne', Emma interjected, reflecting her wealth of experience in her civil engineering background.

A long pause then ensued, and the wall went into a dimmed mode, presumably this turn in the dialogue had not been anticipated by the Gorgass, and they were doing some calculations and having discussions. Then the wall lit to the previous intensity, and a caption flashed.

GORGASS REQUIRED 1,500 TONNE IN TOTAL OF SEVERAL RAW MATERIALS

Then came the list of various materials.

300 TONNE METALLIC HYDROGEN

300 TONNE SILICON

300 TONNE CARBON

300 TONNE PURE WATER

300 TONNE IRON

Andy looked at Emma. 'That's a lot! But do we have any idea about the usual weight of payloads that we normally send out on our rockets?'

'Sort of. For a fact, I know our most powerful rocket ever was the *Saturn V* used for the Apollo program'. She wrinkled her nose as she was prone to do when in deep thought. 'In their heyday, their usual payload was around 140,000 kilograms or 140 metric tonnes'.

'But that's 1960s, so what about our current rocket program?'

'I would guess around 50–80 tonnes, depending on the type of rockets'.

'Why has the payload been reduced? How on earth do you know that much about such things?' Andy was clearly mightily impressed.

'My brother works for a company that specialises in building communication satellites in India'. She smiled. 'He confided in me about how difficult it was to squeeze two satellites into one single payload limited to 80 tonnes on a Chinese-made rocket. That's how I remembered the figures'.

'If that's the case, then we need . . .' Andy paused, trying to calculate mentally. 'Around 20 to more, probably 30 rockets would be needed to carry that quantity of materials!'

'That may be barely attainable but requires full international cooperation amongst every country that has either or both rocket-launching sites or raw material capabilities! We have no idea just where it would be possible to actually obtain something like metallic hydrogen', Emma said but didn't sign this time.

'Yeah, and even then, only if they are prepared to cooperate . . .' Andy trailed off.

'Within the next nine months or so?' enquired Emma, addressing the wall.

Oh heck! They will not understand months. She went on, '12 months is one orbit of our sun. Does that help?'

*WITHIN **9.30** EARTH MONTHS*

'Any leeway? Such as extending by an extra three months?'

UNFEASIBLE AND IMPRACTICAL

'Why not?'

TIMING LAPSED IN JOINING OTHER TWO GORGASS SHIPS

'Time is running out. What's the problem, and why can't you catch up with them eventually, given thousands of years you've been travelling? What's the rush?'

ANY DELAY WILL RESULT IN PROGRESSIVE AND ABERRANT DIMINUTION OF OUR EXISTING PROPELLANT FUEL BECOMING UNFEASIBLE AND RESTRAINING

COUNTERPRODUCTIVE TO DELAY

'Then it comes down to the question of timing that is not on your side, and it's becoming a matter of life-and-death issue for you?'

NOT LIFE-THREATENING BUT PROBLEMATIC

Andy walked toward the wall and with his flat hands, gave it a light slap on it.

'Now you see!' he said. 'Your problem, not ours!'

YOU THREATENING TO NOT COOPERATE WITH US

'We may be warlike and controversial creatures, but we can be reasonable and prepared to cooperate with you if given the chance'. He continued, 'But the last thing we need is any severe threats from you on the basis of your uncompromising attitude of demanding something from us without any balancing benefits to Earth'.

YOU WANT SUBSTANCE FROM US QUESTION

Andy ignored it and looked at the other three occupants, and their eyes were locked on him, expecting him to say something, but he said nothing. He simply shrugged.

Emma looked at Gillian and said, 'I assume you want to be the first to go back to Earth, do you, Gillian?'

Gillian clasped her hands together and nodded, looking pleased. 'I don't want anything from them!' Her response was drastic and short. 'Just get me back to Earth!'

Andy looked around at his fellow prisoners, which was what he was beginning to realise that they were just that. 'I think we could do with an interval whilst we try to get some agreement amongst ourselves as to just what any one of us would be able to say and to whom, if and when any of us return to Earth?'

Hussain snarled at the rest of the humans, 'I do not care what you say or do as it will all be determined by Allah!'

Andy ignored him and addressed the wall and said, 'Can we have a period of rest and food to restore our energy, and then we will communicate more efficiently just how we think we will obtain the most benefit?'

REQUEST GRANTED

The wall faded, and the humans were able to reassemble themselves into a loose circle, as once again, they tried to adjust themselves to the extraordinary atmosphere.

'What sort of benefits or choices do we think we might suggest to the powers on Earth? Medical solution my best choice? They have already shown that they are way ahead with their knowledge of genetics when they took samples of the chimp's blood. It would surely the best opportunity to benefit the whole of mankind, regardless of colour, creed, or country?' said Emma.

'Good thinking', responded Andy. 'Who on Earth would we have to persuade to be the principal points of contact for us to start off discussions, if and when any one of us get back there?' he asked with a chuckle.

'The trouble is, how much tolerance the people on Earth are prepared to have on accepting the limited choice provided to them under these circumstances?'

Andy continued thoughtfully, 'I would have expected there to be so much diversity and resistance on the idea of which proposal is the most beneficial to them!'

The conversation went on for some time, with Hussain deliberately ignoring the others, as they had some food and rested. None of them slept that particularly well, but nevertheless, they were somewhat more relaxed, and they felt that they were in a calmer atmosphere to resume the dialogue, if it could be called that, with the Gorgass.

Andy faced the wall, and as though they were being observed by the Gorgass, it immediately resumed the now-familiar illuminated 'dialogue' scene.

TOLERANCE OF MATHEMATICS IS PIVOTAL

WE EXIST BECAUSE OF MATHEMATICS

BIOCHEMISTRY EXISTS AND WORKS BECAUSE OF MATHEMATICS

PHYSICS EXISTS AND WORKS BECAUSE OF MATHEMATICS

DIVERSITY OF BIOLOGICAL LIFE EXISTS BECAUSE OF MATHEMATICS

EVOLUTION EXISTS BECAUSE OF MATHEMATICS

BEHAVIOUR OF ATOMS EXISTS BECAUSE OF MATHEMATICS

MATHEMATICS CAN BE OBSERVED AND MEASURED

THEREFORE, MATHEMATICS IS THE LOGICAL ANSWER IN EVERYTHING, EXCEPT INFINITY

INFINITY CANNOT BE OBSERVED AND NOT ACCOUNTABLE TO MATHEMATICS

INFINITY WILL NOT PAUSE

IF INFINITY PAUSED, IT WILL BECOME OBSERVED AND ACCOUNTABLE

THEREFORE, INFINITY CAN BE REGARDED AS OMNIPOTENT

THERE IS NO MATHEMATICS IN EMOTION

THEREFORE, EMOTION CAN BE DISCARDED AS ILLOGICAL ANSWER

IDEAS AND BELIEFS BASED ON EMOTIONS AND ABSTRACTS CANNOT BE REGARDED AS LOGICAL ANSWERS

OPPOSING IDEAS BASED ON SEVERAL ANSWERS IS ILLOGICAL AND ENERGY-INEFFECTIVE

THEREFORE, IT CANNOT BE TOLERANT

GORGASS FIND HUMAN MINDS ABSTRACTED AND ILLOGICAL

Paused.

'But surely emotions are created by hormones, which are then created by chemistry!' Emma exclaimed. 'Therefore, it is mathematically justified!'

UNIT RED POSTULATION INCORRECT

DECISION-MAKING AND REASONING ARE IMPAIRED BY EMOTION, RESULTS IN ABSTRACT AND ILLOGICAL CONCLUSION

THEREFORE, IT IS NOT MATHEMATICALLY JUSTIFIABLE

A lengthy pause occurred.

Holy shit! Andy thought but said nothing. Like the other humans, he was gobsmacked. Silence reigned for the next few minutes. They were trying to absorb and make sense of the implications.

'I don't accept all this!' Hussain's agitated voice broke the silence. 'Allah is the logical answer to everything! He is the truth, omnipotent, omniscient, and wise!'

IF THERE IS A CEASE IN OMNIPOTENT, IT WILL BECOME OBSERVED AND ACCOUNTABLE

    THEREFORE, IT IS ACCOUNTABLE TO MATHEMATICS

    THEREFORE, IT CAN BE MEASURED AND OBSERVED

    IF IT CANNOT BE OBSERVED, THEREFORE, IT DOES NOT EXISTS

    NOTHING EXISTS WITHOUT MATHEMATICS

Hussain's eyes widened, and he roared, 'How dare you to insult me saying my god is not that omnipotent! *That is blasphemy!*' He bent down and took off one of his sandals. With it in his hand, he took a big swing and threw it at the wall. 'TAKE THAT!' he bellowed.

It bounced off the wall with a small thud before falling harmlessly onto the floor. No damage could be observed on the wall. But the action itself had shaken up the others. "WHOA!" shouted Andy. But his word had negligible effect on Hussain as he simply walked off to the furthest corner and stood there folding his arms. He was incandescent with rage.

'Let's leave him there! Better we say nothing more! Pointless to carry on this type of conservation!' Andy suggested. 'We're already wasting our time on this futile subject! Let's go back to negotiating some sort of an exchange with Gorgass!'

He paused, trying to recall the last point before they got sidetracked. 'Fine, but let me think of something else, something that we can utilise their extreme level of genetic engineering expertise to our international benefit. So how do we proceed with this?'

Emma looked down at her lap, thinking deeply. Her shirt was partly exposed through the gap of her nanotechnology suit. She noticed there were a few smudges on it and tried to recall where they came from. She tried to brush them off and recognised the nature of colour of the smudges. *Oh yes, they must have bloody rabbit droppings! I must have fallen onto them!*

At first, she said nothing. Slowly, something materialised in her head, an idea.

She looked up at Andy and said, using sign language with which they were becoming much more competent at understanding each other, 'Did we get the impression their level of genetic engineering skills is, excuse my pun, out of this world?'

'Sort of'.

'Could we see how far we are able to use their genetic-engineering capability to benefit us?'

'Like what?'

'How feasible would it be for them to help us eradicate all the rabbits in Australia!'

'What? Rabbits? Why? Say again?' Andy frowned.

'We all know they're real pests and have become Australia's number one problem! Wouldn't it be a major benefit to get rid of them for the Australians, once and for all? But would that upset the ecosystem balance?'

'I don't think so. We already have had some partial success with eradicating specific types of mosquitoes in Africa to halt malaria through genetic engineering. We made sure that only female offspring matured. All the eggs imprinted with male genes were removed artificially, and soon the population crashed into insignificance'.

'Then can we do the same thing with rabbits?'

'Maybe, maybe not?' Andy shook his head thoughtfully. 'We did develop myxomatosis by creating the myxoma virus in the 1950s, and this was introduced to control the rabbit population in England and Australia'.

'But?'

'Well, at first, it did work quite well, but it was not quite 100% effective', he replied. 'The problem with all living things in nature is that just 1% of them always carry some element of mutation that makes them resistant to a specific virus. That is a fundamental law of nature or evolution in practice. No matter how effective the virus created is, initially, it may apparently eliminate them to start with, but over time, the 1% of the population of any animal that survived recovers and starts to breed all over again. No matter how deadly the virus is, it's virtually impossible to achieve a 100% success rate result.

'That's why we still have the rabbits breeding again and back to pestilential and dangerous levels'.

'Well, let's throw down the gauntlet and see if the Gorgass can take up the challenge to surpass the 99% mark?'

Andy nodded and said, 'It'll be most interesting to see if they have the means to deliver the result to meet our expectation'.

He looked at the wall. 'Gorgass, did you understand our conversation about elimination of epidemic infections? Does it pose any insurmountable challenges to you?'

CLARIFICATION REQUIRED HERE

WHAT IS RABBIT

'Ah, it is a small furry animal with long ears and white fluffy tail', he said, putting his hands up, imitating the size of the animal in question.

CONFIRM IF THIS IS THE ANIMAL

The wall came alive with another clip of video being played out of it. This time they could see a dry barren area. In the far distance, through the shimmering images, there was a man with a rifle.

'Oh, that's Nigel!' Emma shouted out excitedly. Considerable affection showed as her colleague's familiar face made a sense of nostalgia take over her emotions for a few moments until she pulled herself together.

They watched the video being played and saw how Nigel was partly obscured by the ground, but the watchers now realised that the camera on the Gorgass drone had followed every action he made with his rifle leading up to the moment he took out the rabbit with a single shot. When he walked away, they could see movement of the image showing how the drone had redirected itself towards the dead animal.

'Yes, indeed, that's a rabbit!' Emma interjected.

Then they observed the tentacle extending and burying the needle into the bloodied creature.

ACCESSED BLOOD AND GENES ANALYSED BY GORGASS

DATA READY FOR USE

'So I assumed we're lucky with our request!' Emma smiled. 'But Australia is a bloody big country! How can you achieve that?'

DEFINE AUSTRALIA SIZE

'Okay, can you show me the image of our Earth?' Emma spread out her hands at the wall.

Accurately and immediately, the image of Earth loomed out on the full breadth of the wall. It was razor sharp, as if it was like 3D projecting out and could be touched. She immediately located Australia. 'There!' she pointed the outline of land all the way around Australia and said with pride, 'That shows the whole size of my country, Australia!

'Gorgass, I know it's a big country, but is it too much of a challenge for you?

But actually, there are about 300 million rabbits down there! Around 300 million!' she repeated how huge the problem was likely to be.

APPLICABLE

'Huh? Even with 100% result?'

AFFIRMATIVE

'How?' Andy was extremely intrigued to see how it could be achieved on this colossal scale. 'You cannot beat nature's 1% survival rules?'

WITH FOUR TYPES OF VIRUSES ACHIEVING 99.999%

INVASION OF DRONES SPRAYING GENETICALLY MODIFIED VIRUSES TO CARRY OUT THE NULLIFICATION OF RABBITS IN FOUR STAGES

FIRST STAGE USING VIRUS TYPE 1 RESULTS IN 99% OF TARGET 300 MILLION EXTERMINATED, LEAVING 3 MILLION SURVIVORS

SECOND STAGE USING VIRUS TYPE 2 RESULTS IN 99% OF THE NEXT 3 MILLION PERISHED, LEAVING 30,000 SURVIVORS

THE THIRD STAGE USING VIRUS TYPE 3 RESULTS IN 99% OF THE NEXT 300,000 PERISHED, LEAVING 300 SURVIVORS

THE NEXT STAGE USING VIRUS TYPE 4 RESULTS IN 99% OF THE NEXT 300 PERISHING, LEAVING THREE SURVIVORS

POTENTIAL CHANCE OF REMAINING THREE RABBITS ENCOUNTERING TOGETHER IN THE LAND AREA THE SIZE OF AUSTRALIA WITHIN THEIR LIFESPAN IS CALCULATED TO BE 0.0015%

'Oh gee, there's gonna be a total wipe out of rabbits!' Emma suddenly felt a speck of guilt on her conscience. 'How do they get wiped out through what? I don't want them to suffer horribly with a long lingering death in the same way they did with myxomatosis?'

'Can you exterminate them, if possible, painlessly?' Andy asked. 'And how long will it take to achieve the result?'

EMOTION IRRELEVANT AND INTERFERES WITH RESULT

VIRUS INDUCES COMATOSE IN ALL RABBITS

'How?'

*BY LOCKING THEIR NERVE BUNDLES INTO PERMANENT STATE OF
PRODUCING HORMONE MELATONIN IN EXCESSIVE SCALE*

'Ah, I recognise melatonin as responsible for inducing all mammals into cycles of sleep!' Andy's eyes widened. 'Which means, in this case, rabbits will never wake up?'

CORRECT

THEIR SURVIVABILITY WILL CEASE INTO OBLIVION WITHIN ONE EARTH WEEK

'Cause of death?'

DEHYDRATION AND DISINTEGRATION

Andy sucked in a deep breath and with a sombre tone in his voice, said, 'I suppose you have the means to do like that with us humans?'

UNQUESTIONABLY

'May the Lord preserve and protect us from these abominable creatures!'

Gillian wailed.

She suddenly spun around and walked towards the corner furthest from where Andy was standing, well out of audible range. She decided she would not be watching any further communications unfolding on the wall.

Andy gave her a brief glance and decided to ignore her. He returned to look at the wall and spoke, almost whispering. 'I know you could infect us with viruses, but you wouldn't do it anyway, after we have reached an agreement to deliver your raw materials, would you?'

IRRELEVANT AS NO BENEFIT

Andy gave a huge sigh of relief.

HOWEVER, IT DEPENDS ON HOW YOU DO HONOUR OUR NEGOTIATION

'Sure, we'll do our best to deliver your message to the top politicians on Earth', Emma interrupted. 'Please have faith in us!'

'Are we all able to return altogether to Earth?'

NEGATIVE

ONE PERSON PER TRIP

'Why?'

RETAINING THREE HUMANS BEHIND FOR TIME BEING

'What for?'

IN CASE OF FAILURE FURTHER COMMUNICATION OR DEVELOPMENT IS REQUIRED

'I get it, like insurance'.

She looked at Andy, and he looked at her and shrugged. Then they looked at the other two figures on the other side of the room. They were still not looking in his direction.

'Which one of us is the first to go?' Andy said in a loud firm tone, signalling to them to pay attention to him. They turned around, but their faces were still unchanged.

Hussain was scowling ferociously, and Gillian, her eyes red from weeping, looked back numbed and obviously very upset.

Andy rubbed his neck and sighed. *I don't know why, but by the look of them, I do not have any faith in their capability to carry out the mission of Gorgass!*

Unless he restored his team's confidence, the possibility of the success vested in this negotiation was evaporating fast.

We've been dealt with stacked cards! Or so he thought.

CHAPTER 20

The Human Consignment

Emma Wilson walked towards the spot where her utility belt was lying and took out a pen. She looked at Gillian Lee and Rahman Hussain. 'Which of you want to go back to Earth first?' she asked them encouragingly. 'You will have the enormous responsibility of delivering the material demands of the Gorgass to the highest levels of international government'.

Immediately, Rahman made the first move by taking several steps backwards.

'I don't want to do anything with it! It is not justifiable for me to cooperate with them at any level! Just get me back to my home!' he shouted aggressively.

'No! I don't want to stay here any longer. I cannot stand it! I will be glad to leave with their messages or whatever!' Gillian was almost beside herself with emotion.

Emma took a moment contemplating but decided to follow her gut feeling in believing that the devout missionary would be highly credible and should be the first person to go.

'But the point is, Gillian, if you do go first, you would not stay any longer, which is exactly what you said. In addition, you will be in a position of huge responsibility to communicate the demands of Gorgass? Are you prepared to do that?'

'Huh? I suppose so', she replied with an air of resignation. 'But to whom?'

'Good question. Let's ask the Gorgass!'

Emma looked at the wall and signed whilst speaking, 'Where on Earth will you be taking her to?'

ANYWHERE YOU CONSIDER THE BEST POTENTIAL

'Well, there you are'. Emma glanced at Gillian. 'If it was up to me, I would go to the United Nations in New York as my obvious logical choice. Or in your case, possibly the Holy Father at the Vatican?'

At this point, the two females were deep in conversation, paying no heed to Hussain's presence. This had infuriated him even more. *How dare they think they can ignore me so completely and make such important decisions? They shouldn't be talking about such profound matters, which affect me, without involving me!*

'Mind your manners!' Hussain bellowed. 'It's not up to you two women to make decisions as to what is best for men and ignoring us! It's your duty to take orders from men!'

He swung round and looked at the wall and shouted at it hysterically, 'Ignore these women! They don't know what they are talking about! It is obvious that you need to listen to me, not them'. He pointed at his chest. 'I instruct you to send me back to my country!'

He was almost incandescent with fury. The Gorgass detected it as a complete lack of self-control. They had been improving their understanding of human behaviour, and they correctly observed Hussain's attitude to be threatening.

HOSTILITY DETECTED FROM UNIT GREY – CONFIRM GORGASS PERCEPTION CORRECT?

'I don't care about what you think of me!' He was reacting spontaneously as he responded to the Arabic script flashed on the wall. 'You've got to learn to obey my commands! Just take me back to the same place from which you've kidnapped me!'

LACK OF COOPERATION DETECTED HERE

NOT HONOURING ON CONVEYING GORGASS DEMANDS

'Nah! You don't need me to deliver your list of materials or whatever it is! You can have these women to deliver your shopping list! But I still need to go before them!'

He pointed at the two women dismissively.

GORGASS NOT TOLERATE LACK OF COOPERATION

'There you are! You did not cooperate with us or discuss our requirements!

You had the nerve to snatch us off from the face of Earth without any prior discussion! Seems you don't care about us. Therefore, why should I consider your interests, whatever they are?'

Silence. A minute lapsed. The atmosphere was becoming extremely tense.

ATTITUDE NOT PRAGMATIC

'So what?'

RECONSIDER YOUR STANCE IMMEDIATELY

'Why should I?'

CONFIRM YOUR STANCE UNCOMPROMISING

'Naturally!'

CONFIRM YOUR STANCE FINAL AND ABSOLUTE

'I don't respond to threats'.

He was glaring through the wall at the Gorgass. He folded his arms, and his whole attitude was bellicose and threatening, and he was muttering incoherently under his breath. Defiance and belligerence were written all over him.

Another minute of silence. The atmosphere was now becoming extremely tense. Everyone was eyeing one another up. They were unsure what to expect next. Andy felt things were going badly wrong after what had seemed to be a constructive dialogue with the Gorgass. His gut feeling was telling him to brace themselves for the worst. *What now?* he thought.

The colouring of The lights emitted by the walls in the room slowly went through a sequence of changes—yellowish, orange, then finally to red. Everything in the room, including the people, were bathed in red light. A sober mood descended on all the earthlings, and even Hussain started to look worried. It was certainly unnerving the humans. They held their breath unconsciously, expecting something to happen.

'What's going on? Why the red light?' Gillian muttered apprehensively.

RESONATE WITH GORGASS REMORSE

At this point, Hussain became agitated and started to walk off to the far corner by himself. He simply didn't like what was happening and felt he was responsible for the effect of the lighting changing but without understanding the significance.

———

GORGASS CONCLUSION REACHED

Suddenly, a long slit appeared, parting the ceiling between where Hussain was and the rest of the humans. It stopped when it was 6 inches wide. Out of it came some transparent substance. It was responding to the artificial gravity and seemed to be an amorphous blob. It became thicker as if some part of the ceiling was melting. A second curtain of transparent material lowered to the floor. A new section of wall was forming between the one figure and the three earthlings. Hussain was being isolated from the other humans. Emma instinctively reached out with her hands and scooped out a handful of the translucent material from the newly forming wall. Hussain was startled but was rooted to where he stood. He could not think what to do, except gape with an open mouth at the new curtain as it materialised.

Emma tucked, squeezed, and pulled apart the pliable stuff in her hands. It had a rubbery and soft feel to it. 'What kind of gooey material is that?' she enquired of herself. It was part of her inquisitive mindset with her architectural background kicking in.

As soon as the gooey, slimy substance touched the floor, the curtain suddenly solidified and hardened into a new transparent wall, which isolated Hussain from the other humans.

Simultaneously, in a split second, the gooey stuff in Emma's hands hardened into a solid glassy lump in an irregular shape. 'Wow, they must be using nanotechnology.

I would love to have some of that for building materials. It is amazing stuff!'

She looked up and realised the new wall had formed across the whole room, cutting Hussain off.

A new adjacent section with a much smaller space had been created, with Hussain standing alone in it. He tried to punch his clenched fists against it. It would not budge. There was less and less space for him to move as the cell closed in around him.

There was no sense of vibration. It had a rock-solid, thick, bulletproof-glass-quality feel to it.

Then Emma dropped her piece of the now-hardened material to the floor with a loud clacking sound, and she joined with others trying to tear the new wall down, kicking, smashing, slamming, thumping. The wall would not budge nor vibrate. Hussain was becoming frantic as he realised there was no sound coming through the glassy wall. Then the material closed in on him, totally inhibiting any movement.

'What's happening? What's going on?' Gillian said with an imploring look at the others.

It was an eerie sight for them to be able to still see Hussain whilst he was still bathed in a glowing red light on the other side of the wall.

Moments later, a new orifice opened in the ceiling above where Hussain was encased. A long tentacle snaked down menacingly towards Hussain. At first, he failed to realise there was any movement from above until it was hanging just behind his head. He sensed its presence and tried to evade it, but it was too late. The transparent encasing held him immobile. It stung him squarely on the back of his neck.

The three people on the other side of the wall stopped their useless hammering on the transparent wall and were transfixed in horror as they each recalled having been assaulted in a similar way back on Earth. They all knew the consequences would be anaesthetisation. But the only question they were asking was, *what now?*

Almost immediately, they had their answer as the drugs kicked in.

Hussain's legs simply crumpled, but he remained half standing as he was propped up by the confines of his newly created cell.

Andy turned his head around and shouted at the wall, 'Gorgass! What are you doing?'

No response.

'Look at the wall!' Gillian's exclamation caused Andy to glance back at the new wall. It had started to become frosty, losing its transparency. Hussain disappeared from their sight.

'What's happening?' wailed Gillian. 'What are they going to do with him? I truly pray and hope he's okay and just being detained temporarily'.

Andy turned around and stood before the wall, and with an uncharacteristic acerbity, he barked, 'What the hell are you doing with him? We demand you to release him back to us!'

It was an indication as to how disoriented they were all becoming as they were not exactly in any situation to demand anything whatsoever. Still a blank wall. No writing.

'Look, Gorgass, you want our cooperation, right?' he said with real anger showing. 'It's important you keep us in full picture of what you are going to do with him!'

No reaction.

'If you don't cooperate with us, then I'm not sure if we can guarantee our continued collaboration, and you will have expended too much energy on this whole enterprise for no gain to you or us!'

Andy had made a huge effort to show some composure and to try to maintain some sort of dialogue, but he was enormously worried at the impasse.

Finally came the response.

HUMANS NOT IN POSITION TO DEMAND ANYTHING THAT OBSTRUCTS OUR OBJECTIVES

Andy paused and said nothing. He rubbed his chin, trying to consider carefully what to say next. *What game are they trying to play?*

'Why can't we know what's happening to Rahman? Isn't that a simple-enough request?'

HUMAN EMOTION ERRATIC AND NOT IN POSITION TO REACH DECISIVENESS

GORGASS MINIMISING EFFECT IRRATIONAL ATTITUDE MADE BY UNIT GREY HUMAN

'Well, let us be the judge of the situation, and we have the right to act accordingly!' said Andy. 'Whatever it is, you still need to give us the full reason for your intention of what you are going to do with Rahman Hussain. From there, we'll understand you more clearly, and then perhaps we can accommodate you'.

Pause. No reaction.

'Look!' shouted Emma. 'Something's happening to the wall!'

The newly partitioned wall had started to defrost and soon by becoming softer as if melting. In a moment, the whole wall had drained away into the slit formed on the floor, exposing an empty section of the room. Hussain was nowhere to be seen. As if by magic, he had disappeared into thin air. Simultaneously, the colour of the lighting was returning to its original bright white.

'Where's Rahman?' Gillian wailed. 'What have you done with him?'

Andy looked at the main wall and took a deep breath. 'Gorgass, it's imperative that we know what's happening to Rahman'. He struggled to keep any emotion out of his appearance and his voice. He wanted to show everyone, including the Gorgass, that he was in control. 'Whatever happens to him, we'll know could happen to us. We deserve to know. You owe it to us to know as we're still the people that you have acquired to help you and on whom have already expended enormous amounts of energy to achieve your objectives'.

Again, another pause, this time an uncharacteristically long one. Finally, a familiar text flashed.

GRANTING YOUR REQUEST AND DISPLAYING

A new image appeared on the wall. It was presumably an outside view of the spaceship. The image seen extended from ceiling down to the floor of the wall. It took them a short moment of contemplation to realise they were indeed viewing the spaceship via an external camera of some kind. It was the first time they had seen the exterior appearance of the spaceship. They could make out long bulging ribs protruding horizontally across the length of the craft. What they did not know was that these ribs were pure iron, with the primary function to create protective magnetic shields cocooning the ship.

'So that must be the spaceship in which we are prisoners', Emma said, signing.

'But what are we looking for?'

'Search me'. Andy kept scanning the wall.

'There!' Gillian squealed, pointing her finger at a barely visible hole that was opening on the outer skin of the ship. It was very small scale relative to the huge bulk of the craft, and if it was not for Gillian's sharp-eyed detection, it would have been easily overlooked.

Andy squinted at it, and suddenly, his stomach sank with anxiety. *It looks like a duct. Something is not going right!* He suddenly hid his head with his arms.

He wanted to shout at others not to look at it, but he was too late. An object was ejected from the hole followed by a thin gaseous vapour propellant. This pale green halo quickly dispersed, and as it did, it revealed what was unquestionably the form of what had been Rahman Hussain.

As a first impression, it resembled a disjointed ragdoll, slowly tumbling around through the vacuum. The images were enlarged and clarified, and on closer inspection, the remains of Rahman Hussain inflicted a sickening emotional punch to their stomachs. His face and hands started to swell up abnormally because of the vacuum. His skin had retained sufficient resilience to prevent him from exploding. A layer of blisters formed on his face when it was exposed to the sun and as his gyrating body turned into shade, then it froze. There was no indication of any suffering as he had been fully anaesthetised. It was a peaceful and painless death. He was still tumbling slowly towards Earth when Gillian screamed, 'May the Lord deliver him . . .,' but she stopped abruptly in the middle of the sentence because she found it too traumatising to continue. Instead, she took a few steps away from the wall and buried her face deeply in her hands.

She wailed and wailed. Then she sank onto her knees and continued wailing.

She was clearly suffering from a severe psychological shock.

Emma's face went pale as she was shocked but to a lesser extent. She said nothing and remained totally silent. She had never witnessed a human death in her life.

Only one word kept going round in her head persistently: *WHY?*

Even though Andy had been unaffected emotionally, he had suspected something was going on with the Gorgass, but he had not expected it to be that bad. *That's bad!*

He let his arms hang loosely by his side. He was clearly dejected. He looked at the wall. 'I know Rahman was an awkward bastard, but why did you still have to kill him? For what reason? He didn't deserve death that way!'

The video image of the exterior of the ship went blank, and the wall resumed its usual frosty appearance. Soon it was punctured by a new text.

UNIT GREEN POSTULATION IRRELEVANT

ACTION OF DISPOSING UNIT GREY IS NECESSARY

'On what grounds?'

ENERGY-INEFFICIENT TO DETAIN A LONE HUMAN ON LIMITED RESOURCES

'Oh, for Pete's sake, get real!' he said with eyes opening in amazement.

'I can't believe you are so obsessed with energy efficiency! You Gorgass are seriously in need of seeing a shrink!'

GORGASS DO NOT UNDERSTAND YOUR POSTULATION

IS THAT ANOTHER TYPICAL TRAIT OF HUMAN MEANINGLESS REMARK?

'I am not going to waste my breath on explaining this to you!' he muttered loudly. 'In other words, I'm conserving my energy by removing myself from the need to explain it to you!'

His form of sarcastic humour was lost on the Gorgass, but at least he felt he had scored a point, which, in their perilous position, was a valuable little morale booster.

He walked away from the wall and joined Emma. He was fuming under his breath. *What now? We must be extra careful with these bloody Gorgass!* His process of thought went into top gear. *We gotta focus ourselves and get out of this hell place!*

A hand landed on his shoulder and squeezed it that stopped him in his tracks.

It was Emma offering mutual support. He saw the depth of concern in her eyes and nodded a thanks to her. He looked over at Gillian who was still sitting down but silently bawling her eyes out. Her morale was at rock bottom, and she was clearly not in a good state to linger any longer in this God-forsaken place.

'Let's try and get Gillian out of here', said Andy very quietly to Emma. He had regained his composure and, what was becoming apparent, his natural leadership. 'The sooner, the better for her, and it will be less of a drag on us'.

'I don't have any issue with that!' whispered Emma and nodded.

She looked at the wall and said with signs, 'Gorgass, how soon can we get Gillian back to Earth with your message?'

EFFECTIVE FROM NOW

'Now?' She threw her head back in surprise. 'That soon!'

'Okay, let's do it then', said Andy.

As he spoke the words, the wall furthest from where they were standing, like the previous instance, started to progress through the familiar process of apparently melting. In a short moment, the wall had disappeared into the floor, exposing another new room. In the middle of it was the drone. It was lying on its back on the floor with its belly fully opened and exposing a human-sized empty space. Though it was on its back in what appeared to be a submissive posture, its presence was extremely intimidating to them. They knew its extraordinary capabilities only too well.

Emma walked slowly to the drone with her eyes darting about and searching out for that foreboding tentacle. She was concerned about its injecting tactics. But she could not see anything that would have alarmed her. It was just sitting like a harmless giant seal on its back waiting to have its belly tickled. She looked at the wall and with her index finger, pointed at Gillian and then at the drone.

'Should she go into that cavity?'

OBLIGE

She sighed. 'Okay'.

She walked to the spot where Gillian was kneeling and praying fervently. She knelt next to her, put her arm around her, and squeezed gently.

'I feel for you, and like you, I'm aghast at what's happened to Rahman. That was a dreadful thing. But the main thing is are you okay? Are you up to going back to Earth to deliver the supremely important message to whichever top people on which we agree?'

Gillian said nothing. She was totally disoriented and displayed no reaction to Emma's comments. With tears still flowing down her cheeks, Gillian looked up at her. 'I know I'm supposed to have become immune to all human sufferings and death as I did with my humanitarian aid in Mongolia, but this! Perhaps it was the immediacy that I simply wasn't prepared for!'

Emma struggled to understand what she was saying through the sobbing, which made lipreading much more incoherent, but she got the gist of it, however.

She said slowly, 'Gillian, I know it's hard to control emotions following what has happened to Rahman . . .'

Gillian interrupted her and made a conscious effort to pull herself together and looked at Emma. 'There was absolutely no need for them to kill him!'

This time Emma could lipread her full face more readily. 'That's true—these Gorgass can be real bastards, and I wouldn't trust my life with them at all'.

Emma nodded slowly. 'B ut can we agree that sooner you get back to Earth, the better opportunity for you to redeem our predicament'.

'I suppose so'.

'Then it's imperative that we can rely on you to make sure Rahman didn't die in vain. Can we?'

Gillian took a deep breath and then scrambled to her feet, wiped her tears, and said, 'Okay, let's do it!'

'Good!'

Emma forced an unwilling smile to encourage the distraught nun. They glanced in unison at the drone. It was simply inert. It did not have a threatening appearance as they'd experienced from their first encounters. They took a deep breath and started walking slowly over to the drone.

* * *

Col Thomas Cooper was introduced to the National Security Team in the Oval Office by the president, surely the most influential set of people for such a purpose in the world.

'I asked him to advise me regardless and whenever he had any update on the alien spaceship. Okay, Thomas, go ahead'.

'Of course, ma'am!' He walked energetically to the other side of the room and using his personal controller, switched on the large TV screen on the wall. A few touches later, a new image of a spaceship filled the screen. 'You know the world is now aware of it and recording any new developments made in, by, or around it. Watch this: It was recorded about 10 minutes ago via the Thirty Metres Observatory based at Mauna Kea in Hawaii', looking down at the team comprised of Secretary of State John Campbell, CIA Director Richard Wagner, Secretary of Homeland Security Kim McCloud.

They also had a videoconferencing link with the chief of National Guard.

As they all watched very attentively, Cooper indicated a magnified image of the hatch on the side of the enormous craft. A whitish object ejected was immediately recognisable as a loosely clothed mannequin with arms and legs flailing about aimlessly. It drifted slowly until it disappeared. Cooper replayed the image twice to the stunned viewers before turning to face them.

'Correct me if I am wrong, but that man was dressed like an Arab?'

McCloud observed, and Cooper replied, 'Yes, it does look like that. However, to be certain, we will need a closer re-examination, and it may take a little while. But at this point, we should assume it's factual'.

'Have we found out the identity of this man?' Pres Rachel Wallace pointed her finger at the screen.

'Not yet'. Cooper shrugged. 'Taking into consideration we do have uncoordinated and unvalidated reports of people being abducted all around the world, and unless these pictures are made public and someone recognises the corpse, I do not think it is significant'.

'But the point is, regardless of whoever has been abducted', Wallace said, grim-faced, 'they do not deserve to end up being murdered and discarded like so much space dross. It amounts to butchery without any justification'.

'Looks like that', Wagner confirmed and then asked, 'Any progress made by SETII on contacts with extraterrestrials?' He was referring to the organisation, the Search for Extraterrestrial Intelligence Institute.

'Afraid not, despite of repeated efforts to establish any simple communication, including all types of radio wavelengths, but so far, no response'. Cooper replied dejectedly.

'But don't forget our respective computers would probably be incompatible, and reconfiguration takes time'. Continued Cooper, he was trying to sound optimistic.

'They must have the means to engage with us, but they choose not to do so. Therefore, they simply don't want to know us. In which case, why in the name of Hades, have they been orbiting us for so long?' cut in Wagner.

'Considering the history of mankind, whenever there was no recognisable communications channel, or government in the first instance of contact, we, since Adam was a lad, simply went in and occupied territories without heeding the interests of the natives. Is that what we can most logically expect?' Campbell reinforced Wagner's conclusions.

Then President Wallace said in a tone that signalled she'd brook no more speculation, 'Enough! Let me run down where I think we are. One, we're assuming we are dealing with a hostile alien. Two, they have undoubted and probably superior technical abilities. Three, these major facts lead me to believe, therefore, that we have to take pre-emptive action and defend our world before they do. Time to take our gloves off and respond in a hostile language that they understand'.

The atmosphere in the room became extremely tense. The president decided to say nothing more. She wanted everyone to take their time contemplating the gravity of the situation. She let the atmosphere build for a short while before breaking the silence.

'I gather you are all in agreement with me that this threat to our beloved country and the world is unprecedented, so we need to put the state of DEFCON to level to number'—she held her steely gaze on the TV screen—'2!'

Without a pause, she looked at McCloud and then rounded at each of her individually selected lieutenants. 'Think it's time to start using our strategic planning operations centre'.

'Yes, ma'am, immediately!'

They all started to make their way down to the SPOC, which was located deep underground below the White House. Its presence was suspected by a few, but the actual location is known to very few. The access was secured with the most up-to-date identification scanning devices. It was always manned. The holographic facilities were limited to ten people at any one time. It had full emergency communication channels with all major international allies via their own emergency command centres.

The president suggested opening communications with the closest allies but questioned adding other countries to the list, those with rocket-launching capabilities.

'That would be Brazil, New Zealand, and recently, Australia. Makes sense to include France as it brings French Guiana to the party and it's involved with the European Space Agency'.

'I concur with your way of thinking', Campbell responded. 'But Germany is also already involved with ESA, so why not invite Germany?'

'Make it so'.

'Which of those countries have nuclear capabilities? What are you planning?' Cooper enquired.

Wallace shot a cold look at him. 'I think it's time to show them something that will make them think twice when trying to hurt us or holding us to ransom'.

'Are you going ahead with firing missiles armed with nuclear warheads?' There was a grave concern in his eyes.

'Something like that, but treat it as a warning shot across their bow. We need to establish some form of deterrent that will cause much greater consideration before treading on our toes'.

'A good way of jolting them into opening up communication with us'. Cooper saw some sense in President Wallace's way of reasoning.

Then Pres Rachel Wallace stood up and walked up to the large TV screen and gazed stony-eyed at the spaceship and whispered to herself, 'Watch this space, you're not getting away with it'.

* * *

'Excuse me, Gillian, don't you have a G-phone with you?' It stands for flexible glass phone, the most recent system of mobile communication. She shook her head.

'No worry'. Emma took out her pen. 'May I borrow this for a moment?' And she proceeded to pull the nun's white cowl away from the nun's head, exposing her short cut hair. 'Can I write down the list of materials on this?'

Gill looked up at her and nodded, and Emma began to jot down the list of materials that Gorgass had made. She was glad she had a remarkable memory and that what she was writing also should be checked by Andy and the Gorgass who were observing the proceedings through the wall.

'There you are!' She admired her handiwork as Gill replaced her habit. 'That should do the trick. Just show it to anyone'.

'Who?'

'Anyone in such a commanding position that you think will listen to you'.

'Anyone? Anywhere? Anyplace?'

'Yup. Anyone you feel is truly trustworthy and, above all, will have the power and ability to make things happen and will protect you and all humanity'.

There was a period of silence as she contemplated the awesome prospects facing her. After deep thought, she came back to the reality of their position. 'I think I know'. She had finally come to her decision.

'So where would you like to go and to whom will you approach?'

'The pope'.

'Sure, why not! As he is the leader of your religion, you will have good credibility'. Emma looked at the wall. 'She wants to go to the Vatican. Can you take her there?' she signed again, but this time she used the finger-spellings, 'V-A-T-I-C-A-N'.

ORIENTATION OF LOCATION INPUT REQUIRED

'Then can you please show me the image of Earth? I will point out the location'.

OBLIGED

A new image of Earth loomed into full view across the whole space of the wall. Emma scanned it for a moment and realised she was viewing the vast blue of sea, the Pacific. 'No, the other side of Earth, please'.

Surely the image of the Earth shifted slowly until it became dark. She frowned and realised it was night-time. She could see lots of city lights but took a while trying to familiarise the outlines marked by the lights. She found it and took a few steps towards the wall and pointed at the region of Europe. 'Can you please magnify that area slowly and with sunlight on it?'

The familiar brownish and greenish image of Europe appeared before them.

Her index finger touched the wall.

'Please magnify that area'.

At her prompting, the image kept enlarging until the unmistakable image of Italy came into full view, following further directions from Emma, by Rome and eventually narrowed down to the place in question: The Vatican.

Gillian Lee nodded in appreciation. Her eyes glistened again with a different sort of emotion. To meet His Holiness was totally unexpected and an experience of a lifetime she never thought she would ever achieve.

'Is that possible?' Emma took a step backward.

FULLY ATTAINABLE

YOUR CHOICE TO OBTAIN MOST EFFICIENT CONTACT

'Are you ready?' Emma looked at the drone and took a hold of Gillian's elbow gently. 'Let's go now'.

Once they were over at the drone, Gillian peeped nervously into the opened cell-like cavity. 'Have I gotta go in there?' She was clearly uneasy at the size of the space she needed to enter. 'It's so claustrophobic! I am not sure if I can cope with it?'

Emma did her best to reassure her. 'Don't forget we have already been in one of these things to get here. They will want you to get back to Earth safely. Otherwise, why would they have brought you here?'

HENCE THE REASON YOU NEED TO BE ANAESTHETISED

The Gorgass had clearly been following the signing dialogue from Emma.

'As part of fulfilling your energy-efficiency requirement?' Andy chuckled.

YOUR POSTULATION CORRECT

STATE OF ANXIETY INCREASED RATE OF BREATH RESULTING IN INTENSIFICATION OF CONSUMPTION OF OXYGEN

'Why can't you install some bottles inside the drone for a supplementary supply of oxygen or air?'

EXTRA WEIGHT INEFFICIENT

He said nothing but sighed. *Well, I should have known better.* He looked at Gillian and nodded. 'Would you be okay with it? Are you prepared to be anaesthetised?'

'Seems I don't have a choice, do I?' She resigned herself to the notion that it was necessary for her to be anaesthetised. She lifted her leg over and sat squarely in the cavity. She closed her eyes and lifted her arm and pulled back her clothing, exposing her forearm. 'Get it done over with'. She prayed.

A hole opened in the ceiling, and out of it came a long snake-like tentacle, sliding towards Gillian and stung her on her arm. She flinched slightly.

'That wasn't painful as I thought'. She rubbed her arm and laid back snuggly into the coffin-sized cavity. 'Okay, I'm ready, take me to the Vv . . .' She couldn't finish her sentence as she was already comatose.

The shutter on the drone slid shut. Immediately, the wall glazed, and the drone was isolated. Immediately, the drone slid sideways into the wall, which had become flimsy and liquidised, absorbing the whole drone. It had engulfed it as effortlessly as if it was submerged into a pool. It was all done within moments, and the efficiency left the two remaining prisoners wide-eyed.

'Time for it to travel there?' Andy enquired.

16 HOURS 26 MINUTES IN YOUR EARTH TIME

'What the hell are we going to do during that time?'

WAIT

'For what?'

YOUR NEXT ASSIGNMENT

He sighed. 'It's gonna be a long wait'.

* * *

Cooper's own communication device had alerted him to another new movement seen on the spaceship. 'Hey, something has come up!'

He looked at the TV screen. 'Computer, playback the new movement detected on the alien spaceship!'

All eyes were already focused on the screen. Lo and behold, they could see an object discharged from another larger hole. Instead of a human form that they feared to see, they were surprised that it had a different form, like a large fat torpedo.

'Must be a drone of some kind!' Wagner conjectured.

'Keep track of that object!' Wallace wasn't asking. She was instructing.

'It's gonna be difficult but possible, as long as we get full cooperation amongst all countries with their tracking capabilities', suggested McCloud.

'Well, make it so!' the president instructed. 'The fate of this Earth rests in our hands!'

'Well, I'm making a start on inviting our international friends to join us in strategic planning'.

She nodded in approval and glanced at the various multi-screens and took a deep breath and sighed inwardly. 'May God help us'.

* * *

Next Day

Cardinal Marcello was sitting on a baroque-style bench, his favourite spot located somewhere deep within the gardens of Vatican City. He was taking advantage of the privacy that could be found with over 50 acres of rolling space, urban gardens, and parks, making up more than half of the papal enclave and is owned by the pope.

To the rear of the bench was an enclosed area surrounded by a thick but well-manicured hedge. In front of it, he could enjoy beautifully manicured lawns rolling down a gentle slope for several hundred yards until they were interrupted by a dense rhododendron hedge. As it was late spring, the flowers were out in full blossom, giving a blaze of colours and fragrances.

Whenever Marcello decided to meditate, he always chose this favourite spot, which he found so tranquil. He loved the sound of bees buzzing around nearby, and he found the whole atmosphere spiritually uplifting. He took a glance at his tablet.

He read the headline news: *Drones and ET's Spaceship-- Link Established.* The title blazed across the viewing screen, with a subheading, reading, *'Apart from Andrew and Emma, how many other abductees out there have been actually snatched?'*

So finally, the cat is out of the bag! He cast his mind back to the fateful and heated meeting held a few weeks previously. He had known it would only be a matter of time. He felt anger in his heart. He knew why. *That Antichrist David Bridgewater had managed to cast doubts on our deeply held beliefs! He had sowed the seeds of distrust and mocked us in the seat of the Holy Father's administration! What effrontery! There must have been a rupture in the secret link from Chile as well!*

He looked at a bee hovering lazily around the flower blossoms a few feet away.

Bridgewater may have managed to sow some seeds of doubt and damaged the credibility of the church's teachings, one way or another, but the scale of this news is horrendous. He looked again at the tablet. *That spaceship is not helping us! Surely it will cast some more unwarranted doubts in people's minds to question our God's existence.*

He closed his eyes and took a deep breath, enjoying the flower's fragrance.

This calls for some form of damage control to be installed! But how?

He noticed that the buzzing was becoming more intrusive, probably that bumble bee flying too close to him. At first, he ignored it. Then the noise really started to irritate. *Surely not because of bees?*

He glanced around trying to get a fix on the source of the buzzing. He realised he could not as the noise was coming in from different directions, and it was getting louder. He shielded his eyes with his hand and looked up. His heart skipped a beat—there was a drone.

It was moving slowly into his full view, a hundred metres to his front, looking terrifyingly menacing. He moved his free hand and instinctively grabbed his pectoral cross.

O merciful Lord, please preserve me! He was rooted to his seat, feeling totally terrified. *What am I going to do?*

The drone continued to lose height, with fins constantly changing angles as it lowered itself accurately towards a spot squarely in the middle of the lush green lawn on which it landed softly.

Marcello watched it, dumbstruck. *What next?*

Suddenly, there was high-pitched whining intruding on his awareness, coming not from the drone itself, but from another source, far away from another direction.

He started looking in the direction of the new source of noise, an additional and yet unidentifiable distraction for him.

A moment later, the serene tranquillity of the scene was shattered by two unmanned remotely piloted weapons screaming towards him at full throttle.

They were of the latest-generation drones, named Raptors, produced by Americans for their air force. The design was a combination of

Lockheed Martin F-22 and pilotless Reapers but included a number of other features of highly classified technology, including the latest titanium/carbon alloys resulting in a supreme lightweight/strength ratio. Their appearance, being apparently pilotless, was hugely menacing, and being in black, gave an overall sinister impression. Their size was at least triple that of the drone of the extraterrestrials. They had been scrambled from a military airfield nearby in Italy in response to the alert triggered by their base radar.

As Marcello watched, transfixed, they swept in towards him; the alien drone, suddenly, with its fins whining loudly, shot up vertically, high into the blue sky.

He was terrified, but he could only watch the gyrations with his jaw hanging open in astonishment.

The Raptors banked in unison before they swerved steeply upward and vanished into the wake of the drone. They had been triggered to engage the mysterious unidentified flying object, which seemed to be heading towards the Vatican, and if possible, bring it down.

With their superior speed, it did not take long before they had a drone in full view. The afterburners were switched off, and they slowed down to match the speed of the drone. The silver radome located in the front nose section of the Raptors housed the multi-aspect sensors and state-of-art video cameras. These compact electronic devices were constantly twitching and rolling as they tracked every movement made by the drone, as if they were literally sniffing their quarry.

* * *

Thousands of miles away at Edward Air Force Base in California, two youthful-looking men in US Air Force military uniform were sitting in front of a large screen. Around them were a variety of arrays of technology. These were the pilots of the two Raptors controlling the two Raptors far away in Italy. They were manipulating joysticks in their right hands whilst their left hands were manipulating, with great dexterity, the banks of switches. They were watching their screens intently, with live images streaming in from the pilotless Raptors.

'I have a target'. The first pilot's voice stated in a matter-of-fact drawl. 'But I cannot get my heat-seeking missile to lock on it. The heat from the target is too diffused'.

'Use radar-guided missiles or cannons', commanded Captain Harrison. He was standing behind the two operators. 'But best use canon to bring it down'.

'Aye, sir'. The first operator nodded.

Few steps further behind Harrison stood Aaron Schmidt, the secretary of defence. His face was taut and apprehensive. He was unsure what to expect on engaging a completely unfamiliar target. He then issued a cautionary command to Captain Harrison. 'Can you be a bit circumspect and observe the behaviour of the drone at least initially as we really do not yet know if it has picked up another hostage or if it has delivered one back to us?'

'Sir', responded the senior operator, 'it looks as though we will have our work cut out to even track the target as it seems to be able to move at the limit of our Raptor's speed. I will try to nudge it with wingtips and get it away from land and head for the sea for a softer landing, but that is a hell of a task!'

'Okay, do that, and if you take an operational decision to shoot, I will back you up. Just and make sure it can be brought down to an unpopulated area or sea'.

'Affirmative'.

The second pilot was manipulating the joystick of his Raptor with great dexterity, and it was flying hard to keep up with the lead Raptor.

* * *

The drone sensed the two aggressive objects were closing in behind it, and its artificial intelligence flight control made a dramatic manoeuvre to escape from the threats conceived on the pilot's screens. It made a dramatic flip into a flying backward position with a laser device extended from its nose cone. This sudden movement has startled the first operator who reacted instinctively with his finger on the firing button. He sensed that the reaction was aggressive. The cannons on the Raptor erupted with a short burst of fire but missed as the drone skipped sideways. The Raptors swerved violently, trying to follow the extraordinary ability of the target drone. It had managed to follow narrowly and stick to the flight path of the drone.

The drone was flying backwards, then swerving sideways, then vertically. It was trying to sense human occupancy inside the Raptors but could not. It realised that the flying objects that were chasing after it were also unmanned. It started flying even more erratically to try to shake the Raptors off its tail.

'Oh boy, it's proving really tough to get a lock on!' the leading operator exclaimed. He knew the time lapse of one second delay of radio communication between Italy and America was not playing to his advantage. 'Putting it on autopilot!'

He flicked a few switches. He was adjusting the instructions to his Raptor to try and lock on the drone and get it to link up with its flight controls automatically.

The colour on the frame of the TV screen clicked in a different colour, indicating it had been switched into an automatic mode. A visionary indicator circle could be seen locking on the image of the drone. He eased his grip on the joystick. He punched another button, and the two heat-seeking missiles were ejected, unarmed, from the Raptor, and they fell harmlessly into the sea. He wanted to make his Raptor slightly lighter, giving it optimum speed and making it a little more manoeuvrable.

He looked at the other operator and nodded. 'You should try that!'

The second operator went into the same procedures by engaging his Raptor to fly on auto mode and ejecting the heat-seeking missiles.

'Done!' He smirked. 'Okay, let's try to splash it!' He kept his finger hovering over the firing button.

* * *

The two Raptors suddenly flew in perfect formation with the drone at the 'V' point. Whenever the drone dropped down sharply or swerved hard, the Raptors danced with it effortlessly. It was now a classic form of dogfight made between the drone and the Raptors—aliens versus earthlings. The drone sensed it and understood the dynamic of the Raptors flying behind in its wake. It braked hard and flipped backwards towards the Raptors and dived under one of them. Instantly, both

Raptors flicked out four large spoilers on their wings to act as air brakes to execute a dramatic 360-degree manoeuvre to maintain their pursuit. They severely stressed the structures of their wings, which were creaking brought about by forces way beyond their design concepts. It was fortunate there were no pilots in these craft as they would never have been able to withstand the colossal g-forces generated and that the aerobatics on display would have maimed or even killed them.

A few seconds after, burners engaged in unison with the air brake spoilers snapped shut into their housings, and they were back on the trail of the drone and continued dancing and waltzing with it.

The drone realised it could not shake them off. It scanned the Raptors for their structural weakness. Quickly, it fired off a few seconds' burst of a high-density laser beam at the leading Raptor, focussing on the radome located at the very front of the Raptor's nose, retaliating aggressively for the first time.

'Oh shit!' said the operator as the screen went blank.

With reflex thinking, he punched another button, and instantly, a new series of images came alive on the screen. It was almost an identical image, differing only slightly off centre. He had linked up with the second Raptor's live video feed into his screen. Both were now relying on the second machine's multispectral sensors.

'Act now!' Captain Harrison gave the order for the operators to start shooting. 'Before it can disrupt the second Raptor's sensors!'

'Let me get it to edge sideways into your pathway!' The first operator pressed the firing button.

The leading Raptor sent a short burst of a few rounds deliberately slightly off the drone. It was intended to herd the target sideways into the pathway of its partner.

It did the trick. A split second later, the cannon on the second Raptor erupted.

The spray of explosive shells was all around the drone until one exploded into one of the three propulsion fins on the drone. The single hit contained sufficient destructive force to be terminal. The fin disintegrated quickly, unbalancing and killing the drone. Instantly, it flipped over and went into a spiral dive with the two victors following hard behind it to ensure its termination.

A moment later, the drone managed to stabilise itself by using extra thrust from the two remaining fins, but it was still severely disadvantaged for speed and manoeuvrability. It had lost its ability to continue the battle on equal terms with its opponents. The Raptors circled as the drone started to break up. It slammed into the Tyrrhenian Sea.

The victors circled around the point of impact, signalling images of success to their controllers in their remote centre in the United States. 'We have a splashdown!' they exulted.

The second operator turned to the captain and in a somewhat subdued tone, asked, 'But what has happened to the body which was assumed to be inside the drone?'

There was concern on his face. 'Have we killed someone?'

Aaron Schmidt stepped forward and squeezed lightly on both operators' shoulders. 'Discard that idea, just treat it as part of collateral damage'. He smiled. 'It cannot be helped, but if it is of any consolation, I'm going to mention your names to the president. Congratulations to you both on a job well done'.

* * *

'Aye, I saw everything'. President Wallace was nodding at Aaron on the TV screen in her command bunker. 'Well done, boys! The world will be grateful for their actions. We owe it to them both!'

She glanced up at Cooper who was standing nearby and smiled. 'Please arrange a live press release now! I'm going to announce this excellent news!'

'Yes, madam, will do so!' Cooper nodded at once. 'And we're gonna play these recorded videos as part of boosting the public's confidence!' He walked away and stopped after a few steps with a look at her. 'Are we still going ahead with the idea of inviting other people into our holographic meeting room?'

'Nothing's changed!'

She looked at the large TV screen, where she had watched all the actions being played out and sighed with relief. 'One thing that has been proven to us is that the extraterrestrials are clearly not that invincible! So far!'

'Yeah! Without a doubt, that concept will instil confidence in all other countries to share and collaborate with us on using nuclear capabilities!'

Wallace leaned back in her chair and smiled wryly. 'I hate to say it, but indeed, you're spot on! That's the spirit!' She looked at the TV screen once again. 'This will hype up our playing card of observable strengths to get them to rethink their strategy or whatever their reason for coming here in the first place!'

Cooper said nothing and exited the room. He had only a few words ringing in his mind: *They're not that invincible!*

* * *

Marcello was still standing with his hand shielding his eyes watching the sky intently as he had been for the last ten minutes. He was in awe of the intense low-level dogfight being fought out briefly around in his district before they went away in the direction of the sea. He waited for a few minutes after they disappeared and started to walk away. *I can't believe that out of all the places, some sort of aerial battle has taken place right here above the Vatican!*

He bowed in deep thought, oblivious to the surroundings. Suddenly, he jerked his head back and hit his chest with his clenched fist. He shuffled a few steps further before collapsing onto his knees. His face went white with shock, and he held out his trembling hand and touched a shapeless heap on the grass.

Is this a sign from God?

It was the warm skin of the nape of an unconscious woman wearing a nun's habit.

A nun?

CHAPTER 21

The Virus Strike

Emma Wilson and Andy Nelson had not exchanged a single word for a while.

With the unasked-for input from the Gorgass, they had a full wall-to-wall dramatic display of the aerial dogfight between the drone and the Raptors. They had been watching hypnotically the extraordinary manoeuvres the drone made in its attempts to evade the Raptors. They gasped involuntarily together at the climax when the Raptors had finally clipped the fin of the drone, sending it into the sea, sending up a huge plume of water.

The viewed scene had shifted sideways and zoomed down to a tiny black figure amongst the greenery of the garden of the Vatican. They could make it out to be a human figure walking towards another apparently lying on the grass, and they recognised it as Gillian. She was inert, showing no signs of life.

Now as they watched, the upright human outline managed to lift her for several hundred metres before two more joined it to provide assistance with carrying Gillian towards the buildings.

'Looks like Gillian might be okay, the first part of her mission accomplished.

Has she survived? Is she in safe hands?' Andy and Emma looked at each other, seeking reassurance. 'But that was a hell of a dogfight!'

Suddenly, the video images faded away quickly, only to be replaced by the unmistakable text Gorgass flashed before their eyes.

ARE HUMANS THAT RELENTLESSLY HOSTILE QUESTION

DECIMATING GORGASS DRONE NOT LOGICAL AND COUNTERPRODUCTIVE

UNIT GREEN REQUIRED TO DECIPHER THEIR MOTIVATION

'Search me!' Andy raised a questioning eyebrow at Emma. 'I admit I wasn't expecting any unwarranted aggression as those Raptors showed. What in the hell were they trying to achieve?'

She responded quickly, 'I think that it was probably something to do with Rahman's demise'.

'How come?' He shot her a searching look.

'I wouldn't be surprised if the defence powers must have seen him ejected out of this spaceship'. She looked at him quizzically. 'From his obvious death, they must have reckoned this spaceship to be hostile. Don't forget the powers that behave almost nothing on which to act based on concrete or scientific evidence. They probably do not yet know that we are up here, and they certainly have absolutely no understanding of what we know and how we have created a system of communication. That is crucial!'

'Perhaps you're right', Andy agreed. 'They're not taking any chances. Furthermore, they fear what they don't understand. Attacking Gillian's drone was probably what they considered to be a pre-emptive strike?'

'Then we need to reassure the Gorgass that this must be a one-off accident', she continued reading the text on the wall.

'I concur with your way of thinking'. He rubbed his neck. 'Let's try and convince them to try some sort of positive action, something as a way of winning trust'.

'But again, I still feel they and our people on Earth are seriously disadvantaged with zero availability of any *practical* communication system in place between us', Emma signed passionately so the ever-watching Gorgass might read her message, even though she was apparently signing and talking to Andy. She was always acutely aware of any communication misunderstandings throughout her everyday life.

She treated it as her own cross to bear.

'There is no doubt that the aerial battle occurred before Gillian was picked up. Therefore, she could not possibly have communicated in any way either that she had been on the spaceship or that she knew that the aliens were seeking some sort of deal for their supplies from Earth. We do not know how far the message delivered by Gillian has been communicated as we, that is you and I, and the Gorgass have had no feedback. The powers that be on Earth obviously have not had any real international dialogue and to what level of decision-making has been reached'.

'It doesn't make sense for the Gorgass to discard the opportunity to strike up an opportunity for direct communication with Earth'. Whilst she was speaking, she synchronised the words constantly with her hands. 'Once they do that, they'll be able to know the particular reason for their drone being destroyed by people on Earth'.

'Yep. We've got an assortment of large and small radio telescopes scattered all over our world'. Andy mirrored his agreement with Emma with signs and speech. 'By now, they should be able to decipher our interstellar messages or mathematical languages'.

He looked at the wall. 'Hey, Gorgass, did you follow our conversation?'

AFFIRMATIVE

'Well, would you explain to us your reluctance to link up with our radio communication systems?'

NON-EXISTENCE OF CONFIGURATION EXISTS BETWEEN HUMAN VERBAL LANGUAGES AND GORGASS OCULAR LANGUAGES

IT TAKES TIME TO DIAGNOSE AND CALIBRATE OUR COMPUTERS TO DECIPHER YOUR LANGUAGE

'But you've already established an effective communication mode with us?'

Andy pointed at Emma's translator device.

ACKNOWLEDGED

COMMUNICATION MODE ALREADY IN ADVANCED STAGE WITH NO FURTHER MODIFICATION REQUIRED

'But why not?' He shrugged. 'At least you can have a further opportunity to establish an improved means to negotiate and gauge potential results about to be conceived with people on Earth?'

UNIT BLUE ALREADY IN POSITION TO CONVEY OUR REQUIREMENTS PLANS

GORGASS COMMUNICATION SYSTEM USING EARTH PEOPLE TO NEGOTIATE ALREADY ESTABLISHED

WHY NO RESPONSE

TIME IS AN ESSENTIAL COMPONENT OF GOOD PROGRESS AND LOGIC

Andy squared his shoulders and faced the Gorgass.

'When you want to deal with the inhabitants on Earth, you have to realise that there are many, many different groups of humans, and they all have different interests. It is almost impossible for the different groups to agree to one policy. There must surely be time allowed for the communication of your requirements to be made amongst all these disparate factions on Earth. You've got faith in Gillian, or unit blue, as you prefer, to achieve the desired result you and we are looking for, but what will happen to me and Emma then?' Andy conjectured. 'For what purpose will you still need us here?'

PRECAUTION AGAINST FURTHER FAILURE

'Huh? Like insurance?' He pointed at Emma and himself and said with suspicion, 'But should Gillian have succeeded, then would it not be energy-inefficient to keep us here anymore. You would throw us into space, discarding us like you did Rahman?'

Emma's eyes glistened with emotion as she watched her colleague's impassioned discussion. There was an uncharacteristically long pause.

UNIT RED POSTULATION . . .

Another long pause and it was exceedingly psychologically unnerving for the humans.

LOGIC AND FACTUAL

'In a way, I am hoping Gillian's mission hasn't delivered any positive results!

That will save us!'

Andy sucked a long deep breath with a sickening feeling to his stomach and squeezed Emma's shoulder. 'Let's keep our wits about us. Think logically and find a solution to save our lives!'

There was a long silence between them as they were contemplating that, sooner or later, they could no longer be around. The possibility of returning to Earth was now extremely dubious. A big black depressing cloud was forming over their heads. Finally, Andy sank into the floor as if he was resigned to the idea that he and Emma were living on borrowed time. *What can we do about it?* He looked up at the wall and considered the options. *How in the hell can we make ourselves indispensable?* He looked at Emma and then at her personal translator.

Why can't they be grateful for Emma's invaluable contribution towards cracking the communication barriers that existed in the first place during the early stage of encounters between them and us?

Then he realised that gratefulness was a human emotion, and that would mean nothing to the aliens. The Gorgass would only respond to anything that would benefit their enterprise.

He looked at Emma and mouthed exaggeratedly, 'Watch my lips, I'm not using my voice'.

Emma nodded in response.

'We'll need to know their level of commitment, especially if they will honour their agreement made with us'.

He then started using a crude form of British Sign Language, which was strikingly similar to Emma's AUSLAN. 'If they have any form of understanding that progress will be made if we can achieve a balance or equal benefits that will save our necks!'

Emma said nothing but nodded nonchalantly. He turned to the wall in a pensive manner before breaking the silence.

'Seems we don't have much choice in this matter, do we? But at least can you assure us that you will hold to the agreement you've made with us with regard to Gillian's cooperation in delivering your message to the people on Earth?'

THE PROBES ARE ALREADY PRIMED WITH VIRUS AND ABOUT TO DESPATCH IMMEDIATELY ONCE OUR POSITION IS ALIGNED WITH AUSTRALIA

'Already? I have to say I'm mighty impressed!' Andy's eyebrows raised. 'You are highly efficient!' Then he stood up. 'We can continue to provide knowledge of how communications and our international systems work. This will enable you to obtain the vital supplies you need efficiently. You have already indicated that you would not be able to work in the gravity prevalent on Earth. This means you will need cooperation, not friction, from our planet. *If* we are assured that we will be returned to our planet, we will do the best we possibly can. You have already indicated that you are losing time and need the supplies to be expedited for you on this spacecraft and for your fellow travellers on your other craft. You need our help, but we need your confirmation that we will be returned to our planet unharmed'.

YOUR WINDOW OF OPPORTUNITY FOR ACHIEVING YOUR OPTION IS BECOMING FUTILE ONCE OUR OBJECTIVES HAVE BEEN ACHIEVED

'But your opportunities will disappear without our full cooperation'.

WHAT POSSIBLE OPPORTUNITIES QUESTION

'We will assist you in negotiating with organisations as we have been given unique insight by you as to what you need. Without your continuing access and willing cooperation between us, you will be wasting huge amounts of energy without it being replenished. This will surely not be acceptable to your other space travellers who are dependent on your obtaining supplies for them as well?'

GORGASS INSTRUCT UNIT GREEN TO PROVIDE EXAMPLES AS A MEANS OF DELIVERING YOUR POINT

UNIT GREEN FAILED TO WARN US THE IMPENDING CHANCE OF HOSTILE ENGAGEMENT BY DRONES

'Exactly the point I am making. You didn't ask us about the possibility of dangers in the first place, did you?' Andy shook his head. 'If you had, would you have considered alternative action to minimise the potential damages to your drones? Think about it'.

He paused. He signalled to Emma by putting his thumbs up to indicate that he was hopeful. A new text sequence flashed on the wall.

UNIT GREEN MAKES A VALID POINT BUT NO GUARANTEE YOUR INPUT WILL HAVE SUBSTANTIAL VALUE TO GORGASS

'But all I'm asking is if you can consider extending our right to live as long as you find our source of information beneficial to you. There are always possibilities'.

GORGASS NOT IN POSITION TO SPECULATE ON ANY UNSPECIFIED AND IMPERFECT DATA PROVIDED BY UNIT GREEN

'Why can't you?'

SUCCESS NOT CERTAIN NOR WITH GUARANTEE

'Well, then welcome to a human's version of Murphy's law!' muttered Andy, smiling at Emma with a twinkle in his eye.

GORGASS NOT UNDERSTAND THE INPUT BY UNIT GREEN AND IN NEED OF DECIPHER

'It's a real possibility that anything that can go wrong will go wrong'. He winked at Emma. 'The loss of your drone is a perfect example of how you underestimated our human's unpredictable responses or our technology capability. Therefore, there is even more reason for you to maintain our cooperation. You need us to clarify unforeseen circumstances arising from humanity's complete unpredictability.

Earth's population does not even have a single opinion or policy on any aspect of their existence, except a wish to live, which is exactly what you are seeking for yourselves!

'There's no guarantee that your plan will be carried out flawlessly according to your expectations! Your intentions are not necessarily on the same wavelength with humans!' He shook his head. 'You have already found the dynamics of humans' thought processes somewhat mystifying and bewildering'.

No response was made by the Gorgass. But he kept up the pressure.

'Let us have the opportunity to provide any hypothesis that may explain what has happened to your drone or something else that may happen unexpectedly later on.

'Having expended so much energy in taking us on board your spaceship, you will want to obtain the maximum benefit from this process. To do otherwise would be inefficient. It benefits you to maximise your energy investment by keeping us in a positive mode for the duration of the exchange of material and knowledge between our respective civilisations.

'In return, can we ask you to guarantee returning us back to Earth alive?'

He pointed at Emma and himself. 'Is that too much to ask?'

There was a pause in the flow of dialogue—a worrying time for them. He forced himself to walk around slowly and calmly in a circle but with his mind in turmoil.

A mental image of Rahman floating out in space continued to haunt him. *Will my body ever be returned to Earth or stay floating out in deep space forever? What a dreadful prospect.*

Then finally came the response. He quickly glanced up at the wall.

PROVIDING UNIT GREEN OR UNIT RED CAN DELIVER ANY PLAUSIBLE POSTULATION THAT CAN CONTINUE TO ASSIST GORGASS

GORGASS WILL GRANT UNIT GREEN REQUEST

'Much appreciated!' Andy exhaled deeply. He turned to Emma, grabbing her shoulders. 'Looks like we've been granted a stay of execution as long as we can continue to liaise with them by providing any useful details for their benefit'.

'But still, I cannot help hoping there are some major setbacks with Gillian!'

There was a troubled expression on Emma's face. 'Isn't it imprudent of me to think of that? But you know what I mean. It would emphasise our value to the Gorgass'.

'No shame in mentioning it. It's all part of our survival instinct', he assured her. 'Let's cast pessimistic views aside and start collaborating with them. I think it's essential if we can get them to consider it's in our mutual interest for them to keep us alive!'

He looked at the wall and lifted his head. 'Okay, Gorgass, can you explain how you will proceed with wiping out the rabbits? With how many drones?'

115 DRONES

'Is that all for the size of Australia?' His interest was piqued. 'But from what altitude will they operate, and how will they return to this spacecraft?'

DRONES ARE CONSTRUCTED IN BIODEGRADABLE MATERIALS AND WILL FLY AT THE HEIGHT OF 50 KILOMETRES

DRONES ARE TO DISINTEGRATE AND DECOMPOSE IN THE SEA AFTER USE

Andy's eyes widened. 'So they're practically on a one-way ticket to Earth?

I didn't think you were that green-minded! But what about . . .' His formidable thirst for more scientific information continued.

* * *

Gillian Lee opened her eyes slowly and stared at the ceiling, which was whitewashed. Her groggy mind started to clear, and she realised she was lying in a bed. She did not move and from under her lowered eyelids, realised that a priest in a black cassock was sitting on a chair positioned next to her bed. He was wearing a deep red sash around his waist, with a pectoral cross on his breast. His red skullcap had been removed and rested on a sideboard at arm's length from where he sat. She found his appearance quite intimidating. She stirred, and he realised she was regaining consciousness.

'Hello there. No need to be alarmed as you're safe here', he spoke in Italian.

'You can address me as Cardinal Marcello. Are you okay? Do you want me to get a doctor to check you over?'

There was a puzzled look on Gillian's face, which indicated she did not understand him. He switched to English. 'Can you understand me? I'm not sure which language to use? Maybe you would prefer Chinese?' He based his assumption on her Asian-looking features.

'My native language is Korean, but English will do fine by me as long as it's plain and basic', she responded in English.

'Great!' He repeated his original introduction in English. 'Do you—'

'Where am I?' she interrupted him.

'Oh sorry, you're in one of the staff's residential bedrooms at the Vatican'.

'Vatican!' She sat up too quickly, and immediately, her head started to spin, and she realised she was still wearing her nun's habit. 'How long have I been unconscious?' she asked.

'Not long. I would say 30 minutes'. He glanced at his watch. 'But do you remember how you came here? But for a start, your name? Where do you originally come from?'

'Those dreadful aliens! Are you aware that I've been abducted and taken aboard their starship?' She buried her face in her hands. 'I'm so glad to be back here on Earth! Oh, my name is Gillian Lee'.

'Gillian, please let me assure you're perfectly safe here with me', he replied in a soothing voice and pointed at the door. 'I've placed a Swiss Guard outside your door. I've made sure no one will approach you without my say so'.

She ignored him for a few moments and continued examining the room. It was sparsely furnished and starkly plain in taste. A simple wooden cross could be seen on the white wall opposite her, and she found this spiritually comforting. He saw her smile a bit. *I still can't believe she's been delivered to me out of all the other possible places!* Slowly, an idea came to him. *How feasible would it be if I could manipulate things for mine and my God's advantage?*

'That's okay. I've made sure you're allowed to stay here as long as you want to'.

He patted her leg through the blanket. 'I'm sure you've been traumatised by the extraordinary encounter you've had with the ETs, Gillian? Take your time and tell me about them'.

She nodded but said nothing.

'Then perhaps you wouldn't be ready yet to face the barrage of questions thrown at you by the world's press? Are you?' He smiled slowly. He was trying to win her confidence and increase her dependence on him. 'Let me assure you, as long you're here, you're safe, away from the prying eyes of all the people around the world!'

Again, she said nothing. However, her attitude was becoming more tense.

He sensed it, but he kept up the pressure.

'I understand your predicament, as I too would dread to face all those people, all with cameras focused on you. You will be famous and hounded wherever you go and whatever you do! Imagine that!'

She looked at him with absolute horror developing in her eyes.

'Calm down, Gillian, I can protect you!' he spoke soothingly. 'We believe our God has meant us to meet for a purpose! By the way, would you prefer that I call you Sister Lee?'

'I . . . I suppose so . . . ." she spluttered. "But what am I going to do whilst I'm here?'

'Apart from relaxation and recovering from your extraordinary experience, just do nothing! It will be just like you are gaining absolution in a confession, except you have absolutely no sins to confess. We will just review all the circumstances and experiences together, and I'll help you find the best way forward for you to see what's required to inform the world. I'll act as your communication agent!' Again, he patted her lower leg. 'How would you feel about that? Wouldn't you be more comfortable with this way forward?'

She looked down sheepishly but still said nothing.

Cardinal Marcello smiled. 'But you'll need to tell me everything from the beginning up to now, especially what have you learnt of the reasons for the ETs to come here and what they expect you to do for them'.

'Yes, Eminence, but it's going to be a long and complicated story because I don't really understand many different aspects of what has occurred!'

'Sure, no problem. Take all the time you want, but I'm sure you understand the sooner you fill me in with the facts, the better position I will be in to communicate and help you to deal with them'. He stood up. 'Before you start, how long has it been since you have had any food or drink?'

Gillian lay back and nodded her appreciation. 'I do not understand the time dimension since I last ate or drank, but I feel that the drugs they put into me have left me feeling weak. I am hungry and thirsty and very tired, so I would like some time to myself. You have been very kind'.

He took out his personal communicator and spoke rapidly in Italian. He turned to her and spoke gently to her. 'Of course. Someone will come and see to all your needs, and when you are happy and rested, use my communicator that I will leave you, which is connected only with me, and we will continue'.

Some five hours later . . .

'Okay, let's start. Take your time. Where are you originally from?'

She took a deep breath and started her story. He smiled and nodded earnestly. *Whatever the information I get from her, I'll be the one to filter and broadcast them to the world and put whatever slant on her story that I see fit.* His eyes narrowed slightly in response to a sensation building up inside him. *That means I'm in control of the world! That must be God's intention! I failed to realise until now how wise God is in his wisdom to allow me to act as a credible messenger . . .*

He stopped thinking and started listening to her story.

* * *

Five ports opened on the side of the alien starship, and five drones were ejected simultaneously, followed by a total sequence of 115 drones all dispatched towards Earth or, rather more precisely, to Australia. At a glance, they were all the slightly different designs and colour to the previous drones that were originally used to obtain human samples. These new objects' size was markedly different by being at least three times bigger and were for a completely different purpose.

Their launch was being carefully monitored on the large screen by several people in the oval room.

'Mrs President, that is the most unprecedented view we have of the alien starship!' Dr George Clark shot a perturbed look at Pres Rachel Wallace. 'Seems with the skirmish we've had over in Italy, we've made it worse! We've stirred up a veritable hornet's nest!'

Pres Rachel Wallace quickly responded, not at him, but at Col Thomas Cooper.

'Is the hologram meeting room ready?'

'Yes, it should be in 30 minutes, but expect the meeting to be up and fully operational in an hour'. He inspected his tablet. 'All leaders from nine countries have indicated they'll be there for a full assembly. So let's go there now'.

President Wallace stood up and glanced at Doctor Clark. 'Can you please keep monitoring where in the hell all these drones are going? And keep reporting to me whilst I'm in the hologram room, got it?'

'All of them? At my last count, there are probably more than a hundred of them!'

'The destination of mankind's survival may depend on the availability of accurate details'. She shot a cold look at him. 'Do you have any problem with this?'

'Oh, none at all, ma'am'. George's neck became sweaty. 'It's just I'm trying to coordinate the logistics of getting all the people to report to us what and when they can see them. We have absolutely no idea at present. I'll need to alert all the chains of radar stations to coordinate with one another and start monitoring these new drones'.

'Then get on with it!' she instructed abruptly before walking off with other people following her in wake. 'We need to increase our level of brinkmanship!'

George muttered under his breath, 'All right, for you, ma'am, it's my balls that are in the mangle, and you don't have any to worry about!'

* * *

A chain of perfectly coordinated drones was flying in synchronised flights towards the extreme western part of Australia. At first, they were flying closely together, but as they arrived at the attained height of several kilometres, they started to spread out at intervals of 50 kilometres between each of them.

A contrail of whitish vapour could be seen forming behind each of them. They were essentially a mixture of water vapour condensation and genetically engineered virus. The Gorgass had the virus infused with sulphur hexafluoride gas, which, as the main characteristic of its physical chemistry, apart from being odourless and colourless, was six times denser than the Earth's atmosphere. This would enable the virus to not only spread out far and wide but also sink towards the ground. Once there, it would penetrate any impressions of the ground, including any openings of rabbit burrows.

In a couple of hours, the effect of the virus would start to kick in by conditioning the rabbit's pituitary gland to lock itself into a permanent state of producing and releasing a large dosage of hormones, melatonin, and vasopressin, which conditioned the brain into a comatose state. Another type of virus would also infect the brain by inhibiting any cells that produced neuropeptide hormones responsible for promoting wakefulness. The result would be a constant state of deep sleep without any chance of waking up—an extremely lethal comatose condition.

The effect of it on rabbits became visible immediately as they started to get sleepy and lumbered slowly into a sleeping position. In a few days of not eating nor drinking water, the body masses of the whole colony of rabbits started to wither away until they reached a critical point where their body could not sustain any means of survival. Rabbits cannot endure water deprivation for more than 24 hours, even less during hot weather, without serious health consequences. The outcome would be simply death within two days at the most.

The effect on the rabbits was noticed immediately by the farmers around in Australia after they had been alerted by the news of the drones that had plunged into the sea after more than two days of flying. Their feedback had an enormous impact on the media, sending it into a frenzied state with a consequence of creating a massive fallout of fear amongst the public. Their curiosity as to the reason why the drones had inflicted such a catastrophe only on the rabbits but sparing all other animals had proved too much for many leaders and media to cope with. Was it a threat? For what reason? Was there any threat to humans? Or was it a blessing in disguise? Getting rid of the rabbits has been their number one feral pest for many years? Or was it carried out as part of some sort of diabolical experiment by the extraterrestrials, and for what purpose? Should it be regarded as a hostile or friendly gesture? Or was it a stark warning gesture to say they would do the same thing to humans unless their demands were met?

Whatever it was, they demanded one thing, to be precise, a scientific explanation and soon.

* * *

Back in the Vatican, Cardinal Marcello was back in the room again with Sister Lee. Since he had formally broken the news to the world a few days ago, he was under constant pressure with round-the-clock surveillance imposed on him by the press and, indeed, the scientists. The demand for Sister Lee's exposure to the public and scientific scrutiny was increasing by the minute. Verification if there was an element of scientific truth in his summary of her story, which he narrated more than a few days ago, was not forthcoming. But he stood firm, saying he wanted Sister Lee's request for seclusion and a degree of anonymity to be respected.

But there was another pressure on him from an unexpected sector. It was the pope himself who had insisted if she wanted to see him, then she must waive her right to remain anonymous as the only way of granting some credibility to her story. He said she owed a duty to the world to disclose any vital information to the scientists and leaders if they were to come up with a better understanding of how to deal with the ETs. The essence of gaining knowledge could give them an edge over the ETs.

The survival of the world was the utmost priority, not at her personal whim or quest for personal privacy.

However, on other hand, the pope understood the concept of using the Vatican as sanctuary as sought by Sister Lee. Sanctuary, in any form, is a sacred place to the Catholic Church. No force would ever be permitted by the Catholic Church. The pope insisted Sister Lee could stay indefinitely.

That alone had given Cardinal Marcello some breathing space. He had to consider what next move he could take to keep the wolves at bay. In his metaphoric sense, the wolves were the media reporters. Unfortunately for him, there was an exceptionally large pool of reporters and people that had formed outside the forecourt of St Peter's Square. They had been waiting patiently for any glimpse of the ever-reclusive woman with the name of Gillian Lee. The red-capped cardinal had a natural hostility to them as they were forever at him like a dog for a bone. For a start, they were not satisfied with his source of information as it was clearly lacking in form of coherence and rationality. What they had not realised is he had already withheld a vital piece of information from them.

He had informed them of everything Sister Lee had told him but only up to a point. He had failed to divulge to them the missing and essential part of Lee's extraordinary saga. The shopping list delivered by the ETs was critical. She had given him her white cowl with the list of supplies that were the key to the whole concept of potential cooperation written on it. He had thanked her for it. He then took it from her to his own office. Whilst he was there sitting in his chair, he decided to give it a weighty thought. *What am I going to do with this list of demands by the ETs?* He leaned back. *With all the communication technology at our disposal, yet still, they cannot communicate with us, and they've resorted to sending a puny human as a messenger to deliver the details to us, isn't that strange? Perhaps the ETs are not that sophisticated a race or species that we have estimated them to be?* Then a new idea dawned on him. *If they are not that advanced, then we can defend ourselves with the confidence that we can annihilate them. Totally. And that would give us an opportunity to restore so much of the faith in our God, knowing that it has been declining over the last several years. Our Lord has once again come to our rescue—it was the perfect answer to David Bridgewater!* He looked at the scribbled writing on the white cloth and smiled. *Nah, we don't need it.* He then cast it into a trash bin next to his desk.

Marcello had since then installed additional Swiss Guards outside her room.

They were much beefier in appearance than the other usual guards. These gave 24-hour security. He could not afford any lapse in security as it would have him disadvantaged with no leverage to use against the suspicious world, never mind the extraterrestrials.

A few days ago, he had faced the barrage of questions from the press, and it had taken him more than an hour reading the story off the tablet in his hand in front of the banks of microphones that weighed heavily on the lectern. Whilst he was orating, he had failed to notice one man standing in the sea of reporters directly in front of him. Brett's face had achieved almost superstar status, having one of the most recognisable faces in the world of media, in a matter of a few days since his visit to Hawaii. He had flown into Rome when he heard of the major news breaking out about the woman in question being holed up deep inside the Vatican. He was observing Cardinal Marcello intently. He wanted a chance to lure him into his local TV interview studio. He had not travelled alone as his companion was a very attractive woman, 'the cub reporter' had joined him from his office in Los Angles. It turned out it was a mixture of pleasure and business trip. For her but benefitting him mainly.

Since then, the global situation had taken a turn for the worse with the news coming out of Australia about the decimation of the rabbits, which had raised huge international concern. It did not quench the media's insatiable demands for the latest news; instead, it had created a feeding frenzy.

In the absence of any positive understanding of the assault on the rabbits, there was a growing demand for more positive retaliatory measures to be taken against the extraterrestrials. This was a mirrored viewpoint that many leaders of the world shared as evidenced at the holographic meeting.

* * *

Later that evening, Brett was lying on a lofty king-sized bed in a plush hotel near the Vatican. His travelling companion, Sarah, the cub reporter, was scantily clothed and lying on her back next to him but in an upside-down position. Her feet were stroking his bare chest. They had steamy fornication since they entered the room in the late afternoon. They had thrown themselves at each other in a frenzy brought about by frustration, using sex as an outlet when they had failed to secure an interview with Cardinal Marcello. 'He was one really reclusive bastard!'

'Mmmm . . . So is this what you've promised me? A real Italian adventure?' She was twirling her long auburn hair. Her voice was husky and very alluring. 'If it is, then I've already forgiven you for the treatment you gave me back in our office!'

At this stage, Brett was only half paying any attention to her. His mind was drifting somewhere else. He was trying to find a way of gaining access to Gillian Lee. He knew from gossip gleaned from other sources that Gillian Lee was secluded and under guard, somewhere deep inside the Vatican and away from the public's prying eyes.

Something was bothering him—that Cardinal Marcello. *Why does he need to be so inaccessible? What's he hiding from us?*

He surmised that there were some deliberately created gaps in his version of the story that he circulated to the world about Gillian Lee's plight on her trip to and from the Ets starship. His gut told him there was more to it than met the eye.

Something doesn't add up!

His instinct had never failed him. It was just the same as it had been at the Hilton Hotel. He just knew there's something lacking in credibility with Cardinal Marcello's version of the nun's fantastic story. He felt there was a strong need to have his story checked out and, if possible, verified. He only believed in one thing: nothing but the truth.

He understood, wherever possible, the public needs to be informed accurately.

For too long, the world has been misled and polluted with so much misinformation that the public was becoming very wary of what to believe. They deserve some information, the factual type. *Only if I could gain access to her . . . only just for a few minutes, that is all I need! But how?*

Why would the aliens go to all the trouble to kidnap four humans and send one back and launch a huge assault on the rabbits in Australia?

It was not until Sarah's toes touched his nose that he snapped out of his reverie. 'Huh? Sorry, Sarah, say that again'.

She said, 'So far, we have only had an Italian starter!'

'Well, not really! This is only an I of the real Italian adventure yet to come!'

He grabbed her foot and gave it a soft massage and lifted her limb high to admire her shapely leg.

Suddenly, whilst he was holding her leg, an idea came to him. 'How hungry are you for any juicy news from that female abductee sector?' He was still admiring her leg. 'I've got an idea for a plan on gaining access to her. But unfortunately, I would still need your help!'

She lifted herself and crawled towards him. 'If you are saying there's a bigger adventure out there for me?'—her lips were hovering close to his—'Then I'm yours . . .' She kissed him passionately.

But only for a fleeting moment, until he broke away from her and said, 'Yes, but how far will you be prepared to go, even if it may cause some damage to your professional reputation? That is my real concern!'

'My reputation? What reputation? It's already been severely damaged since I met you!'

He looked into her eyes. 'Then I'll take that as a compliment . . .' He chuckled.

Her devil-may-care attitude aroused him. He grabbed her and wrestled her into a different position on the bed from where they made love again enthusiastically.

And once more an hour later.

* * *

Cardinal Marcello was up again before the crowd of reporters and TV crew in the St Peter's Court. Under the order of the pope, in response to the latest development of the rabbits being wiped out, his instructions were to restore the public's confidence with a plausible explanation for the reason as to why the rabbits were being annihilated.

An hour beforehand to his appearance before the reporters, he had the opportunity to discuss this extraordinary incident with Sister Lee.

"Sister Lee, letting you know I've been getting all the news with all rabbits in the whole of Australia being annihilated, whilst sparing all other animals, isn't that amazing? But I don't recall you telling me anything about this turn of events. Did you know anything about it?'

'Oh, I've forgotten about that! I'm not quite sure what that was really all about, as I wasn't paying much attention to the conversation of Andy, Emma, and the aliens. I did recall Emma having some sort of dialogue about it in return for my being returned to Earth'.

'You mean your task of delivering the list to us? But what has that got to do with this rabbit business?'

He realised the danger of her finding out about the list not being mentioned.

He knew about her finding out what's happening out in the world. After all, there was a TV in her room where she could access the latest news daily. *I gotta find a way of reasoning with her should she ever find that I've withheld that vital piece of information from the world!*

His mind was toying with ideas and any possible plausible justification he could deliver to her. But there was a problem: She had access to TV, which had been installed in her room to counter the monotony of her isolation, though she said she did not watch it that much nor understand what's going on with the world because of the fact the news delivered was all relayed in Italian. She had been offered a 'glasscomm' tablet that could enable her to access other news channels via the Internet in any other language she specified. But she loathed media networks as she found their commercial dynamics not in line with her mindset and teaching. She had been given a glasscomm but had left it on the sideboard collecting dust. She, therefore, had no way of monitoring the information that had been delivered by Marcello. Her only access to the outside world's latest situation was through Marcello. This source of information was manipulated in any way he chose, and she had no way of verifying what was in accord with her message. He knew this but needed to be careful of supplying her any information beyond what he thought she needed to know. He understood, sooner or later, she would find out the truth. Even at the present time, he did not really know how much awareness of the current situation she had.

He did not even really want to ask her as this might provoke her into asking awkward questions.

He decided he just had to try and test her out and see if she was still being kept sufficiently in the dark as he wanted her to be. She broke into his train of thoughts.

'Not sure, Your Eminence, but I think they want to demonstrate their supremacy in the use of genetic engineering that no human has ever been able to match or surpass'.

He sensed a window of opportunity to manoeuvre her. 'Let me clarify this for you, Sister Lee, you mean they're threatening to use this rabbit business as an example of what they could do against humans?'

Sister Lee shot a look of horror at him. 'Then you must warn the world that they are really evil creatures and not to be trusted!'

'Absolutely! I feel it's my duty to warn the world of what these extra-territorials are capable of!'

'But hang on, I think, as long as we can deliver on their requirements, then we should be okay. Better to be on the safe side and heed their demands, isn't that the best way?'

Damn, the List! he thought. Quickly, he reasoned with her, 'Perhaps not!

But don't you think it's more important we need to prioritise it by worrying about the potential threat to our life on Earth than'—Marcello gesturing his hand up in the air—'with their demands! The sooner we get the world to be equipped to safeguard against this biological warfare, then we can worry about the list later! We should be able to argue from a position of strength!'

Sister Lee saw his reasoning and looked down and nodded. She did not want to argue with him further. She was grateful to him for giving her every opportunity to stay in her quarters, out of the limelight. 'I don't want to think any more about it!

So you'd better do what you think best!'

'That's very understandable. No worry, just leave it to me, and I'll think of something to say to the media'. He exhaled a sigh of relief. 'But thanks anyway for your faith in me'.

An hour later, Marcello was now up before the media people once again. He took out his tablet and laid it down on the lectern in front of him and started to read his carefully prepared statement.

'In response to the situation being developed with the rabbits in Australia, I have had the opportunity to discuss this matter in depth with the female abductee to try and find the reason for this extraordinary event. Unfortunately, as expected, it is not the good news that we are hoping to hear'. He looked up briefly and could see a sea of expectant faces looking at him before he continued.

'It is simply their intention to demonstrate their supremacy in genetic engineering. They've started demonstrating and testing it out, our rabbits being one of most populous animals that can be found in every continent, except for Antarctica. That is their first step to be undertaken before carrying out further "treatment" on the human population!'

'Their core reason being what?'

He looked slowly up and found himself looking into Brett's face a few seats away and recognised him. But he kept his place and went on. 'It is solely to eliminate all humans before undertaking the next step of invading and occupying our world.

Our deepest fear of this happening has been affirmed to show how indisputably inadequate we are, whilst they are unquestioningly formidable and superior. At this stage, it seems that short of a miracle, we have no technology to retaliate. I have discussed this with His Holiness for his esteemed guidance on this matter . . .'

He had managed to continue for a few more minutes, summarising his statement before being swamped by salvos of questions aimed at him by the reporters. He was not sure which reporters to choose as they were all practically screaming at him for his attention. He realised only one reporter remained seated in his chair with his arms folded. He recognised him above all others as the one and only Brett Fielding. He lifted his finger and pointed at him. 'I assume you have a question, Mr Fielding?'

Brett smiled and stood up. He was glad his tactic of remaining seated in the chair had paid off. All he wanted was to grab his attention, and he did.

'Your Eminence Marcello, thanks for this opportunity, and indeed, I do have a question!' He looked down at his tablet briefly before locking his eyes with the cardinal. 'The most important question remains to be answered: Why didn't the female abductee use the opportunity to warn us last week about this absolutely monumental threat? Why wait 'til now? Surely it would have given us a critical time window of an extra week for us to consider on how to formulate effective countermeasures against the ETs?'

'You are, indeed, correct in your observation'. Marcello kept his cool. 'But as we all only now know how traumatised she was by her close encounters with these ETs, so it has clearly affected her emotionally'. He looked straight at Fielding and assumed a teacher-like pose dealing with a favourite but naughty student.

'Let me put it this way, any severe psychological trauma can also affect your memory. This includes violence, sexual abuse, and other emotionally traumatic events, which can lead to dissociative amnesia. This helps a person cope by allowing them to temporarily forget details of the event'. Marcello smiled in a superior manner. 'So in many cases, this person has unfortunately suppressed memories of traumatic events until they are eventually recovered sufficiently, ready to handle them. This sometimes, unfortunately, may never occur'.

'Until now . . . ?' Brett smirked. 'How convenient it is! It clearly showed how irresponsibly you are behaving!'

'I beg your pardon!' Marcello kept his cool posture. 'Your point being what?'

'By professional occupation, you are clearly not a psychologist, are you?' There was a sarcastic tone in his voice. 'Who are you to determine her well-being, never mind decide how she should not be entitled to a professional help, such as a counsellor or psychologist?'

'Of course, I'm fully aware of her needs!' Marcello was clearly getting really rattled at the line that this public debate was following. 'It was Sister Lee herself who has declined my offer of professional help!'

'Your offer?' Brett gestured towards Sarah who was sitting next to him. 'Then why not offer her properly qualified psychological professional help? She could reconsider any other offers from another source if she knew they existed?'

This was the prompt that Sarah had been waiting for. But it was not Sarah who had been warming Brett's' bed recently. This was an immaculately groomed professional in a pinstriped business suit. Her naturally fulsome bosom was neatly suppressed.

Her pace of walk was slower than usual to give Cardinal Marcello more time to survey her up close. Her presence was electrifying enough to arrest his response and rendered him speechless. She took out a plastic business card from her breast pocket and slipped it into Cardinal Marcello's side pocket and patted it. 'There you go, please do give this contact card to her. It's up to her to decide whether to contact Brett or me'. Her voice was soft and inviting. 'And you . . . maybe?'

She turned around and walked back again in a slow pace, knowing he would have no choice but to keep admiring her shapely backside swaying so alluringly. Up until now, Marcello had been transfixed hypnotically to his spot and remained unmoving. The vision moved away, and she finally sat down. The hushed atmosphere was punched by a sudden outburst of laughter by the crowd. They had watched everything and thought it was exceedingly hysterical to witness a cardinal having succumbed to his very human nature by allowing himself to be bewitched by a wholesome female person.

Cardinal Marcello was suddenly rattled by the chorus of laughter and found it insulting. He shot a sharp look at Brett as if he was about to shout at him but decided against it. He simply turned his heel and exited quickly. His action had the immediate effect on the crowd as their laughter was even louder.

Only Brett and Sarah were not laughing but smiling a satisfied and victorious smile. They had got him to dance to their tune, unwittingly, by planting the plastic card on him. A sophisticated homing device had been incorporated into this plastic card.

He was hoping Marcello would lead him straight to the female abductee in question. That was his first step of creating a snare. But the next step was how to benefit from the ruse, and that would be even more challenging.

Brett understood that with the current mayhem in Australia, action was required sooner than later.

CHAPTER 22

The Holographic Meeting

Located deep inside the White House, the large room was windowless. There were plenty of lights located in the ceiling, but they were remarkable as they appeared dim, but this was an illusion as there were no shadows. Their design was part of the integrated capability of the whole room. The walls had a black matt finish. Sited in the middle was a large round table, with its colour echoing the same shade as the wall. This was also specifically designed to give optimal holographic imagery.

The striking difference in the layout of the table was that there were only three chairs at the end of the table. The central chair was occupied by Pres Rachel Wallace, between her two lieutenants on either side. Secretary of State John Campbell was sitting on her left side with a large tablet positioned in front of him. Col Thomas Cooper occupied the third seat on President Wallace's right.

There were eight cylindrical glass devices spaced equally around the table.

These glowed with a hint of an eerie bluish colour. Each measured 3 feet in diameter and 4 feet in height. The resulting imagery was of people in spectacular 3D format.

The leaders from each country could be seen individually on each holographic device.

Five bulbous video cameras were seen installed inconspicuously on the ceiling in semicircles and were focussed on the American president. These were transmitted simultaneously to the other collaborative countries, all of which possessed the same layout as this room in the White House. The only difference being that in each of the participating countries, the chair was occupied by its president or prime minister. Subtitles at the foot of each glass cylinder gave out the identity of each person and the country they represented.

The United Kingdom's prime minister, Tony Turnbull, opened the conference by welcoming the members and spoke out with a welcoming bit of humour.

'Sorry that the timing of the meeting does not suit all the members, and I am sorry to get some of you out of bed! Please blame our friend, the American delegate! However, please let me remind everyone that under the constitution outlined for the use of this international holographic conferencing, we take turns to chair and facilitate the meeting according to the year. As it is 2028, it falls on me to chair this meeting'. He looked around at the others and continued. 'The seriousness of the situation facing the whole of our civilisation is unprecedented, and above all, we do not seem to have any clear view of the intent, benign or adverse. I open the meeting to ask for considered opinions as to how we, that is our civilisation, should respond'.

'As long as you don't handle it biasedly in favour of America, then I don't have any problem', the Russian president, Vladimir Popov, spoke first, his facial expression exhibiting his usual thin smile. He spoke in Russian, but the international translation filter automatically translated and relayed his words through each country's holographic hub.

'That is mandatory for anyone officiating in this chair', Turnbull addressed Popov brusquely. 'I'm fully aware of the special relationship status that exists between the United Kingdom and America, but let me assure you all that anyone occupying this chair has a duty of impartiality, and I will try my best to follow this dictate. However, that is exactly why the Holographic Meeting Constitution article number 3b has been inserted, to instil confidence that impartiality will be practised throughout'.

'Exactly, and don't forget France does too have a special relationship with America anyway', Pres Sabina Paquet cut in.

'Then I will suggest we get on with our consideration as to what (a) the ETs actually want and (b) how the heck we are going to respond'.

Turnbull looked directly at Wallace and said, "Madam President, I've noticed all nine countries presented at this table have nuclear capabilities, so what is your reason for calling this extraordinary meeting, rather than going through the usual channels, such as the United Nations?'

The president cleared her throat and began a clarification and condensation of the situation.

'We believe that the ETs have already demonstrated an unacceptable threat to humankind. We must demonstrate a unified resolve and to respond with great urgency, which would take far too long if we went through the lengthy debates and procedures automatically involved with any decision process if we tried to work through the United Nations. Essentially, the threat from the ETs has been demonstrated. They have technology that has already been demonstrated that is beyond anything we have on our planet. They, in all probability, have even more, which has not yet been in evidence. Without a doubt, these beliefs have been underlined as seen from their abduction of at least four people. We now believe the mounting evidence gleaned from JPL that our *Voyager 1* had been destroyed deliberately!'

Wallace took a deep breath before she continued, 'We know from bitter experience that the usual rate of progress made through the United Nations is all talk and no action, a very much self-restraint in the form of "wait and see" handlings. To follow the usual procedures would, in fact, greatly increase the threats to our planet, and that this fully justifies taking urgent measures. I would have no objection to keeping the United Nations informed as quickly as we can *after* we have taken whatever retaliatory action that we can justify'.

Turnbull cut in, 'Then we will make absolutely sure all other countries will be kept well informed'.

Half the gathering nodded acceptance, amid a general muttering of unease.

'Then can you lay out exactly what you are planning to do, particularly with regard to our combined nuclear capabilities?'

Wallace looked around at each delegate carefully before finally responding, 'Yes, you are correct, Tony. As far as I can judge, the waiting game is over! It is such a major issue that we felt that a pre-emptive retaliatory strike, using whatever resources are available, is the preferred option'.

There was a completely stunned silence.

The Chinese president was the first to break it. 'Firing our ICBMs at the ETs spacecraft? Is that possible? Please wait whilst I consult my military weapons specialists'.

President Wallace had already anticipated this situation and knew that it was not feasible without serious technical questions being answered. She spoke out.

'For example, when the alien starship is orbiting this world at the distance of 20,000 kilometres. It was far out of the range of current ICBMs, regardless of the nationality of the designs, which was usually of only around 10,000–14,000!'

'There is clearly a need for us to modify our ICBMs or create new much bigger missiles!' Vladimir cut in. He had a very relaxed, almost nonchalant attitude as he stirred his tea. 'But we don't have the time!'

The American president was not disconcerted by her Russian counterpart.

'I'm fully aware of the technical limitations of all our current ICBMs, and that they are absolutely not designed for the situation with which we are now faced, but still, I think it's beneficial for us to fire a missile or maybe two missiles and then have them detonated well before they reach the Ets without doing any damage to their spaceship. In other words, we would wish to make them think again because of our spectacular fireworks display, and that might act as a warning or a deterrent'.

'Then we need to supply them a bucket full of popcorn! Such a contrived effort would only show our weaknesses', Ms Paquet commented sarcastically.

There was a short period of various other delegates joining in, trying to add their own arguments. The chairman was forced to re-establish some form of control on the meeting and switched off the delegates microphones in what was an electronic form of a gavel. The effect was immediate, and the atmosphere became quieter.

'We need to be calm about all this and think rationally'. He turned and spoke directly to President Wallace. 'Are you suggesting we need to fire our missiles at their orbiting spacecraft, *if* we can overcome what at present seem to be, that all our various rockets have pretty significant technical limitations, regardless? And to what purpose? Care to enlighten us on your ulterior motivation?'

Wallace responded with some difficulty in restraining her temper. She was not used to being challenged in such a way. 'We have to make them at least come up with some way to establish a dialogue and to meet us and explain what they actually want. Blasting our space probe into particles, abducting our citizens, massacring millions of rabbits all sounds like threatening behaviour to me, but what for?'

'Yes, madam, I get your drift, but still, I'm not convinced'. Vladimir took a sip of tea. 'How can that achieve any specific purpose? With your typical gung-ho attitudes, you are inviting them to be very confrontational, aren't you?'

'On the contrary, we need to show them something of our capabilities and get them to pause or reconsider their handling or whatsoever their intention will be'.

'In order to achieve what?'

'To buy ourselves with time!'

'But for what?'

'To build a bigger missile or find ourselves a more feasible way of defending ourselves?'

Paquet interrupted, 'Whether they occur on Earth or in space, nuclear detonations are never good news! We need to reassure the public of our reasoning. Not only that, but we also still need to consider the effect of several nuclear detonations, in space, on us'.

'Then precisely what constitutes a valid reason?' Turnbull looked at Wallace questioningly.

Wallace pointed her finger slowly and deliberately around at them. 'I can understand your concerns, and in a way, I've expected you to come up with them. I do share your uneasiness about creating nuclear detonations in space and in what amounts to uncomfortable proximity to our planet. In fact, I've got Dr George Clark on standby to provide you all with answers. He's our director of the White House Office of Science and Technology Policy'. She looked up and said, 'You can question him directly'.

Colonel Cooper vacated his seat to enable Doctor Clark to address the meeting.

'Hi there. You can please call me George. I've been expecting to be called up to explain in layman's terms the potential impact of large nuclear detonations made out in our bit of space'. He suddenly looked serious. 'Can we refer to the actual experiences in the most dramatic stages of the Cold War, where Russia and the United States were testing nuclear bombs left, right, and centre?'

He took a quick breath and continued, "And because of fears of a long-range nuclear missile or a satellite delivery system for a nuclear warhead going AWOL'—he pointed his finger upwards—'the United States had launched a series of tests code-named Project Fishbowl, which were high-altitude nuclear weapons tests.

'The most impressive and historic test in this project was Starfish Prime. In 1962, a 1.4-megaton nuclear bomb was detonated approximately 250 miles above the surface of the Earth'.

'What was the effect?' enquired Paquet. 'How bad was it?'

'Please bear with me, I'm coming to that'. He looked at her. 'First of all, since there is no atmosphere in space, there was no iconic mushroom cloud nor a blast wave. Instead, there was an intense outpouring of not only heat and light, but also high-intensity radiation in the form of gamma rays and X-rays, with no atmosphere to interrupt their path. Visually, the blast was roughly spherical, and the wave of radiation and light expanded to light up the sky'.

He waved his hands and waggled his fingers in the air graphically. 'From the surface of the planet, vivid aureoles of light would be seen for thousands of miles within minutes of the blast because the charged particles from the blast would immediately begin interacting with Earth's magnetic field. Imagine the aurora borealis, more commonly known as the northern lights, except, in this case, the vivid display spread across thousands of kilometres above the Pacific Ocean'.

'But what about the radiation?' the president of Israel questioned. 'Wouldn't that be shooting ourselves in our collective feet?'

'Not as much of a danger as you might think'. Clark shook his head. 'All radioactive material created by the blast was, in fact, absorbed by our atmosphere, which dissipated it around the entire planet. Our atmosphere has rendered it somewhat harmless. Great to have Earth's magnetic field coming to our rescue again as it has been doing for hundreds of thousands of years!'

'If that's not a worry, then what is?' the Israeli persevered .

'Without a doubt', Clark responded unfazed, 'it's the effect of the electromagnetic pulse that was interesting to us and should be the one to worry us the most'.

'Then why, and in what way?'

'Essentially, those highly charged, rapidly moving electrons will create a small and incredibly powerful magnetic field, also called an EMP (electromagnetic pulse). It did happen in this case of the Starfish Prime project. The blast had managed to cut off all the electronic power within this area, bringing disruption to the nation's electronic communication system and effectively crippling the nation's infrastructure!'

'Then wouldn't it have an inverted effect on our communication satellites?'

Paquet retorted with a distasteful look on her face. 'We are practically shooting ourselves in our feet!'

Clark quickly threw his hands up before the others had the chance to join in the chorus of objection. 'Hang on!' he barked. 'You have overlooked one thing!'

'What is it?!'

'You have failed to remember that I mentioned this nuclear donation was made approximately 250 miles above the surface of Earth!' He held his gaze unflinchingly.

'I was speaking of what has actually happened! But this time there is, indeed, a big difference. We can detonate our missiles much further out, something like 7,000 miles out, far enough out and much more into a safe range for us but close enough to give the ETs a jolt.

'And at that distance, the effect on our communication satellites will become minimal, as most of our communication and GPS satellites are orbiting at the distance of between 12,000 and 22,000 miles, well beyond the range that our nuclear missiles could inflict any collateral damage'.

'But can you guarantee that?' asked Popov. 'I'm sure there are a few satellites that we haven't charted that are still orbiting somewhere in this range?'

'I have done my homework, and believe me, there's relatively empty space at around 5,000–10,000 miles'. George waved his hands. 'Nothing out there for us to be concerned about'.

But Wallace interrupted quickly, 'President Popov, look, I can understand your reservations on if there is any constructive benefit to detonating our missiles, only if you are prepared to join me in sharing the global responsibility of protecting this world, but my point is, we need to increase our level of apparent technical retaliatory abilities somehow or do whatever else is required to respond to the critical threat unfolding on our collective doorsteps, such as the kidnappings and not to forget the rabbit issues in Australia! If you have a better idea, then I'm listening. But for now, I'm sure you couldn't help feeling compelled to agree with me. An immediately available drastic measure of reaction is essentially the best way forward'.

The meeting went on heatedly for a few hours. That was two days ago. A different meeting was held one day later. It achieved a much more productive result.

* * *

Cardinal Marcello knocked and waited for Sister Lee's response before entering her room. He found her sitting in a traditional Victorian leather antique armchair holding the tablet. Her face looked haggard. There was a look of profound concern on her face.

He hastened to comfort her. 'I see you are familiarising yourself with some of the latest technology?'

'Well, not too good so far'.

'Something is still bothering you?' Marcello was gesturing in askance at the tablet she was holding. 'Found something that you were not comfortable with?'

'Nothing to do with it'. She put it aside on the table. 'The world is already in trouble, and I don't want to know any more about it. It's already too disturbing for me'.

He moved closer to the table where the tablet was and picked it up to examine it. He did a quick scan of her previous searches. He was satisfied the contents were, indeed, irrelevant, and there was nothing that would alarm him. All accesses were in the form of card solitaire and word scrabble, alongside a few other games not worth mentioning. Marcello smiled with relief inwardly. At least it was the answer he was hoping for.

'Then is it a health or maybe mental stress problem? After all, you have been through, it would not be surprising?' He was inviting her to converse and open an outline of her thought processes.

'Well, frankly, I'm starting to find it rather claustrophobic being holed up in this room for far too long! Though I'm grateful for the occasional walks around the garden, never in my life have I felt so restricted, especially with a Swiss Guard shadowing me a few steps behind. Don't you think you're a bit overzealous with your protection?'

'If the Swiss Guard bothers you, I can instruct him to be much more discreet and keep at a greater distance from you. Would that help you?'

'Nothing to do with him, but the point is I feel so unproductive with nothing to do. I long to go back to my post in Mongolia and resume my useful work there. I'm afraid to say I find the boredom here is stifling me! Am I a prisoner?'

'Of course not! I do not want to be overprotective or intrusive to your well-being. On the contrary, you're free to go to any place'. Marcello's suave manner demonstrated his years of practice in a confessional role to dampen her concerns, but he felt trepidation building up inside him at the thought of this extraordinary asset slipping away from his control. 'But forgive me for saying this, I've always thought it's for your protection and peace of mind to keep you from being hounded by the people out there. You are so vulnerable. Am I wrong to consider this?'

'Thanks for your concern'. She looked up at him. 'But I'm quite a mature woman, and I want to serve my Creator, and I am quite capable of deciding what's best for me. Perhaps it's high time I face the grilling from the reporters and be done with it. Sooner the better for me, as I want to get back to my normal life'.

Marcello nodded and slid one of his hands into his side pocket. 'I do sympathise with you. Don't blame you for thinking like that . . .'

He realised there was something in his pocket. He pulled it out and realised there was the plastic card and remembered the minor incident he had with Brett. He toyed with the idea of giving it to her but paused for a moment whilst contemplating and gauging the possibility of exposing her to mainstream media. *Imagine her alone with Brett, and he'll be able to dismantle her so ruthlessly in his usual quest for a story.*

A form of horror was materialising slowly in his head. *Sometime soon he'll find out that I've been rather selective with my statements, which have been broadcast around the world. Full disclosure would have been a catastrophe to me and the church! I can't have that!*

He looked out of the window and could see the thin clouds drifting in the deep blue sky. Their shapelessness and apparently totally unrestrained movement always had a soothing effect when he was troubled and sought inspiration. *Up to now and against all odds, I'd managed to keep her level of anonymity intact, but for how much longer? A ticking bomb indeed!* He glanced at her furtively. *Wouldn't it be better if she could disappear from here for good and the world would not be any wiser?* He could hear a shifting of the sentry's feet through the door. *But first, I will still need to deal with these Swiss Guards. But how? Their original purpose and duty were to keep intruders away from his 'exclusive collaborator' to protect her. From whom? Now they seemed more like gaolers. I could dispense with them quite easily.* He looked at the card and slipped it back into his pocket. *Technical help from a psychologist? No need for that! Need to think carefully! Of course, there is no real issue.*

He quickly took a seat squarely in front of her and looked straight into her eyes.

'I have utmost respect for your right to the life that you've longed for, a right to live in peace and in relative anonymity'. He leaned over the table and lifted the tablet.

'But speaking about anonymity, I still need to know if you've contacted anyone whilst you're here? Your relatives for example?'

'No, no one, and I don't have any relatives, only a distant cousin that I am not too familiar with'.

'You live a solitary sort of life, do you?'

'Only physically'. Her eyes went glazed. 'I am never alone in the presence of our Lord . . .'

'Bless you'. He waved a hand at her. 'If I can assist, wouldn't you like the opportunity for you to travel out of this country with total anonymity to a location of your choice?'

'Nice idea, but how? Too many eyes around this place'.

'Not if we arrange it carefully'.

'Like the spy agents in the movies using alias names?'

'It doesn't have to be like that, but close enough!' He chuckled. 'Can you assure me you won't be using the tablet anymore?' He lifted the tablet.

'What's the problem?'

'Just to maintain your degree of anonymity. Last thing we need is having people accessing it and finding out about you and giving you a hard time.

Constant harassment is something you will not want'. He frowned at her.

'We can't afford any unforeseen exposures, can we? The less you contact the outside world, the less chance there would be of them finding more about you'.

'How can they?'

'You would be amazed to know the lengths to which they can penetrate personal data with the latest technology in their hands. They could easily hunt you down without you having any knowledge as to just what they know . . .' He let his words hang for a few moments, increasing the threat in a subtle way.

He spent several minutes trying to reassure her with the pitfalls of using the technology before retiring to his own office.

Once he got there, he sat in his chair and took out the card. He took a lengthy look at it before he decided that he knew what to do with it. He flipped it into a bin tucked in the corner of his room. *That should be the end of him.* Or so he thought briefly.

Then he realised there would be other unidentified problems lurking in the world waiting for when he least expected them. It would only be a matter of time before another person would appear on the world scene. The nun from Korea had already mentioned one, and it had a name: Emma.

From what Sister Lee had already told him, Emma had already selected the United Nations in New York as the best potential location for her to make her own monumental reappearance on the world stage. This would blow away all attempts that Cardinal Marcello had made to maintain any form of secrecy, with the intention to deliver the details and with it the ultimate truth of Cardinal Marcello's secretive handling of Sister Lee's disclosures would prove to be most inflammatory and damaging to him personally and the international reputation of the Catholic Church.

He could foresee her as his very own personal paradox. He had created a really urgent need to act, but to do precisely what, before his situation and, of course, that of his beloved church became untenable. *But how?* He thought, his brow deeply furrowed.

He looked at the glasscomm on his desk and instructed, 'Computer, please find the mayor Bianchi of New York . . . and arrange a video conference with him'.

'Request acknowledged and processed . . .'

* * *

Back in the private lobby they had booked in the basement of the hotel, Brett and Sarah were sitting either side of the extremely experienced IT technician they had hired. He sat with his shoulders slightly hunched, but his eyes were focused intently on a large thin glass screen in front of him. His unkempt greyish hair gave his age to be midfifties, but Brett was praying that he would be justified in paying him the extortionate fee for which Brett had secured a budget from his boss and which only covered a few hours of his time. The technician was already showing his value.

A large schematic illustration of a building in 3D format could be seen on his monitor. His fingers danced across the keyboard at an extraordinary rate. He kept muttering under his breath, 'Mmm, ha yeah, there . . . mmm, well, well . . . ha . . .'

He stopped abruptly but said nothing, except for nodding and shaking his head for no apparent reason.

'Well, Troy, any luck?' Brett couldn't contain his curiosity. 'Any success with our homing card?'

'Virus app planted and secured!' Troy looked at him and started to smile slowly. 'Not only that, but I've also been monitoring the routes the card has taken around the building! An impressive piece of GPS that piggybacks off the Wi-FI in any buildings and yet remains undetected!'

Sarah slapped Brett a high-five over Troy's head. 'Okay, Troy, stop pussyfooting around. Tell us what you have come up with?'

'You should be thankful that whoever holds the linkware-card needs to be within a few feet of another Internet device, and not only that, but it also needs to stay there for several minutes!' He glanced at her. 'Just enough time for me to hack into the Wi-Fi whilst taking advantage of the card's linkware to establish a relay station!

I've planted a trojan virus on the tablet that will enable us to operate a remote control on it!'

'From such a distance?!' Sarah looked at him suspiciously. 'You are seriously that good? You are not having me on?'

He looked at her in dismay as if he was insulted and with a sarcastic tone belied by his grin, answered, 'Don't ever question my experience! My name speaks for what it is! My specialisation is purely the world of the Trojan virus!' He pointed his thumbs at his chest. 'Get it?'

'A nickname or a real name, I wonder?'

'Is that the room where the suspected person is located?' Brett pointed his finger at a particular spot on the layout of the building on the monitor. 'Or is it the other one? Which one?' He insisted that they get back on track, which was what he was paying for.

'My gut feeling is that it's the first one'. Troy scanned the monitor. 'It's due to the length of time the card has been located in that room and the length of inactivity or the lack of movement of the card in the final room, so hence, I assumed he left it in a drawer or even discarded it in the rubbish bin'.

'So in spite of all my technical qualifications, he did not find them sufficiently important to contact me!' She grinned to herself.

'Okay, can you tell me what you want me to do now?' Troy interrupted. He had no patience with any form of horseplay. His electronics world excluded any escape into human social interactions.

'I think the best thing is to make sure Marcello is well clear of her room, and even more so, she's on her own in her room'. Brett broke off his study of the screen.

'When we are ready, then I will personally . . . oh no, on second thought, you, Sarah, will create a video conferencing with her'.

'Why me?'

'Female to female, a less threatening environment for her'.

'Fair enough'.

'But first, let's try to activate the camera on that tablet, can we?' He looked at Troy. 'Is that possible?'

'Aye, nothing is impossible!'

'We need to try to see what the person in this room likes, first, before proceeding to the next step of alerting her to the possibility of video conferencing with us!'

'Why the caution?' Troy queried.

'To make sure it's a female for a start, and I need to study her dynamics in silence. A requirement is for me to build up some idea about her psyche'.

'Such as?' Troy was puzzled.

'For example, does she act briskly or timidly or aggressively?' Brett rubbed his chin. 'It will help me prepare my style of questioning in advance'.

'Your call . . .' Troy shrugged.

'Can we start tomorrow, early in the morning?' Brett stood up. 'We need to be bright-eyed and bushy-tailed!'

* * *

The atmosphere in the second holographic meeting was intense. From the outset, Turnbull outlined that the main purpose of it was to treat it as a primary decision-making process. The major decision was to be about if ICBM missiles would be fired without understanding the likely reactions. But as it went on, the flow of the meeting was disturbed by several smaller countries who had been consulted in the aftermath of the preliminary discussions and wanted a bigger input into the debate. There was enormous unease at the superpower's apparent attempt to ignore the considerations of the wider membership of the United Nations.

Early on during the meeting, it had been proposed that each country would have the opportunity to fire a single missile, but thanks to Turnbull's extensive diplomatic experience, he had skilfully steered them into understanding it would be an overkill and a counterproductive act to send nine missiles.

As the debate went on, he found it heading toward a type of problem-solving meeting he was trying to avoid. He used his diplomacy and managed to get it back on the track he had laid down when formulating the agenda. In a nutshell, he wanted to avoid any retaliation risk posed by the ET's spaceship. He wanted to establish a dialogue, but this was an avenue that had, so far, been only very lightly touched upon.

Turnbull had eventually not only got them to harmonise with one another's philosophy on the principles of integrity and spirit of comradeship, but he had also managed to get them all to agree that it would need only two countries to fire one missile each. They had voted for only Russia and America. The rest of the other seven countries, Pakistan, India, Israel, France, China, United Kingdom, and Iran all had agreed to wait for the consequences to follow before taking the opportunity to fire their own missiles, if there was a need caused by any kind of retaliation by the ETs. The main reason for the decision selecting the two major countries was down to the reliability of their missiles based on their far-greater resources developed over a much greater time frame. The smaller nations did not have sufficient resources to carry out the reconfiguration of their missiles to carry more fuel and use smaller nuclear payloads.

An agreement had been reached that the timing of the missile's launch would be in a synchronised sequence. From the location of their ICBMs underground silos in both countries, both missile-launches would be at the same GMT, detonating both missiles at an altitude of 7,000 kilometres. Whether the detonation had been performed at night-time or daytime, the exhibition would be equally spectacular and seen by most people on Earth and, as intended, the ETs residing in their starship.

CHAPTER 23

The Missiles

It had been decided that the missile's launch would be monitored closely by the holographic meeting members, with the additional presence of all their key government members from each country. This unprecedented, coordinated action was made after consultation with the United Nations. Also in the agreement was the provision that the United Nations would have continuous and full access to the progress made with the flight path of the missiles.

The atmosphere at the meeting was totally muted and tense. No one dared to interrupt the complicated and delicate strategy of the simultaneous launches of the ICBMs. In reality, it was their first experience of monitoring the progress made with the flight of the missiles. In other words, they had no idea what to expect, apart from sitting in all-encompassing awe of all the complex data, facts, and figures being continually rolled out before them.

The synchronised launch of the two missiles, with their ballistic trajectory reprogrammed, ensured they were on one-ticket flight plan towards outer space rather than the usual pathway of 'arcing over' to the traditional and more obvious targets on the continents. To achieve escape velocity by breaking away from the Earth's gravity, they were required to blast off at the speed of 25,000 kilometres an hour. Within a few minutes, they had flown out of the Earth's mesosphere towards space. However, this came with a price tag: The short but intense rate of fuel burnt in each of the three stages of boosters left no options for reconfiguration of their trajectory.

'Final stage of third-stage thrust completed', a computerised voice came through. *'All systems green. Flight path calculated and followed correctly'.*

'As I had previously advised you all, the usual triple nuclear warheads in each missile have been reduced to a single warhead', Doctor Clark reassured the world audience. He was still sitting next to President

Wallace. 'Absolutely every measure required to lighten the payloads has been taken to obtain escape velocity'.

'Countdown to first detonation, 3 hours 23 minutes and 46 seconds. Followed by the second nuclear detonation in 3 hours 25 minutes and 56 seconds'.

'From what I see, it's taken a few minutes to blast them off from Earth but still taking much longer to fly towards the alien spaceship? Why is that?' the Israeli prime minister enquired.

'All the fuel in both missiles has been used up completely and with no chance of reignition for further course alteration. They are simply floating off towards the target', Doctor Clark responded. 'All we can do is just wait. Perhaps we can take a comfort break for a few hours before we come back to review progress'.

'Computer, please confirm both warheads are armed and primed', instructed Wallace.

'First warhead is primed and accounted for. Unable to account for the second warhead. Need to seek additional input from another source'.

'Then can you please confirm if there is a malfunction, President Popov?'

Wallace looked at him.

'Da, I can assure you it's primed and hot'. A slight smirk could be detected on his thin lips. 'There was a minor defect in the operating systems brought about by the unexpected violence of the acceleration process. My team are already transmitting the relevant data inputs to yours'.

'Thanks, Vladimir'. Wallace nodded. 'It is great to see us working as an international team'.

* * *

Emma had just woken up and sat up slowly whilst stretching her arms. 'Seems we are getting used to sleeping on hard floors, aren't we?' She saw Andy still on his back on the floor with his eyes fully shut. 'It's a great thing about this low gravity! A real bliss about it!'

Her now-familiar voice alerted him. 'I'm not really sleeping'. He turned his head sideways, opening one eye and smiled. 'Well, the floor doesn't really bother me, but your snoring does!' He signed in the basic way that he and Emma were becoming very used to using between them.

'I have no idea if you snore'. Emma laughed. 'In a way, it can be blissful to be Deaf when sleeping! The outside world just does not bother me'.

Suddenly, the room darkened, and a new display of images flashed across the wall, followed by new reading superimposed squarely across it in the middle. At first, a full image of Earth embraced the whole wall, but it quickly enlarged drastically when the images focussed towards two new flying objects.

UNIT GREEN AND RED ARE REQUIRED TO DECIPHER THEIR INTENTION AND OBJECTIVE

With minimum effort, Emma flipped her hands on the floor to push herself up into a standing mode and tiptoed gracefully like a ballerina towards the wall to get a closer look at the objects in question. 'Looks like a missile or rocket of some kind?' she gestured at Andy. 'Can we treat it as a good sign that Gillian's message has been delivered successfully, and it's the first run of new supplies being delivered to us?'

'Not sure!'

'Then what is it?'

'I think the best way is to search out the place where it came from!'

Andy scrambled up quickly and gave the instruction to the wall. 'Gorgass, if you want us to identify the rocket flying towards us, then please play back to the time when it was blasted off. From there, I may be able to identify the type of rocket!'

UNIT GREEN REQUEST ACKNOWLEDGED AND PROCESSING

The image froze instantly and rewound quickly until the rocket could be seen launching from the middle of America.

'Can we zoom towards the site? Until I say stop?'

The image magnified slowly showing the launch. 'Stop!'

'That's clearly a silo!' Emma exclaimed. 'Therefore, the rocket must be the same type that would normally carry a nuclear intercontinental ballistic missile!'

Suddenly, another new video image washed over the wall, and the first images were deleted before their eyes. A second missile could be seen heading towards them. Again, the images were frozen, and without being asked for by the humans, the images were wound back to an obviously different terrain of a second launch site.

'I believe that must be north of Russia! That is the only place from where they have their intercontinental nuke missiles sites!'

WHAT IS NUKE QUESTION

'Oh, just a slang word for a nuclear fusion weapon . . .' Andy made a gesture of his hands showing the indication of an explosion. 'Pooofpt . . . like a big boom!'

'Hey, you know the meaning of nuclear fusion concepts?' Emma stepped in.

'Fusion reaction is used to release the massive nuclear energy'.

GORGASS COMPREHEND PHYSICS OF FUSION

'Are you saying you've also got a nuclear bomb?'

NEGATIVE–- GORGASS FIND THEM CRUDE AND INEFFECTIVE

'Then how are you going to stop them from harming us?'

UNIT RED TO CONFIRM THE INTENTION OF THESE TWO MISSILES ARE HOSTILE AND HARMFUL TO GORGASS

'Oh possibly!' She signed. 'Any of these missiles detonating is dangerous and harmful! You need to stop them from coming at us, if possible, now!'

Andy threw his arm around her in a protective gesture and shouted in a way that he had never before exhibited. 'Gorgass, I believe these two missiles heading towards us would destroy you and us together. I don't really know why they have shot off the missiles in anger and still have no idea of their intention on achieving the result by wiping us off . . .' He didn't finish his sentence when Emma broke in.

'I don't understand why they shouldn't care about us! Perhaps they are not aware of we humans being still trapped in this spaceship? Maybe Gillian has failed to explain, or maybe she did not survive her return ordeal?' she said.

'I think you need to take a preventive measure against these missiles now before they get too close to us'. Andy let go of Emma and continued, 'Do it *now*! Just destroy them with your lasers or whatever other defensive weapons you have in your possession!'

GORGASS PROGRESSING WITH ACTION

'Doing what? What is it to be?'

GORGASS TO EVALUATE THE COURSE OF ACTION REQUIRED

'Aren't you wasting your time?'

GORGASS EXECUTE ACTION IMMEDIATE

No further writing could be seen on the wall. All went quiet, except for the video on the wall that continued displaying the missiles drifting slowly through the space towards them.

Andy's and Emma's eyes locked on each other. They were speechless and terrified, as they had no real understanding as to what to expect.

Andy muttered, 'For a start, the dogfight that happened over in Italy did not give us much encouragement or any indications as to what additional retaliation to expect, and certainly, we have never had any previous knowledge of missiles, such as these, being sent into space!'

GORGASS EXECUTING ACTION WITH INTERMEDIARY ORBITOR

'Huh?' Andy was at loss to understand just what message the Gorgass were spelling out. He decided to say nothing, except staying close to and supporting Emma in silence and watching the drama unfold on the large screen.

* * *

'A new movement was detected there!' Cooper said, checking the display on his large tablet. It had full access to a live feed being streamed in continuously from the communication centre based in Houston. It had been monitoring all the data inputs from a mixture of long- and short-range radars. He could see a whitish blip materialising and moving steadily towards the American ICBM, which was still drifting slowly further out of proximity to Earth.

'What is it?' Turnbull snapped. 'Please relay your findings to us all!'

'Done!'

All their eyes were immediately focused on their individual communication tablets.

'Cooper, I can't comprehend it, so please care to enlighten us about what you are seeing?' Turnbull's eyebrows furrowed. 'Is that one of ours or theirs?'

'Probably one of their drones that have been orbiting our planet discreetly until now . . .'

'Why weren't we aware of it?'

'It's a relatively small size and difficult to track, especially if it is deliberately concealed, and it deliberately blended in amongst our own satellites orbiting at a relatively low altitude', Clark replied.

'Then are we seeing it's chasing and closing up on our American missile?'

'Looks like it'.

'Can't we steer our missile to another path away from it?'

'Afraid not. I've already told you, all the rocket fuel on our missiles has been used'. Clark shook his head. 'Nothing we can do apart from watching where it is going'.

'Can't we detonate our warhead now before it gets too close to our missile?'

'Pointless and dangerous when our missiles have not yet cleared out of our satellites' orbits. We need to wait 'til it's beyond their orbiting range. To detonate it prematurely before then would be catastrophic to our own global communication satellite systems'.

'Length of time before it will be a likely threat to our missile?' Wallace requested. 'We do not know what their object is or what it will do'.

Clark pressed a button on his tablet and then altered the signal on the screen. 'Computer, please confirm if the trajectory of the foreign object is on the same pathway that will lead it to encounter with our missile number 1'.

'*Request noted and calculated*'. There was a pause of a few seconds before it was announced. '*Confirming the pathway of the foreign object is on track to encounter missile number 1*'.

'Computer, please state the length of time for the rendezvous to take place'.

'*Calculated and confirming the rendezvous of a foreign object and missile number 1 will take place in 17 minutes 27 seconds, with a leeway of 1.5 seconds*'.

'That doesn't give us much time to detonate our warhead, does it?' Wallace grimaced.

'Nope'. Clark sighed. 'All we can do is to sit tight and watch what this alien spacecraft is going to do! We'd better hope it's not going to do anything with it at all!'

The next 15 minutes proved to be their longest nightmare. It was not the exertion of waiting that bothered them; it was their utter impotence to affect any outcome that caused the entire earthly contingent to realise they were witnessing an event that would harness the disunited powers on Earth as never before. A thousand questions flashed across their minds on what kind of movement to expect with this mysterious object.

'Computer, please detect any new movement made with the alien mother spacecraft', Clark instructed. He wanted to be in the position of preparing for the unexpected.

'Negative. No additional movement detected. It's still orbiting in its usual path'.

'Computer, please relay us a close-up image of the impending encounter between our missile number 1 target and also report every 2 minutes the position of this unidentified object'.

'Unable to comply with the request. Requires input from an observatory site not yet integrated with the current programme as of now'.

Clark shot a look at Cooper. 'Can you please alert the teams at any observatories scattered around the world, starting with ours in Hawaii . . .' He didn't finish his sentence.

'Already on top of it, and new information streaming will come in a minute', Cooper cut in. 'Transmitting it to you all'. He reprogrammed his tablet.

* * *

A close-up of the movement made by the intermediary spacecraft could be seen on the wall in full view of Andy and Emma.

'Hey, Gorgass, what objective have you programmed for your spacecraft?'

Andy addressed the wall. 'I can see it's closing up on the American missile, and then what?'

GORGASS DETECTED NO ADDITIONAL MOVEMENT OF THE MISSILE OF WAR

OUR SCANNING SHOWS IT HAS NO FUEL AND IT IS DRIFTING

'I'm not surprised as it's relatively a small rocket and takes time to reach here!' Emma said.

IT MUST BE MOVED OUT OF DANGER ZONE

115

'Then how?'

IT WILL BE PUSHED BACK TO EARTH

'Why do it when you can blast it out of harm's way?' Emma was intrigued.

HUMAN NEED TO BE TAUGHT A LESSON BY MAKING THEM ACCOUNTABLE TO ANY ACTION THEY HAVE ADMINISTERED

'What? Are you giving them a taste of their own medicine?' Andy conjectured but stopped as he knew Gorgass would not understand.

* * *

Rendezvous of a foreign object and missile number 1 taking place now.

'Computer, please magnify the video image three times'.

Request acknowledged and complied.

They could see the larger bulbous and unusually shaped spacecraft drifting slowly towards the smaller object for a few minutes before two tentacles could be seen shooting outwards and slinging around the object. The tentacles had started to winch the smaller object towards the larger object until they made contact.

'What's it doing?' Turnbull shot a look at Clark. 'Any idea?'

'Looks like it's lassoed our missile, but that's only my initial observation'.

Foreign object and our missile have been combined into a single unit.

The object in question suddenly made a dramatic new movement. It flipped over and continued flying backwards until a new shimmering cloud could be observed trailing behind it. The alien spacecraft was applying a reverse thrust to alter the combined units' course. The effect of this was to reduce their speed, which resulted in the object being pulled back to Earth.

Detecting a new trajectory of the joined foreign object.

There was total silence in the room. No one was sure of what to expect with the new movements now being made evident on the screen. They were watching the events unfolding, transfixed like rabbits caught in headlights.

The next phase in the saga evolving to the dumbfounded audience showed the alien spacecraft releasing its tentacles and withdrawing them back into its ports. Then it moved away from the missile and started steering itself into another new trajectory but this time flying away from Earth.

'What the hell has happened?' Wallace screeched. 'George, do you think our missile has been nudged back towards Earth? Are those crazy sons of bitches retaliating with our own goddamned missile? Has it been pushed back at us?' It was more of a statement than a question.

'It looks like it, but now I'm not sure of the trajectory of our missile', Clark replied icily. 'Based on the angles of entering our Earth's atmosphere, there are always three options as to where it will end up: (1) If the angle of trajectory is too shallow, our missile will bounce off from our atmosphere into empty space. Or (2) if the angle proved to be correct, it will enter our atmosphere with minimum friction made, with the result of it landing relatively undamaged somewhere on Earth. Then finally, option (3) is if the incidence angle is too steep, it will cause intense friction to our missile and create a fireball, rendering lethal damage to it'.

'Then will it still detonate?' Sabina Paquet questioned with an obviously highly agitated voice.

'Technically and theoretically, that is possible!'

'Give me an unambiguous answer!' Wallace's voice had become much more highly pitched compared with her usually measured stance. 'Just give me the factual details!'

Clark scratched his head and nodded. He reconfigured his tablet and gave instructions. 'Computer, please calculate the trajectory of our American missile and then confirm us the destination of where it will arrive. Now!'

If specified to give you the immediate result, the probability of delivering the accuracy of the result based on a calculation of the missile's trajectory will be 52.5%'.

'Computer, then please advise us how long will it take to deliver the result with the accuracy of at least 90%?' Clark rolled his eyes.

Achieving a result with 97% probability of accuracy will take 14 minutes 43 seconds with a maximum of 95.7 seconds achieved in 19 minutes 37 seconds'.

'Why will it take so long?' Wallace threw her hands up. 'Aren't these computer systems supposed to be ultra-fast latest technology with their calculations?'

'The longer it can compute the timing of the trajectory pathway from one point to the next point, the more accurate it can deliver the conclusion to us', Clark replied. 'Isn't that what you want? A more solid and accurate answer before making any decision?'

'What decision?'

'I think regardless of where our missile is going, our best immediate action is to have our warhead disarmed', Clark replied. 'My advice is to have it aborted now, and by doing that, it will render it harmless and let it go anywhere with minimum worry about the damages it will inflict when it's hot and primed. By the time the computer delivers the result to us in 15 minutes, it will be around 200 miles away!

It's coming too close for our safety!'

'That sounds right!' Turnbull cut in. He glanced around at the other people in the meeting. 'We need to take drastic action now, so does anyone object to having our missile mission aborted?'

No one raised any objection. Turnbull looked at the American president.

'Then please proceed with aborting it now, Rachel?'

'No question about it, I think that's the most pragmatic action we can make'.

Pres Rachel Wallace tapped in her password, and then Dr George Clark followed with his own security verification procedures.

'Deactivate warhead immediately'.

All the eyes of the world's leaders were on them. They were all involved with a threat from barely understood technology, and their levels of confidence in the Americans' leadership were being severely tested.

'Facial and voice recognition of Rachel Wallace and George Clark have been confirmed as bona fide and true. Continuing with deactivation procedures as instructed'.

All eyes were on the video display on their own tablets. They could see the missile as it rotated slowly but was still drifting towards the Earth.

'Confirming the warhead has been disabled and neutralised'.

No new movement could be detected on the revolving missile, and that did not help reassure the major players of the world that their instruction had been executed successfully. Yet they could see it drifting closer and closer to Earth's atmosphere.

They waited for another 15 minutes before the unmistakably familiar computer voice came up. *'Trajectory of the American missile calculated. It will enter the atmosphere in 8 minutes 30 seconds. The probability of it breaking up and dispersing at the latitude and longitude zone of 33 degrees 17 minutes north and 47 degrees and 15 minutes west will be at 95.7% accuracy. The sector of dispersion will be 70 miles long by 2 miles wide'.*

'Where the hell is that?' Wallace yelled. She was already reaching her own upper limit of tolerance of the computer's constant insistence on meticulous procedural details that were becoming terrifying to her.

'In the middle of the Atlantic Ocean!' Clark exclaimed, with no trace of a smile on his face. He remained calm and detached since he was more aware than all the others of the terrifying risks that still existed before they could relax.

'That's a relief!' Prime Minister Turnbull hollered. He cast a searching look around at the other people at the table until he saw President Popov burying his face in his hands. 'Hey, Vladimir, you okay?'

'I've just been informed only 10 seconds ago that whilst you were all so engrossed about the American missile, the same thing has happened to ours! Apparently, the alien spacecraft has managed to reach my missile and have pushed it back to us only a few minutes ago! I have been informed it's now drifting back at the height of 430 kilometres!"

'Oh, roughly 220 miles!' Clark cut in.

'That's bloody close!' Turnbull's eyes widened. 'Then deactivate the warhead now! Just like Rachel has done!'

President Popov looked back at Prime Minister Turnbull with his steely eyes.

The idea of someone instructing him what to do angered him. He was not used to it, and his immediate response was to argue, but he realised that these circumstances were a time for demonstrating his authority. He took a deep breath before responding, 'I've already instructed the commander of the Russian armed forces to proceed with getting our warhead disarmed'.

'Computer, please focus on the Russian missile and then provide us with the updated readings of its trajectory at five-minute intervals', instructed Clark.

'Instruction acknowledged and processed'.

'Excuse me, I need to disappear for a moment', Popov announced. 'I need to confer with my team. Something is happening that is not quite right!'

The holographic image of him was switched off unexpectedly and without warning.

'What's his problem?' President Wallace turned to Doctor Clark as she hated surprises.

'Search me!' Clark replied. 'Just give him time, he surely knows what the score is with his systems'.

All went quiet as no one knew what to say apart from staring in silence for a few minutes at the blank screen. They were willing it to come alive. Suddenly, they were startled by a synthetic voice piped up so unexpectedly: *'The trajectory of the Russian missile has been calculated to enter the atmosphere in 26 minutes and 24 seconds. The probability of accuracy stands at 76.8%'.*

'That's good enough!' Wallace declared. 'But we need to know where it will land!'

'Computer, please pinpoint the zone where the Russian warhead will land', Clark gave the instruction again.

'Calculating'.

And then they were caught off guard by a pop-up holographic image of Popov.

His face looked stern and grim. His steely eyes rested on Wallace before he sighed aloud. 'I'm afraid we have a real problem'.

'What is it?'

'Our attempts to have our warhead disarmed . . .' Popov paused. 'Have failed!

All attempts to connect it with communication signals have been unsuccessful! It's still programmed to either detonate at the time given or at the height of 100 metres over land'.

'So it is still hot and primed to detonate?' Wallace was dismayed. 'But why can't you get it aborted? What's the problem?'

'We suspected a technology malfunction on our missile'. Popov shrugged. 'It's an old one using 1980s technology'.

'But . . . why did you use the older model that you know is less reliable than the newer one?'

'On contrary to your belief, we haven't made any new missiles after the year 2000 because of the economic shackles that Russia has been experiencing. And we thought it better to discard the older missiles by sending it off . . .' He did not finish his sentence as he was interrupted by a familiar synthetic voice.

'Trajectory of the Russian missile calculated with a probability of 81.7% accuracy, and based on this leeway, it will enter the atmosphere in 28 minutes 32 seconds.

The probability of it breaking up and dispersing will start at 38 degrees 50 minutes north and 124 degrees 50 seconds north and ending at 37 degrees 53 minutes north and 132 degrees 55 minutes east. The sector of dispersion will be 310 miles long by 6 miles wide.

Doctor Clark punched in details furiously on his tablet. He knew President Wallace would baulk at the monotonous detailing of data intoned by the computer.

'Got it . . . !' He looked up slowly at Wallace and then at the rest of the team at the table.

'Well, where in the hell is that?' Wallace gripped the edge of the table. It was more of an instruction than a question.

'The pathway of dispersion starts at the Yellow Sea . . .,' Clark answered quickly. 'Near Pyongyang and continuing across North Korea towards the Sea of Japan.

But remember the inaccuracy of these details means the danger zone could extend into Japan as well as China!'

Suddenly, there was an uproar at the meeting with everyone shouting in their views on the detrimental effect it would have on the world alliance that had united to combat this major incident. They knew the touchy situation with the Korean peninsula had never been promising for years and was far from solved. Back in 2018, they announced they were to dismantle all the nuclear missiles and hoodwinked the world into believing the action of reunification with South Korea would be accomplished within a few years. As time went on, with no solid evidence of progress to show, the United Nations was becoming impatient and decided the sanctions would remain in place until the real evidence of reunification had actually taken place. North Korea accused the United Nations of postponing the peace incentives and went back on their words and recommenced their own nuclear missiles programme. A mini version of the cold war has resumed again between North Korea and the rest of the world.

President Wallace took a deep breath, and her mind was racing furiously on what action to take. But Prime Minister Turnbull beat her to it and with his distinctive clipped English accent, pointed his finger at Colonel Cooper. 'Can you please raise a communication link with the prime minister of Japan for President Wallace to alert them of a small possibility of a nuclear warhead falling on their land . . .?' He then looked towards the Chinese president, Yongrui Yang. 'You are still the only country that maintains the usual diplomatic channels with North Korea, so can you please raise the attention of Kim Jong-un to this unfortunate situation that could endanger his country? Do it now, if you don't mind!'

'What a mess!' Yang exhaled deeply. 'It's not looking good as you all probably know. Kim's already greatly angered and has lost many faces from his country's exclusion from this meeting, even though his country has considerable nuclear capabilities.

This situation will greatly aggravate an already-tense political—'

'Forgive me for interrupting you', said Wallace. 'We already know about his position, and we don't have time for your lecture, as we're wasting our time on talking. The question I'm asking is, can you alert him now? Immediately as of now? Please use your considerable influence'.

Pres Yongrui Yang glanced at PM Tony Turnbull with eyes narrowed. He paused for a short moment as he gauged the situation that was unfolding. He suddenly announced with a small but curt bow, 'You have a point. Say no more. I will proceed with top priority. I will keep this meeting informed'.

His holographic image vanished abruptly. The unexpected alacrity of his response was so out of keeping with the usually extremely restrained Chinese president that the entire membership of the meeting gave a small, spontaneous, but well-meant applause.

This was interrupted as a synthetic voice punched into their awareness. *'Data input received 7 seconds ago confirming dispersion of an American missile has been detected in a fireball located in the Atlantic Ocean at 35 degrees 26 minutes north and 47 degrees 25 minutes west'.*

Elated by this, President Wallace ordered Doctor Clark to get the nearest US naval vessels to the site and to start the process of salvaging the warhead from the depth of the seabed.

The French president interrupted, 'Forget it! You're wasting your time when we have much more pressing matters to deal with. It's the Russian warhead that needs to be taken care of as of now!'

Wallace was not used to being challenged in such an abrupt manner, but she realised the validity of the comment and made a visible effort to control herself.

'Fear not, I'm still fully aware of it, and I can assure you I've got several naval task forces on standby . . .'

A heated debate ensued over the next few minutes until they were interrupted by the holographic image of Chinese President Yang. All eyes were focused on him, expecting him to be the bearer of good news.

'Well, any luck with Kim?' Turnbull questioned. 'How did he take it?'

'It is contrary to my name Yongrui, which, in Mandarin, stands for *forever lucky*', Yang scowled, unsmiling. 'I'm afraid it's not what you want to hear. Indeed, it is very bad news! Despite my presenting the situation in a logical and methodical way to President Kim, he insisted that it was the threat from the American missile, not the Russian, that he was convinced would be the threat to his region. He even accused Russia of collaborating with America using the situation with ETs as a ploy to attack North Korea!'

'But come on, he should know we're trying to deal with ETs!' Wallace was flabbergasted. 'It's very much a global matter!'

'I did point out exactly that'. Yang shook his head. 'His argument was that since it's not been discussed and endorsed by the United Nations, it's an American manipulation'.

'Then what is he going to do about it?' Wallace held her breath.

'The worst we can imagine!' Yang looked down. 'As long as the warhead explodes in proximity to any part of his country, he was very clear that he will fire off his newest missile armed with a nuclear warhead at Hawaii. This is not a new policy, but he has repeatedly warned the USA that he would retaliate—always! He is only upholding his country's declared defence policy'.

'He *what . . . ?!*' Wallace screeched. 'That's absolute madness that we cannot put up with!' She gripped the table so hard her knuckles went white. 'If he does that, then using that same medicine he understands, I will respond by unleashing several missiles at his country, resulting in total obliteration—'

She was interrupted by the emotionless detached computer-generated voice. *'Trajectory of the Russian missile calculated with a probability of 85.7 percent accuracy will enter the atmosphere in 17 minutes and 31 seconds—'*

'Computer, *shut up!*' Wallace screamed. She had clearly lost her self-control.

'Instruction noted'. There was no emotion in the flat impersonal tone of the computer.

'I don't care where it's gonna be detonated, but I'm not having *him* second-guessing us! We all know he's always looking to grab every opportunity to fling a nuclear missile at us, no matter what the situation is!" Wallace yelled. "Get all the Pacific fleets to be diverted at once towards North Korea!'

'Hang on, *hang on!*' Turnbull bellowed. 'Last thing we need, to become too emotional with our decision-making! Just take a deep breath! For god's sake, get a grip of yourself, Rachel!'

Wallace opened her eyes wide in disbelief at Turnbull, but she said nothing.

She was clearly seething at the idea of someone taking the control at the meeting, undermining her leadership.

'Thank you, Rachel!' Turnbull's tone dipped down a little. 'Let's be pragmatic with our decision-making! Before we do that, can we ask, Yongrui, if there's any chance of Kim not hitting Hawaii or any American land?'

'Yes, possibly', Yang responded, not taking his eyes off Wallace. 'A slim chance, but nonetheless, it is only if the Russian warhead is detonated in the Sea of Japan, away from North Korea. If that happened, he would still fire off his missile at the Pacific Ocean at the same distance away from Hawaii, a means to uphold his tit-for-tat status'.

'Then that is it?'

'Yes, that's about what we are expecting to see'.

'If so, we need your assurance you will not take any further action, will you?' Turnbull leant sideways towards Wallace. 'Pointless to hype your action up apart from letting it go! All we pray that the warhead will break apart or, at worst, detonate somewhere in the Sea of Japan.

'I have to concur with Mr Tony Turnbull', agreed Sabina Paquet. 'Just sit it out and wait for it. It's about keeping our nerve in this situation'.

Out of the corner of her eyes, President Wallace caught President Popov nodding in agreement, and then she shifted her focus to President Yang, who also concurred. She continued her surveyance and realised all the team were nodding in agreement before finally resting on Doctor Clark. He looked back but displayed no trace of acknowledgement of if he was in agreement. She understood that such was his level of loyalty that he could not create any doubts. He suddenly ignored her and shifted his attention to his tablet and was startled to see the details now being displayed.

With great vehemence, he muttered only three words, 'Oh my god!' He looked around before fixing his attention on his president. 'Whilst we've been arguing the toss, we've lost track of time! The warhead has just detonated'.

The expression on his face was unreadable. Everyone at the meeting suddenly held their breath.

'Then where?' Wallace yelled at him.

'It's at . . .' He put his mouth practically in the president's ear, whispering something to her.

Her eyes widened a bit, and she nodded, relaxing her grip at the edge of the table.

'Where exactly?' Turnbull repeated his question. He looked at Popov who could be seen talking through his phone.

He looked up and announced, 'Confirming my warhead has been detonated in the middle of'—he took a deep breath—'the Sea of Japan. A radio message from one of the fishing trawlers has witnessed a huge splashdown followed by an enormous explosion apparently under the sea with water rising to a height of several thousand feet.

That shows that there was a slight malfunction with the Russian warhead as it has been detonated under the water rather than in the air!'

There were audible sighs of relief from all the delegates, followed by involuntary cheers and clapping hands, as the reality of the situation sank in.

'It will be only a matter of a short time, and Kim will fire off a missile to land it somewhere in the Pacific Ocean, probably around 700 kilometres away from Hawaii as he threatened', Yang said and threw a searching look at Wallace. 'But can you please assure us all you are not going to escalate this situation with any further action from you, are you?'

Wallace simply stood, and with her head high, she said, 'What choice do I have?

It looks like I'm the one who has made a real shambles of our plan. It is with my understanding that our attempts to shoot a warning shot across the bows has backfired badly. We have practically shot ourselves in our collective feet, so to speak! It has shown I am personally not capable of managing the responsibilities that my country entrusted me with. For that reason, I have no excuse but to hand in my resignation to the House of Congress, which I will do tomorrow morning. I wish you all the very best of luck in finding a solution in dealing with the ETs. I sincerely hope someone of considerably higher calibre will handle the situation better than I did'. She lifted her tablet with her as she stood up. 'It's been an honour to work alongside you all'.

She strode out of the room, leaving everyone speechless.

CHAPTER 24

Human Consignment. Second Time.

The two remaining residents aboard the spacecraft were wide-eyed and dumbfounded. They said nothing for some time. They were unsure as to what to expect, never mind understanding the implication of the dramas that had unfolded before them. As the drama developed, they had watched the video display on the wall in complete silence. The clarity of the visual display of the missiles being redirected back at Earth, leading up to the two separate detonations of the nuclear warheads, astounded them. They muttered to each other and deduced that the explosion that could be seen in the Sea of Japan was caused by the Russian warhead. Another surprise to them was to see a third smaller eruption, not exactly an explosion, that could be seen at some distance from Hawaii in the Pacific Ocean. That was unexpected and highly disturbing.

They continued watching the wonderful vista as night followed day as they watched planet Earth from their position in space. The Gorgass spacecraft continued orbiting it for some time as they watched in total silence. No further untoward events were observed. The scene had a serene quality as the tranquillity of the display of the greenness and blueness of Earth, with constantly changing vistas of changing patches of clouds, mesmerised them.

Andy finally broke the silence. 'Thank goodness! It looks like there won't be any retaliation after all, but that was really shocking to see the two, possibly three, nuclear detonations happening on our dear old Earth!'

'I still cannot believe they've taken such an extreme action to launch two missiles at us! Why on earth did they have to do it?' Emma was shaking her head and talking to herself. She was so totally immersed in the memories of what she had just witnessed that she had not realised her faithful translator was operating whilst it was lying on the floor at her feet. Immediately and as ever dutifully, it had picked up her comment and conveyed it via the wall to the Gorgass.

Andy realised it when he saw it, and he sensed that they were themselves in a very delicate and vulnerable situation. The ever-threatening death sentences were still hanging over their heads. He nudged her discreetly and urgently and signed to her that 'walls have ears'. Emma was taken aback by his abrupt action but quickly cottoned on to the intent and regained her composure.

He pointed at the translator device on the floor and gestured by slitting his throat, indicating that it was possible to carry on conversing in sign language rather than verbally. Emma nodded but shrugged at him as a way of inviting him to explain his intention.

'Okay, I'm not using my voice', he signed slowly and mouthed silently.

'Remember our potential death sentences! We need to maintain our side of the bargain. We need to assure them we are able to provide them with some credible and essential information as a way of assessing the situation and aiding them to determine what's in their best interest . . .'

A new text flashed across the wall, and Andy practically stopped his signing.

GORGASS DEMAND UNIT GREEN AND UNIT RED FULLY DECIPHER CONVERSATION

'Well, all I wanted to do is exchange ideas with her about our views about these unexpected events', Andy said convincingly. 'But the last thing we want to do is to alarm or misinform you. We had not anticipated the inexplicable reaction from Earth, and we needed, as you do, to try and interpret the reactions from Earth so we can give you our considered response. We do not want to mislead you until we are sure that our opinions are properly thought out'.

GORGASS ACKNOWLEDGED COMMENTARY PROVIDED BY UNIT GREEN TO BE PLAUSIBLE

Andy gave a big sigh of relief.

HOWEVER, HOSTILE ACTION BY HUMANS ON EARTH PROVED ILLOGICAL AND WITHOUT FOUNDATION

GORGASS NOT TOLERANT OF HUMAN HOSTILE ACTION

GORGASS DEMANDS UNIT GREEN PROVIDE FULL DECIPHERING OF THE ACTION BY HUMANS

'I agree with you that it's really unacceptable, what they have done by sending two missiles at us, but can you at least give us some more time to discuss and, hopefully, come up with a logical theory for their action?'

GORGASS NOT TOLERANT TIME DELAY

TIME DELAY NOT ENERGY-EFFICIENT

Andy was swift to counter the issue raised. 'If we give you the wrong interpretation because you did not give us sufficient time to give the most logical explanation, it will be Gorgass behaving inefficiently, and we are not sure you would want to do that'.

A most exceptional delay occurred in the time the Gorgass usually took to respond.

THERE WAS EVIDENCE OF FAILURE OF YOUR PEOPLE TO UNDERSTAND MESSAGE DELIVERED BY GORGASS

PROPOSE NEXT ACTION

Andy signed again to Emma, 'We need to shift emphasis', then asked the Gorgass, 'How much time do you estimate you will need to load your essential supplies?'

WITH NO SUPPLY OF MATERIALS, GORGASS CALCULATED SIX EARTH MONTH

THIS IS THE POINT OF NO RETURN FOR THIS GORGASS UNIT TO REJOIN OTHER GORGASS

'Oh yeah, I do recall that from our previous conversation. But still six months!

I don't know if that is enough time left for humans on Earth to construct several rockets to supply you with materials that you require before you go off to meet your other Gorgass space travellers'. Andy looked questioningly at Emma. 'If you get some materials delivered to you within that time span, would that make any difference to you?' He held his hands open. 'Would that help you extend the duration of your time in your Earth orbits?

CALCULATING TO BE IMPROBABLE AND IRRELEVANT

'Why not?' Emma injected, an alarmed expression on her face. 'Is it something to do with the question of energy-efficiency?'

SUPPOSITION CORRECT

LONGER WE REMAIN IN PROXIMITY TO EARTH, THE MORE ENERGY OUTPUT REQUIRED TO CATCH UP WITH OUR COMPANIONS

Andy squeezed Emma's shoulder softly to alert her that he wanted to say something. 'Okay, you've made your situation clear'. He looked at the wall.

'But wouldn't the extra supply of fuel you get from us help you accelerate your travel speeds?' He tilted his head. 'Don't you happen to have plan B in place in case things don't meet your initial objectives?'

CLARIFICATION REQUIRED FOR PLAN B QUESTION

'Another word for a backup plan or second plan, to prepare to take corrective action'. He sighed.

AUXILIARY PLAN ALREADY FORMULATED AND IN PLACE

GORGASS CONSIDER EXECUTING AUXILIARY PLAN AS LAST RESORT

'Then what is it to be?'

ACCUMULATING MOST OF THE ARTIFICIAL SATELLITES ORBITING EARTH

'*What?!*' Andy's eyes widened. '*You're retrieving most of our satellites as something to compensate for the lack of materials not delivered to you?! How convenient!*'

'There's about 4,000 of them'. Emma slapped her forehead with her hand. 'Most of them are communication and GPS satellites! Removing them would plunge us back to 70 years ago, into a dark age in terms of Internet or technology capability! All our Internet servers will become obsolete!'

'It would become a real technology nightmare to us all on a massive scale!'

Andy shook his head.

'Then it's really imperative that we . . .' Emma could not finish her sentence as her emotions got better of her. She looked with horrified eyes at Andy.

'Huh? That is it? Nothing in place as an alternative plan if something completely unpredictable ruins the original intentions?'

Andy interrupted. 'Don't you make any allowance for anything that can go wrong, such as the failure of the Earth powers delivering your materials because they did not understand your intentions?'

PRIMARY AND AUXILIARY PLANS FORMULATED IN PLACE

GORGASS WILL EXECUTE THEM IMMEDIATELY AND VACATE REGARDLESS OF THE RESULT

'What about us?' Andy raised his eyebrows. 'Will you return us to Earth as you said before?'

ONLY IF YOU CAN DELIVER THE RESULT THAT MEETS GORGASS REQUIREMENTS

'In other words, when there's been a failure, then the conclusion is that you will have no further need for us and that we have failed in some way?' Andy stared at the wall. 'Therefore, you will dispose of us, like you did with Rahman?'

AFFIRMATIVE

'We already appreciate that he was not cooperative, but . . .' Andy sucked in a deep breath. 'Why are you not keeping to our agreement? We have not failed!'

THE AGREEMENTS HAVE TO BE CHANGED IF CIRCUMSTANCES CHANGE AND ARE AND NON-BINDING

YOU HAVE FAILED NOT GORGASS

'Only because you and we have no understanding yet why our communications failed'. Andy shook his head. 'This is more harmful to your interests than if we try to re-establish another link with Earth. I'm sure we, the humans, have not only harmed but also pissed you off more than you expected. Now you want to punish us, is that right?' Andy's face was becoming lined with worry. 'You only wanted to make us accountable for our action as it is not in line with your reasoning, is that it?'

AFFIRMATIVE

'I cannot believe we puny humans managed to make Gorgass respond illogically and irritated you to such a degree!' He started to clap his hands slowly and softly.

'You Gorgass are not such cool unflappable sons of bitches that we've judged you to be!'

GORGASS REQUIRE TO DECIPHER THE MEANING SON OF BITCH

Andy continued clapping his hands at the same rate and smiled. 'Why should I? I'm still going to continue to irritate you even more by not explaining the meaning of our words!'

Emma interrupted, 'What about the humans on Earth? Do you have any plans for further dealings with them? It is they, rather than us two puny humans who are completely under your control, that must have irked and frustrated you so significantly!'

AFFIRMATIVE

There was a long unnerving and frustrating pause.

'Then please enlighten us'.

Emma couldn't hide her irritation with Andy's continual hand clapping, which stopped her constructive thought processes, and at her prompting, Andy stopped clapping.

'What are you going to do to them?'

Another long unnerving pause.

'I don't like the way this is all leading!' Andy cautioned her.

HUMANS NEED TO BE DECIMATED

'*WTF!* Partly or all of them?!' Emma cried. 'But *why?!*"

ACQUISITION FOR THE RIGHT TO EXISTENCE FOR HUMANS NOT ACHIEVED

'Yes, but your intended response is not logical. The top people might appear to need punishing, but it is most logical for you to assume they do not understand what your intentions were. It is equally logical that further attempts to obtain their cooperation will still benefit you. You do still need to be sure that the Earth people would understand your desperate needs for supplies. Otherwise, why the hell did you spend so much of your resources in proximity to our planet? You could still benefit from a cooperative dialogue but without the need for such extreme measures!"

Emma collapsed into a heap on the floor, and she continued on her knees.

'You're actually punishing us for the action that you took by extracting the four of us without any explanation! You cannot punish the entire planet's population for the mistakes you made in not explaining in a cooperative way what a desperate need you have for supply of materials!

Don't you see your threatening presence was more of a totally undefined threat, resulting in our . . .' Emma paused, trying to find the most appropriate words. 'Unprecedented retaliatory behaviour!'

ACTION BY HUMANS DEMONSTRATED THEIR LEVEL OF REASONING PERCEPTIVENESS TO BE LACKING

FURTHER COLLABORATION WITH HUMAN IS BECOMING FUTILE AND INEFFECTIVE

Andy interrupted, 'Look, you have already achieved some success in establishing contact with us and are able to maintain a level of reasoning with us four original abductees, in spite of our psychological differences! Can't we use that kind of success to recognise the level of probability was very much in your favour to continue the effort to establish positive and effective communication links with our people on Earth?'

PROBABILITY OF OVER 50% CHANCE OF FAILURE NOT ACCEPTABLE TO GORGASS

'Are you saying you're giving us one more chance of success?' Andy slowly looked up at the wall. 'Or the gloves will be off?'

GORGASS REQUIRES PRECISION CLARIFICATION ON THE LAST COMMENT MADE BY UNIT GREEN

Andy rolled his eyes. 'In other words, in the case of any failure on our part, you will start decimating the human population on Earth! Even if we two humans did not cause it and the events were caused by lack of proper understanding by you?'

AFFIRMATIVE TO UNIT GREEN POSTULATION

PROBABILITY OF 75% OF FAILURE NOT ACCEPTABLE TO GORGASS AT ANY LEVEL

'You're putting an unwarranted pressure and enormous responsibility on us!'

Andy gesticulated and thumped one fist into his other palm.

'You're trying to terrify us with the idea that just the two of us are responsible for the extermination of humanity'. He stared hard at the wall.

'The way you're trying to inflict such pressure and responsibility on us seems like you are acting out of desperation. Your mission to obtain supplies from planet Earth is going to fail entirely because your requirements have not been clearly understood because neither you

---

nor the powers on Earth have understood each other's requirements. Wiping out humanity will not explain what you actually want to obtain. Trying to save your own group of people with a fresh supply of materials is clearly your highest priority. To destroy us would be the one remaining opportunity to restore some credibility with your purpose of investigations of resources to enable your onward voyages strategic intentions. We remain your major asset in retaining the success possibility or indeed, the probability of success!'

He flicked his head at the wall and continued, 'We *can* be reasonable, if given a chance! Believe me, we will help you when the situation is right for us both!'

GORGASS HAVE REACHED CONCLUSION YOU HAVE REACHED THE POINT OF NO RETURN

FUTILE TO HOLD ANY HOPE WITH HUMANS

CONSIDER DECIMATING THEM THE BEST SOLUTION

'All of the humans or just 99% of them?' Emma was referring to the eradication of the rabbit incident. 'How did you get the virus engineered from human blood in the first place?'

99% OF YOUR ORIGINS KNOWN

Andy looked around and realised with a sickening feeling in his stomach, 'Do you mean you've already taken *our* blood samples whilst we were being brought here against our will?' His face sagged. 'That means my being from the black Negro people, Emma's being from white Caucasian people, Gillian's Chinese people, and finally, Rahman's ethnic people, namely the Arabic people, are all threatened?'

AFFIRMATIVE TO UNIT GREEN POSTULATION

'Hang on, let me clarify this'. Emma took a step forward. 'You mean *both* sexes of each race, such as both women and men of Andy's own race?'

AFFIRMATIVE TO UNIT RED POSTULATION

Andy's and Emma's eyes widened in horror at the concept of genocide about to be imposed on the humans on such global scale, a replication of the Holocaust many times over.

'That leaves only the indigenous people of South America, Australia, and possibly few others like the Māori of New Zealand and the Pacific islands?'

QUESTION MARK TO CROSS BREEDS

'Crossbreeds?' Andy scratched his forehead, and then it slowly dawned on him. 'Ah, you mean the mixed people who were born by the interrelationship between different races of people. The effect of the virus would be somewhat diluted on them according to their own pool of genetic mixture?'

AFFIRMATIVE TO UNIT GREEN POSTULATION

Andy responded in a conjectural manner as he thought things through. 'Still, whatever happens to any of these four major races of humans, it's guaranteed there'll be a total collapse of infrastructures in all continents, except possibly South America!'

'Gorgass, you *cannot* be that *serious!*' Emma yelled. 'Without any infrastructures in places, how can you expect us to construct any rockets, never mind launching them to supply you with the materials that you badly need in the first place! It's illogical'.

There was a pause. An uncharacteristically long one. No response from Gorgass.

'Well done, Emma'. Andy threw an admiring glance at her. 'I think you've got them to reconsider their stance carefully!'

'I hope so!' Emma nodded. 'It would be awful to know you've become a liability or responsibility for the decimation of your own race!'

GORGASS DEMAND INPUTS FROM UNIT GREEN AND RED

DECIMATION OF WHICH ETHNIC GROUP MADE WITH MINIMISING DISRUPTION TO THEIR ROCKET LAUNCHING CAPABILITIES

'*Huh*? Again, you cannot be that serious by forcing us to select which ethnic type of people for you to start decimating!'

There were dark shadows in Andy's eyes as he paused to give a prolonged consideration before he replied, 'All humans on Earth are very much interlinked with one another through every conceivable level of infrastructures! There'll be a massive uncontrollable effect throughout the world, no matter which ethnic groups you try to obliterate!'

GORGASS INSIST ON UNIT GREEN REACHING CONCLUSION

His eyes widened. 'I am afraid it's gonna be an impossibly difficult question for either of us to answer or even to try and hypothesise!'

Then he took a deep breath before going on. 'Look, as far as I know, if you obliterate all the Caucasian white people, that means America,

Europe, and Australia will be affected. Without infrastructures in place, there will be no supply of high-quality rockets available to launch from Florida and New Zealand who have recently become deeply involved in the technology of research rocket sciences. And the same thing will happen with the black people, whose genes are very interwoven with white people, especially in North America, not to forget the vast number of materials that are being mined in Africa for the purposes of exporting to all over the world. Remove the workforces in Africa, you'll be guaranteed the global infrastructures will collapse, and not to forget there's a large community of African Americans of direct ancestors from Africa living in the south of the USA, *so removing them* will still affect the launching capability at the Kennedy Space Centre.

'Then there's Rahman's own people. Arabic countries alone supply over 80% of the world's oil needs. Remove them, then the entire industrial capabilities in America and China will be severely disrupted! No question about that! And finally, the Asian people, which consist of around 20% of the world's population! China is now a world's superpower with its industrial production cranking out to meet 80% of the world's manufacturing processed goods. It's already surpassed America with two large rocket-launching pads. I believe it's very capable of putting more rockets into space than all other countries combined!

'So there you go. It's no brainer to have one ethnic group decimated without affecting others!'

Beads of sweat broke out on Andy's forehead. Emma took a step forward and whispered with a sign, 'We sincerely wish and beg for your understanding that there's no need for you to inflict a sickening genocide on any race on a global scale. That'll be a real unforgiving nightmare on an unprecedented scale, which would totally inhibit any further cooperation either from us or, more importantly, any group or organisation on Earth'. She could not continue. Her freckles darkened with emotion as she continued amid her sobs, 'It's totally contrary to everything we have achieved whilst we have been here in your alien environment!'

Andy gave her firm morale-boosting hug as he sank slowly to the floor alongside Emma without uttering a word. They were aware of a new message appearing on the wall, but they couldn't bring themselves to read it as they were mentally drained.

They were staring at the floor for a few minutes until Andy grudgingly peered through his hands to look at the wall.

Silence for few minutes.

GORGASS HAVE CHANGED CONCLUSION BASED ON YOUR INPUTS

IN THE INTERIM UNITS GREEN AND RED WILL DECIDE WHICH OF YOU IS TO RETURN TO EARTH

Andy took a long slow deep breath before he prodded Emma to look at the wall. With reluctance, she forced herself to focus on the wall once again.

'Are you saying one of us will remain as a hostage? And then what would happen to the person left behind?'

ENERGY-INEFFICIENT TO DETAIN A LONE HUMAN ON LIMITED RESOURCES

'But you said last time you would consider returning both of us back to Earth if we produced the results you need? Why have you changed your plan?'

Andy's emotion was guarded, and he spoke in calm measured tones to hide the turmoil that seethed in his brain.

SITUATION CHANGED

'What has changed?'

SITUATION WITH NUCLEAR MISSILES

'So it's these bloody missiles that have made you question our level of authenticity and integrity?'

UNIT GREEN POSTULATION CORRECT

'But no harm has been done to you yet!'

Andy was feeling totally frustrated at the ability of Gorgass to discount any constructive discussion and to disregard the value of human lives at their sole discretion.

HUMAN INTELLIGENCE ALREADY SHOWN NOT ABLE TO FOLLOW LOGIC

'But, but . . .' Andy was stammering to find the right words. 'Don't you think we should be given a chance to continue to learn from you as we have already shown a considerable measure of positive results between us?'

ON THE CONTRARY

THE HUMAN FAILURE TO ACHIEVE PSYCHOLOGICAL COGNITIVE UNDERSTANDING OF WHAT IS RATIONAL IS FUTILE AND NOT ENERGY-EFFICIENT

'I think you're being unfair to us by grouping us with other irrational humans on Earth with the senseless action they've made so far!' Emma interjected with her signing movements, noticeably exaggerated to match her level of resentment with the Gorgass. Andy muscled in, mirroring Emma's concerns.

'What we are asking is to be able to be put in a position where we can evaluate the reasons behind the reactions so far from the people in control of the responses from Earth. So far, we have only been able to only guess, reading the same signals that you have seen across the distances of space.

'We have certainly not yet been able to explain what your very reasonable requirements are for supplies of materials. We have seen no evidence any more than you have that your ability to benefit in a reciprocal manner has been fully understood. The list of requirements written on Lillian's cowl may not have even been seen and understood. That clothing may have even been destroyed or washed without realising its significance.

'All I'm asking you is *not* to put us in the same camp as these humans on Earth, and we don't want to be made liable for their actions. Just give us a chance to use our communication skills that we have developed between us in the short space of time that we have been held here by you!'

He knelt on one knee as if he was begging. He eyed the wall. He was willing to give him a glimmer of hope, hope for life, their lives to be spared, regardless of whoever would be left behind.

There was a lull in writing on the wall, a significant pause. The Gorgass contemplated the long and logical plea from their two prisoners. Finally, a new sequence of sentences developed.

GORGASS REMAINS UNCONVINCED ABOUT HUMAN BEHAVIOURS

GORGASS NEED MORE ASSURANCE

UNIT GREEN OR RED TO BE TRANSPORTED TO EARTH AND BE GIVEN THREE EARTH DAYS TO PROVE GORGASS HUMAN CAN BE DEPENDABLE AND REASONED WITH

'Aren't they still forcing us to decide who's to commit suicide by staying behind?' Emma's eyes glistened with emotion as she conferred with Andy. 'Regardless of the result achieved by us?'

'Not quite, I think they mean they would only spare the humans on Earth as long as they can deliver the materials to the Gorgass'.

Andy was trying to verify everything logically in his mind. He readdressed the wall, 'However, by forcing us to make a decision, you have inadvertently put us at disadvantage. There is no way we can decide who's ever going to go or stay behind.

It's not within our psyche to gamble our lives away'.

'They can't force us to play wrap-rock-scissors!' Emma interjected.

GORGASS UNABLE TO DECIPHER THE MEANING OF ROCK AND SCISSOR. INTERPRETATION REQUIRED

'A game of wagers using our hands'. Emma sighed as she was not in the mood to explain fully the meaning of it.

'We are not in a position to abide by your instruction'. Andy clasped Emma's hand. 'You have to decide here and now then'.

There was a trace of authority in his voice. He turned her around tenderly so they faced each other. He looked deeply into Emma's eyes in search of consolation, but instead, he only admired the rich colour of her eyes. *I haven't noticed until now just what a beautiful green they are.*

'Hate to say this, but I'm afraid there's nothing we can do about it'. He mouthed in an exaggerated way. 'In a way, I was hoping you should go first as you probably deserve it more than I do'.

'Why me? I hate it here just as much as you do! But I don't know how much longer I will keep my sanity. I really don't think I can cope with it all much longer!'

Emma muttered. 'Whichever of us it will be, I'm still really afraid for you and me!

I don't like the idea of nothingness and the emptiness that would come after my death!'

'Those are exactly my thoughts!' Andy was trying to find words to alleviate her fears but could not. Instead, he uttered much to his regret, his voice croaking with suppressed emotion. 'That's the really frightening aspect of this whole affair. I think the best way to deal with it all is to think about the time before we were born.

We don't remember anything about it, except for the peacefulness that comes with emptiness!'

'How reassuring is that but there's a difference'. Emma's emotion hyped up a notch. 'The richness of life that comes after the birth itself has alleviated the fears, but this time there'll be no afterlife to contend with!'

'How true', Andy said dejectedly.

They said nothing for the next few minutes until a new sentence flashed.

BASED ON COMPUTATION, GORGASS HAVE REACHED CONCLUSION THAT UNIT RED HAS BEEN SELECTED TO GO BACK TO EARTH ON A MISSION TO ENSURE DELIVERY OF OUR MATERIALS

Andy's face drained of blood with a nauseatingly heavy punch to his stomach.

So that is it! My time's come up! Shhhiiit . . . ?

There was no comment from either of them for some time as they each tried to gather their thoughts, both thinking of the other's best interests. Emma broke the silence and addressed the wall, 'Based on what? Is it 'cos I'm better-looking than him?'

There was no sarcasm in her voice as this is an aspect which is not universally well practised amongst Deaf people. Still, it made no difference to Gorgass as it was clearly out of their range of comprehension of the humans' customary trait of quirky humour.

PHYSICAL APPEARANCE NOT TAKEN INTO ACCOUNT

IRRELEVANT AND FUTILE

Emma lamented, 'Oh, forget it! Whatever it is, I don't think I'm going and leaving him behind to his fate! No, I *cannot* do it!'

GORGASS DETECT ELEMENT OF DISSENT IN UNIT RED

Andy grabbed her shoulders. 'Emma, don't make a martyr of yourself to end up like Rahman. It's pointless as our two deaths would achieve nothing! Just go and rescue the world! Do not concern yourself with me. I will be truly happy if you were to succeed, and I think you would have a better way of presenting the essence of the Gorgass requirements than me'.

'But it's totally unfair on you, knowing you have had no choice in this matter, did you?'

'Yes, life's a bitch, isn't it? Maybe I shouldn't have said that to a woman!' This quip lightened the atmosphere between them. Andy let go of her shoulders. 'But at least I would feel better leaving life knowing that I did my bit by helping you in your endeavours!'

She brushed him aside and looked directly at the wall, drew a deep breath whilst searching for some inner strength to maintain her level of stoicism. She found it.

'Look, Gorgass, you have us seriously disadvantaged'. A tear broke out and trickled down her cheek. 'But is there any way you can give me a glimmer of hope, something to motivate me on my journey back to Earth, knowing there's a slight possibility of saving him'. She took another deep breath. 'One thing I've noticed was your decision to have him discarded is based on a policy of energy efficiency and conservation that you need to adhere to, is that right?'

AFFIRMATIVE

'Then perhaps it would make a real difference if I could get a rocket blasted off within a few weeks or months with a rescue capsule or craft attached to it and send it off in your direction'. She wiped away her tears and took a deep breath before continuing, 'You can then use it to get him transported or transferred to it at close range. And most important of all, treat this rescue rocket as a signal that the Earth powers have finally understood and accepted your request for materials to be sent up to your spacecraft? How about that? Would that make any difference to our situation?' Emma lifted her chin and continued her combination of speech and signing, 'Perhaps it's an answer to your energy-efficiency dilemma?'

There was no immediate response from the Wall.

'I think you've got them thinking and, hopefully, reconsider their aggressive attitudes'. Andy patted her shoulder.

SUGGESTION PROVIDED BY UNIT RED ACKNOWLEDGED AND ANALYSED

A pause. The very moment had forced both occupants to hold their breath briefly in anticipation.

GORGASS HAVE REACHED CONCLUSION

———

UNIT RED HAS PROVIDED A WINDOW OF ATTAINABLE SOLUTION
GORGASS HAVE GRANTED UNIT RED FOUR WEEKS TO VALIDATE HER POINT AFTER RETURN TO EARTH

At first, both said nothing, apart from looking at each other. Andy then pointed his finger at the wall. 'Seems you've changed your mind. Therefore, this proves one thing: You were previously not thinking positively and critically! Your attitudes or conclusions can be swayed by whatever the objective evidence is presented!'

He took another step towards the wall, maintaining his confrontational stance.

'If you think you are entirely rational, then your beliefs would be grounded in logic and evidence! She has proved to you one thing: You are not totally fixed in your expectations!'

He stopped abruptly as he realised that his confrontational stance could be counterproductive to their situation. He swiftly changed his tone. 'However, I do recognise a very welcome willingness to try and understand different reasoning'.

He flicked a step backwards. 'That is a major and positive change in our understanding of each other's requirements. Indeed, you have given us some hope that we will now be of benefit to each other!'

ABILITY TO RECOGNISE THE REQUIREMENT TO CHANGE THE INITIAL DECISION MADE BY GORGASS IS PART OF GORGASS PSYCHE

'Whatever it is, that is still the same difference and a good thing!' Andy beamed. 'Something that is sadly lacking in many people on Earth! That is the problem with us, basing on too much of our self-importance to consider we could be wrong with our own beliefs! No wonder there are so many squabbles and conflicts going on around the world. Anyway, if there is a slim chance for us to be spared, then there's a reason for us to be optimistic and positive about it'.

He looked at Emma who was still reading the writing on the wall. 'Does that help you? Are you prepared to go back to Earth with full knowledge that there's a strong possibility of me being spared, Emma?'

'No doubt, that's very helpful. Okay. I really am much more comfortable with this exchange of views. That was constructive. I'm ready!'

'Then let's go now as we know time is of the essence! The sooner you get the attention of the top people at the United Nations, the quicker they can get their acts together with a view to sending material supplies to Gorgass—and hopefully not forgetting to send a rescue rocket for me!'

He looked up at the wall and asked, 'Can we have a bird's eye view of New York, where the United Nations headquarters is based?'

REQUEST ACKNOWLEDGED

A large image of Earth gleamed brightly on the wall, followed by a wording superimposed on it.

GORGASS REQUEST UNIT GREEN TO ACCURATELY INDICATE THE PRECISE LOCATION

'Righto, here we go . . .'

He started the proceedings of locating the East Coast of the USA. After a few moments of magnification, he was grateful there were no clouds covering New York. An image of the UN Headquarters was clearly seen.

'Ah, a little more magnification . . . yeah . . . little more . . . there!'

A clear bird's eye view image of the rooftop of the United Nations skyscraper, complete with its heliport, could be seen. He recognised it as it was very fortunate he had visited New York a few times while attending scientific conferences. Once he was satisfied there were no armed police that could be seen on the rooftop, he announced, 'That should do the trick. I think we can get the drone to land you directly on the heliport . . . Any problem with that, Emma?'

'Bu . . . but . . .' There were some concerns in her eyes. 'Isn't there a real possibility of me being shot down by the Raptors?'

'How true!' Andy looked up at the wall. 'How can you assure us that won't happen?'

LOCATING HOSTILE DRONES LAUNCHING PAD

Instantly, a large bird's eye view of New York filled in across the full wall. Then the picture moved away from the United Nation in the northeast across the land until it homed down to an airport. A few military aeroplanes could be seen on the tarmacadam adjacent to their protective silos.

'I think that's somewhere in Connecticut, about a 20-minute jet flight away from New York'. Andy rubbed his chin. 'That is something of an unquantifiable threat that I'm not comfortable with'.

'Then how can I get there safely?' Emma questioned. 'Wouldn't it be better if I can arrive there under the cover of darkness?'

'That's a good possibility!' Andy nodded cautiously. 'But I believe they can operate in any condition, regardless of if it's day or night-time. However, I think the best solution is to just go straight to the top of the heliport and stay there! Don't think the Raptors would have time to arrive at the United Nation building before your drone does. I do not think the Americans would be prepared to fire at or interfere in any way with the drone whilst it's in stationery on the heliport for fear of causing too much collateral damage to the building and people'.

'I think that's the most logical answer!' Emma's confidence was obviously bolstered. 'Gorgass, can you arrange the drone to simply fly straight there and drop me off there but needs to remain there throughout? I can then alert the people not to inflict any damage to it'.

GORGASS NOT CONVINCED IT PRACTICAL SOLUTION

GORGASS NOT UNDERSTAND HUMAN REACTION AND BEHAVIOUR

THEREFORE, NEED TO HEED RECOMMENDATION SET BY UNIT RED

THAT CAN BE ARRANGED

'Then that's it'. Andy slapped his hands together enthusiastically. 'Emma, do you have any problem with this arrangement? Any other issues about it?'

'None at all, I think that's a great idea . . .' Emma kept nodding. 'Sooner I get there, the better your situation will be!'

'Attagirl!' Andy gave a soft congratulatory grip on her shoulder. 'That's the type of Dunkirk spirit we need!'

* * *

Three people were sitting in a semicircle around the large monitor.

'Keep reminding yourself that we have to win her confidence to gain her trust.

After what she has been through, she must still be very disoriented'.

Brett gave the appearance of calm leadership, but he was inwardly highly excited at his ingenious use of technology to gain access and crack the Vatican's apparent censorship.

'Okay! Don't ya worry ya pretty head, honey, chill! Ahm giving it mah best shot!' she replied as she put on a fake Deep Southern American nasal drawl. This did have the effect of relaxing the intense atmosphere.

Brett smiled and looked at Troy. 'Okay, let's go!'

Troy said nothing but tapped a few keys on his ultra-slim customised keyboard.

His eyes were focused intently on the monitor. His concentration had not wavered off it for the last half an hour. An image of a white ceiling with a hanging lighting fixture came up on the monitor. They all stared at it in spellbound silence.

* * *

The tablet which up until then had been resting almost invisibly on the bedside table piped up with a melodic wake-up signal followed by a soft female voice.

'Hello there. How are you? I hope Cardinal Marcello has been treating you well so far? Is there anything you want that would help you in your situation?'

Gillian had been sitting quietly sipping a cup of coffee whilst she was deep into reading a book Cardinal Marcello had obtained with some care. It was written in Korean, and she was totally absorbed. She looked up suddenly and almost spilt the coffee in surprise. *An American woman? How did she access this glasscomm?*

Gillian was bewildered but did not feel threatened as soon as the name 'Cardinal Marcello' was pronounced. 'Hullo? Who are you?' she reacted involuntarily. 'Who am I speaking to?'

'Oh sorry, I didn't mean to startle you! My sincere apologies! How rude of me not to introduce myself. I'm Sarah Smith, a reporter from the *Las Vegas Sun* based in Las Vegas. Just giving you a friendly call to see how you are. I am hoping you could give me an exclusive story of what it was like out in the alien starship, and . . .'

Sarah prattled on quickly before taking another short breath and was about to continue when Gillian cut in.

'I am not supposed to talk to any reporters! I don't want any aggro from them or have them prying into my personal life!'

She stood up and went over to the side of the table and looked down on the glasscomm and saw a video image of a single female face. She was about to switch it off when Sarah continued quickly, 'Yes, I really do have great sympathy for you.

I don't blame you at all for your reluctance to talk to the press in general, and my editor has told me that I must not pry into your personal life. On the contrary, it's not about you. It's just I'm more interested in the other occupants on the starship and to see how they are. Their families are truly worried about them and are asking after them, so here I am, hoping you could give me some assurance they're all okay and in relatively good shape'.

'I thought I've already relayed my details through Cardinal Marcello who must have informed you all fully about the situation on the spaceship!'

'Yes, of course, but unfortunately, there are some missing gaps in the story that the families are clearly anxious to know. Hence, I was hoping you can provide me something to assure them . . . especially after the spell you've stayed out there . . .'

'Like what?' Gillian sat down in the other chair next to the glasscomm.

'I don't really know much about their personal lives that well, especially Rahman. Oh, poor man!'

'Yes, exactly! Take him as an example. It would be nice to know if he had any last message for his family, his last words, his outlook on life, and so on . . . and most important, if there could be any clues as to the reasons why he was jettisoned apparently so needlessly?'

'Well, he was just being stubborn and refused to heed the aliens' demands for cooperation on supplying materials for their needs . . .' Gillian didn't finish the sentence. Her emotions were still raw, and she wasn't thinking clearly.

'Excuse me, what materials? What sort of materials are you referring to?'

Sarah quickly homed in on the hitherto undisclosed aspect. 'We need to be able to have a clear understanding of what you mean. Only you are in a position to give us a clear picture'.

Gillian frowned at the glasscomm and said, 'Oh, the usual raw materials, such as pure water, raw carbon, irons, and so on. Can't remember them all, but there's a list of them that were written on my habit, and I'm sure Cardinal Marcello has it. But . . . but hasn't he already informed you about it?' She was becoming alarmed.

'Oh, you mean that!' Sarah lied very convincingly. 'Oh yes, we weren't sure what materials you were referring to!'

She glanced sideways at Brett, but this was not picked up by Gillian. Out of the picture, Brett was scribbling down a single word on a piece of paper, which he thrust into Sarah's view. It was simply 'rabbit', and that was the cue for her to move on.

She nodded and continued, 'However, there's something else we're not sure about and if it's in any way related to the issue of the rabbits that we're facing at this moment? We know they're being eradicated, but can you at least confirm if there's any connection between the materials and the issues with the rabbits, or was it something else that we're not aware of?'

'Sort of, it was an agreement reached between them and us . . .'

Unwittingly, under Sarah's subtle guidance, Gillian had started unfolding the story in full and filling in the gaps in the story that had been created deliberately in the first place by Cardinal Marcello. A goldmine of information, which had been so far inaccessible to Brett, was finally becoming available.

In spades.

* * *

Andy and Emma were standing in silence. They were examining the very same drone that had snatched them off the Earth. They did not really appreciate just what a technically advanced device it was since they had been unconscious when they were abducted. It was lying on its back in another adjoining space that had been opened to them. The human-sized cavity could be seen in the belly of the drone.

Emma muttered quietly to Andy, 'So here we go. This is it'.

She was still wearing the shining red-coloured bodysuit provided by the Gorgass, plus the bulky bright fluorescent orange cross belt she wore over it. She had also been given a bright orange helmet to protect her head. She took a deep breath and nodded at Andy and then glanced at the far side of the room at the wall, where a video image of the UN building was still being displayed. She could see several tiny black figures patrolling around in the grounds of the United Nations building. She realised that they were probably armed police but in great numbers. She could not help wondering why the unusual amount of security had increased so significantly compared with the images previously recalled by her in newscasts. *Perhaps it was down to the presence of the alien starship that they had apparently stepped up the levels of security?* she pondered.

She looked at Andy and asked, 'Don't you think it's safe to go there when there are so many security people around on the ground?'

'Frankly, it also crossed my mind about the security issues', Andy said guardedly. 'But as far as we can see, apparently, there's no one that can be seen on the rooftop of the tall tower building, so it should be safe for you to go and have yourself landed there directly. If you present yourself to them as being unarmed, then there shouldn't be any problem?'

'I suppose so'. She nodded. 'Probably the safest place out of all the nearby places, and given the limited time we have, it's still the quickest way to address the influential people head on in the UN conference room'. She stopped her sentence abruptly as she walked back to the wall. She had already formulated a request in her mind. 'Hey, Gorgass, wouldn't it be possible for you to anaesthetise me but with a slightly smaller dosage? I want to wake up just before your drone drops me off on the rooftop.

Is that possible?'

GORGASS CONSIDER UNIT RED REQUEST RISKY

GORGASS DEMAND UNIT RED TO PROVIDE REASON

'I do understand the danger of asphyxiation if I breathe too fast, but the difference this time, I will be fully aware that I am inside the drone and will do my best not to panic that much and, hence, be able to control my breathing rate'. she responded with an air of self-confidence. 'A few minutes before your drone drops onto the landing area of the heliport is all I need as it would help me be fully prepared and be able to handle the situation quickly, such as facing the people coming up to meet me. They will need to be told not to do any harm to the stationary drone. We hope it will be needed for at least one more return ticket!'

Andy quickly added his support. 'It's a real possibility they would find her unconscious and feel impelled to take her straight away to the hospital! That is, indeed, an unnecessary trip! Sooner she's up on her feet, the better she's in control of her destiny, especially when my life, never mind the rest of the world, is at stake!'

GORGASS CONSIDER INPUTS FROM UNIT GREEN PLAUSIBLE

WILL ARRANGE FOR ANTIDOTE TO BE INJECTED FROM DRONE AS LANDING PROCEDURES COMMENCE

'Thanks! That is a more accurate method', Emma beamed. 'Okay, let's make a move . . .' She turned around but was stopped by Andy.

'Hang on . . . What about that personal translator, aren't you taking it with you?' He pointed at the device on the floor.

She saw it but shook her head. 'Nah, you can have it as you may need it to continue your correspondence with Gorgass. Once I'm back on Earth, I can get the battery for my CI charged, then I should be okay!' She smiled at him. 'Plus with interpreters available out there on hand, though I understand the American interpreters are fluent in American Sign Language, which are markedly different from my AUSLAN, I'll find a way around it, no worry. I can get them to use the video conferencing and hook up with AUSLAN interpreters from Australia! So there, no big deal! I can function out there!'

'Cool!'

Once again, she turned around, walking back to the drone when she spotted a glassy chunk lying inconspicuously on the floor and realised it was a remnant piece of the pliable material that she had scooped off the wall during the liquefaction incident. She looked up at the wall and said, 'Hey, Gorgass, do you have any problem if I can take this with me back to Earth as a souvenir?'

UNIT RED REQUEST GRANTED

'Thanks! But wondering if I can get it to become liquefied once again so it can be shaped snugly somewhere inside that drone? Is that possible, and how?' She was tossing it up and catching it with her hands.

DOUBTFUL BUT POSSIBLE

IT CAN ONLY BE INDUCED AND FUNCTIONED WITHIN PROXIMITY OF THE SAME ROOM WHERE HUMANS ARE RESIDING

'I don't understand you, but are you saying it's still a possibility?' She continued tossing and catching it. 'It would be of much use if I can apply it into the building materials . . . but how? Please explain'.

* * *

It had taken Sarah more than two hours to complete the interview with Gillian, and with her skilful handling, she had managed to glean much more information than she and Brett had bargained for. Finally, Brett broke the silence. 'Well done, Sarah, that is abso-fucking-lutely a goldmine of information that we have come across, never even imagined!'

'Sure thing! Seems there are several glaring gaps of the story that Cardinal Marcello has refrained from passing on! Was that intentional, or has he overlooked it accidentally?' Her eyes locked with Brett's. 'Especially that list of materials that the aliens have been demanding! Why the hell didn't he tell us? What exactly was his plan that we aren't aware of?'

'Yeah, the extermination of rabbits was carried out essentially as a favour in expectation of some kind of trade-off!'

Their sheer excitement mounted as they batted ideas of the importance of their mind-blowing revelations, and as their realisations grew, so did the level of decibels. Brett suddenly stood up and held up his hands, an action that stopped the further conversation in its tracks.

'From what we have already gleaned, this is the news scoop of the century, and we have to make the absolute most of it and bloody fast!' He looked at his watch. 'I think we should catch the next flight back to America now to deliver our exclusive! Live TV footage from here will not work as we do not have the full technical backup we need. We can work on it whilst we fly, and baby, we fly fucking first fucking class'.

'All the way to LA?' she queried.

He paused momentarily. 'Nah! New York, my honey child! I doubt if we could last the pace all the way to LA!' he said with a salacious grin. 'As Gillian mentioned, I've got the gut feeling Emma or Andy will probably go straight to the United Nations. Then why not be there during the drone arriving, and we'll be there on time to witness and report the whole story!' He put up his two fingers. 'By killing two birds with one stone, we'll have a double dosage of exclusives!'

'But still I think we need to make it our foremost duty to alert the world leaders that their assumption of the ETs' dynamics and intentions up to now were completely misinformed!'

'Exactly, whilst we're there, at the same time, we can raise their level of awareness!' He kept smiling. 'Where is a better place than the United Nations?'

Sarah was speculating inwardly about his level of ethics and integrity, which can be somewhat dubious even for a reporter, but could not help being drawn by the pull of his charismatic and magnetic personality. She was clearly appalled by the prospect of the immense journalistic kudos with which she would be associated. All she could respond unconvincingly was 'Yeah, yeah, let's go there then!'

* * *

Cardinal Marcello was sitting in Sister Lee's room, critically observed by her. Though he was sitting quietly, his face told a different story, an impression of seething fury and exasperation. She had just informed him when he came in about the interview that took place some time ago with an American woman reporter.

'Dei gratia . . .' His eyes were wide open. 'Quid hoc fecisti mihi'.

He gripped the side of the table hard, the white knuckles betraying the intensity of his normally carefully controlled image. His mind was zigzagging all over the place and fell back into using Latin, a language with which Gillian was not familiar.

'Sorry?' Her face was blank.

'By the grace of God, what have you done to us?' His eyes bored into her.

* * *

151

'Are you comfortable and ready?' Andy asked. He was kneeling on the floor next to the drone with his hands grasping Emma's hands. She was sitting inside the drone's cavity.

'Yes, I'm ready!' She was eyeing, with great apprehension, the tentacle hanging from the ceiling directly in front of her. 'What choice do I have?'

In a few minutes, she was in suspended animation. Andy caught her and nestled her carefully into the cavity as any mother would do with their babies into cots.

'I meant to tell you . . .' He paused, trying to speak clearly despite the lump in his throat. 'You are, indeed, one of hell an amazing woman, and for that reason alone, I sincerely hope I will see you once again!'

He stood up and took a few steps backwards, away from the drone. Emotion welled up inside him, and he was trying to find the right words, but all he ended up saying with a voice strangled with his intense feelings was 'Good luck, Emma'.

The orifice was sealed by a multilayered shutter. After a short while, he was watching the image of the drone relayed on the wall shooting out of the port towards the Earth. The view of the Earth was magnificent and transfixing as he longed to be there. He knew his life was entirely in her hands, and he realised he was now totally impotent. He took a deep breath and simply said whilst watching the image of the drone getting smaller as it followed its flight path, 'Bon voyage Emma!'

CHAPTER 25

The Final Reckoning

'Listen to me, my lads', the team leader, Captain Martinez, barked at five other men. Like him, they were all similarly dressed in black NYPD-style uniform. All were wearing dark and mirrored goggles fitted tightly on their helmets and black riot-control armour, including face masks. This sinister and threatening appearance they presented was intentional.

'A few minutes ago, I was online with someone closer to God than any of you are ever likely to get! We have been handpicked to carry out this special mission ordered by high-up . . .' He went on and pointed his index finger up in the air. 'All the way to our goddamned mayor of New York'. He had to shout because the environmental noise was deafening. They were inside a helicopter with both side doors wide open.

The warm air from the slipstream buffeted them as it was in the late afternoon in the early autumn.

One of the team was sitting on the edge of the floor close to the open hatch. He was hooked to the floor of the cabin by a safety strap. 'Yes, sir. But what in hell's name is all the flap about this time?'

'We're now in a state of emergency level 1. He's been tipped off by a reliable source that it's now very probable that an alien drone may be taking a trip to this place'.

He thumbed a sideways gesture at the internationally recognisable tall skyscraper to which they were fast approaching. 'It's now our highest priority to protect and secure the United Nations building'.

'But shouldn't the task of protecting it fall to the National Guard or Army?

That's the proper way of maintaining the armed response to this sort of threat posed by an alien drone?'

'Yes, but we're the rapid-response team in proximity, so we need to get here first and hold the fort until the army gets here'. There was a degree of irritation in his voice. He detested anyone questioning his authority. 'They're, as I've been told, about few hours away from getting here. We were instructed to keep our eyes peeled for anything we judge as threatening acts and to use our judgement to take any precautionary or preventative measures to nullify it'.

'What is the specific order once we encounter it?'

'Our orders are to shoot to immobilise it, and it does not matter how we do it!'

The corner of Martinez's mouth twitched noticeably. 'If possible, neutralise it before it can pose any threat to anyone in, on, or around the UN precinct. It's been declared officially as hostile in any form. Do you have any questions? And any objections?'

All the team, except for one, shook their heads and shouted in a chorus of acceptance. Martinez shot a steely look at the lone figure who was looking rather reluctant. 'Hey, Davis, what's your beef?'

'There's a strong possibility there could be a human inside the drone, or so I've been told'. He stared back at the captain through his goggles. 'Don't we have any concerns about what will happen to it?'

Martinez retaliated aggressively. 'Davis, you need to take into consideration the significance of this threat'. His eyes could not be seen as they were masked by the mirrored goggles. 'I repeat, a very real threat posed to mankind as was proved with the rabbits in Australia!' There was a noticeable irritation in his voice. 'Doesn't it occur to you that this human, whoever it is, inside the alien drone could be carrying deadly viruses that could wipe us all out?' He snapped his fingers. 'Like that!'

He pointed at a small chest cradled in between his legs. 'This is the temporary biohazard control kit box, made specifically for this job! If we find a human inside the drone, then we need to contain it in this special biohazard bag'. He looked outside at the skyscrapers and pointed at them. 'Millions of people are living out there, so it's no contest to put the value of this one person's life over them!'

'Aye, aye, I got it'. Davis waved at him. 'I should have known better than to question our tactics. I concur your point, it's a no-brainer!'

The pilot suddenly gesticulated and attracted Martinez's attention. 'I've just been informed that there's been an eyeball sighting of a drone descending towards the heliport on the roof of the United Nations!'

He banked the helicopter steeply and flew between two adjacent tall skyscrapers in the direction of the United Nations.

'Oh, fuck me! Already?!' Martinez cursed. 'We're not expecting it would be there that soon!' He looked at the direction of where they were going and considered the options of approaching the drone. He looked at the pilot. 'Can you fly much lower than the height of the UN building? Say 20 or 30 feet over the water? Once we get close to it, then we can pop up and over to the top of the building?' It was more of an instruction than a request made by Martinez to the pilot. 'We need to maintain an element of surprise!'

'Roger that!'

The helicopter dived steeply. The waist-gunner shifted his weight behind the machine gun and switched the safety clip off.

* * *

Emma's eyes flickered briefly as she started to waken. She was startled to see it was dark and tried to lift her head in reaction but bumped her forehead. She sensed some odd movement in her body and quickly remembered where she was. *Hang on, gotta calm! Won't be long before I will be free from this drone!* she thought and started to fumble around, trying to make sense of space around her body.

She realised there was hardly any space for her to manoeuvre. Claustrophobia started to swell up inside her. *For god's sake get a grip on yourself! Won't be long!*

She grinded her teeth and tried to visualise the image in her mind of the beaches as her favourite places to go, as she found the sheer vastness of the open sea so soothing and appealing. The pace of her breath started to slow down. *Lovely sea! lovely beach!* She kept focusing on them in her mind.

* * *

The fins had deployed automatically once the drone entered the Earth's atmosphere and continued to hum and pulsate in different pitches. It was coming down at a more controlled rate towards the middle of the United Nations skyscraper complex and swiftly slowed to hover about 50 feet above the heliport.

Its laser device snapped out from its sliding hatch underneath the front of its fuselage as a precautionary procedure. It started to circle slowly as it was surveying if it was safe to proceed with offloading Emma. Its internal perception apparatus confirmed there was no threat that could be detected.

The NYPD helicopter was already approaching the base of the building at low level over the Hudson River when Martinez yelled, 'Get up now! Now! NOW! Up! UP!"

The pilot nodded and pulled the control stick back and with his left hand, reset the side thrust control. At once, the helicopter's engine and the rotor blades whined in response, and the whole body of the helicopter was yanked hard upwards. It took a mere 15 seconds before the window of the cabin could be brought into eye level with the heliport landing area. He made a deft change to the stick, and the helicopter moved around, exposing its port side to the full view of the drone, which had remained stationary some 50 feet above the surface.

The pilot saw it and decided to pull the helicopter further up until it came into the same height as the target. The drone suddenly swerved around as soon as it sensed the new presence and alien threat from a flying machine. Instantly, the laser device, which had already been triggered down earlier, was powered up, an amazingly fast reaction to the perceived threat; its sensors confirming that there were several weapons being aimed at it.

It immediately focussed on the helicopter's crew eyes, and its incredibly fast analysis identified that almost all of them were wearing mirrored goggles, which made its laser weapon ineffective. Quickly, it homed onto the pilot as he was the only one not wearing goggles of any kind. His face was naked apart from a helmet strapped snuggly to his head. He was looking directly at the drone in awe.

Martinez saw a new movement underneath the drone, which unnerved him into taking premature action. 'Let's splash it!' he yelled.

He quickly swung his assault rifle over the sitting waist-gunner's head, clicking off the safety button and pulling the trigger. His gun spurted out a deafening rattle, which was instantly further amplified with several other rapidly firing assault rifles joining in a cacophony of noise. They were all aiming in a totally uncoordinated blast at the drone.

Its high-intensity laser was aimed with unbelievable accuracy at the pilot's eyes, instantly destroying the retinas. He screamed and involuntarily pulled the control stick back causing the helicopter to sway back and sideways into the heliport area.

The co-pilot immediately took over the control and wrestled with it whilst the helicopter swayed erratically.

In the midst of that chaotic scene, an intense crossfire of bullets and laser beams ensued, with several bullets finding their mark and straddling the drone, especially on the area of where propulsion fins and the belly were located. It screeched out a throaty roar, trying to compensate for the sustained amount of damage and lost power. It could not. It yawed sideways, then tried to regain height, and it suddenly dropped down like a stone and crashed hard on the rooftop adjacent to the heliport marked landing zone. The mortally injured drone bounced twice, and at the second impact, the belly burst open, ejecting a human being with its limbs flailing about like a ragdoll before landing on its back with a sickening thud.

Emma's head whiplashed hard on the ground, but fortunately for her, she was wearing her bright orange industrial helmet, cushioning the impact convincingly. Still, she was stunned and groaned incoherently. She rolled over and landed on her knees and hands before making any attempt to stand up. She did so but very unsteadily.

Her bulky belt pouches were hampering her movements. Simultaneously, the helicopter crashed with a mighty metallic thump onto the edge of the heliport, but with a stroke of luck, it managed to right itself, rocking back up squarely on to its landing skids. The six uniformed policemen scrambled out of the safer open side of the cockpit onto the heliport with Martinez out in front of others with his assault rifle, blazing away indiscriminately at the wrecked drone.

Emma finally stood up, very unsteadily as if she was punch-drunk. She was located several feet away from the drone and staggering away from the approaching SWAT team, continuing towards the severely damaged drone but with a little more caution. The laser device was impaired, and the drone was lying on its side, and it kept jerking from the impact from the hundreds of bullets impacting its toughened outer shield.

Martinez saw her out of the corner of his eye and shouted at her, 'For god's sake, GET DOWN!' He pointed at her and waved down to the floor. 'GET DOWN AND STAY THERE!'

It was typical police by-the-book directive aimed at any person encountered at the scene for all incidents. But she glanced at him and shrugged as if ignoring him deliberately. What he had failed to realise was that without her CI processor, she has no inkling of understanding him. All she saw was the drone continuing to take a punishing hail of bullets. This sight alone had infuriated her, and she took a deep breath and shouted at the top of her voice, 'FOR GOD'S SAKE, STOP IT!' But it was too late.

Several bullets ricocheted off the drone into the path of Emma. One hit her helmet, causing her to jerk her head backwards, whilst another landed squarely in the middle of her chest, causing severe damage to her helmet and her travelling overall.

The double impact she received had flung her backwards, and she landed on her back once again in a spread-eagled position, motionless. The floor surrounding her continued to spew out fragments of concrete as the bullets kept ricocheting off the drone, causing splinters of lead and concrete to fly everywhere. One landed on Emma's thigh and grazed it.

Martinez saw what had happened to the human clad in a strange metallic overall, and it took only a few moments for his previous experience as a GI to analyse what was happening. He threw his clenched fist up in the air and screamed, 'HOLD YOUR FIRE!'

But the deafening background of noise from the helicopter and guns rattling, coupled with the thunderous rattle of bullets slamming into the drone, his order was barely audible. This time he screamed louder, 'CEASE YOUR FIRE!'

Finally, the policeman nearest to him heard him and stopped firing his weapon.

He repeated the instruction nearest to him. A domino effect was now in full swing.

One by one, the guns went silent.

Martinez walked slowly towards the human lying apparently lifeless on the floor. He was keeping a wary eye on the bullet-riddled drone and paused a few times as he contemplated any possible threats. Finally, he came up to Emma and looked down at her. He could see blood trickling down from her forehead to the corner of her eyes and forming a small pool of blood next to her head. He could also see a small but noticeable dark fluid oozing from her chest, darkening the metallic fabric of her overall.

He looked at the policeman nearest to him, and he pointed at the helicopter.

He barked, 'Go and get that bloody biohazard box outta the copter NOW!'

'Yes, sir!' Davis acknowledged the order. He turned around and looked at Martinez. 'But don't you think we need to call for the paramedics as she's looking bad?'

'Fuck the paramedics!' Martinez swore at him. 'First, contain the risk of virus, and then we'll worry about the paramedics later!'

'Yes, sir!'

Davis sprinted towards the helicopter, which was still resting with its blades rotating. When he got there and climbed into the cockpit, he grabbed hold of the box, ready to haul it out, but he could see the pilot cupping his hands over his eyes, howling in agony. He looked across at the co-pilot who was totally inexperienced and appeared to be numb with the chaotic scenes he had just witnessed and shouted at him, 'We've got two injured people here, so please call for the paramedics!'

The co-pilot made a visible effort to pull himself together. 'Roger that!'

Davis rushed back with the box to where Martinez was standing and dropped it onto the floor. Martinez immediately knelt and opened the box and took out a large bright yellow package. He tore off the plastic coverings and spread the overall alongside the inert Emma on the floor. Then he and Davis lifted her gently onto the wrapping and quickly zipped it up.

He shouted over to his team to form a perimeter around the drone. The propulsion fins were flicking erratically and powering down slowly.

* * *

Andy's face drained of colour as he watched in horror from a bird's eye view of the actions being played out on the wall. His legs buckled down to a kneeling position and putting his hands over his eyes, uttered with a soulless voice, only one word, 'Emma!'

The image of the rooftop was moving slowly out, and soon he was viewing the side of the tower and followed by a vast blue of the sea in the Atlantic Ocean.

'When's the next time we can come into the view of the rooftop?!' he pleaded in desperation to have another viewing of Emma. He was fully aware of the reliance of the starship's position to gain the best viewing of any place on Earth, but unfortunately, it could not sustain the same viewing of a place for more than a few minutes as it continued its orbit of the Earth.

1 HOUR 22 MINUTES IN EARTH TIME

'Can't you use your other drone to relay the video image whilst we're out of range?'

NEGATIVE

He ignored the last comment as he knew it was not practical as Gorgass did not have their own satellites in position to relay any communication of any kind to the other side of Earth.

'Aren't we humans well organised to have so many of our communication satellites in place around dear old planet Earth?' he muttered, rocking rhythmically whilst hugging himself in his anguish. 'I wish the damned Gorgass had a similar range so I could continue watching, and . . .' He paused as he realised he was talking gibberish to himself whilst he continued rocking. 'See if Emma's okay in spite of this unwarranted attack! I should have foreseen that!'

GORGASS NOT IMPRESSED WITH HUMAN HOSTILE MENTALITY

The resumed writing on the wall brought him back to the grim reality of his situation.

'I know that! Sometimes I feel embarrassed to be human!'

WINDOW OF OPPORTUNITY FOR YOU TO REMAIN HERE HAS PROVED FUTILE

NOT SUSTAINABLE TO CONTINUE STAYING HERE

NOT SUSTAINABLE TO CONTINUE HOLDING UNIT GREEN HERE

HOWEVER, YOU HAVE PROVIDE US A NEW ALTERNATIVE STRATAGEM

Then there was a long pause. A strong sense of foreboding was left hanging in the air. He could not assuage his curiosity. He felt a strange mixture of grievance and mournfulness at the idea of Emma's bloodshed ending the whole saga of the stupendous interface with the Gorgass. He could feel his stomach sinking when he realised it was only a matter of time and he would meet his own end. A mental image of his own lifeless body drifting away into space was materialising in his head. *So my time's up now? How soon will that be?*

Slowly, his rocking came to a stop, and he took a deep breath and shot a daring look at the wall, as if he was inducing a challenge at it. 'Can I have a last request?'

He exhaled out slowly. 'Let me take a last glimpse of Emma as I want to bid her a farewell. Then I'd like a last look of Earth for a while so I can also say my farewell as well'. He tilted his head up. 'Then you do whatever with me. I'm ready'. A tear trickled down his cheek.

REQUEST GRANTED

WHAT CAN ACHIEVE WITH VIEWING EARTH QUESTION

'Well, it's quite mesmerising and hypnotic to view Earth as a beautiful planet and hope to achieve some tranquilising and soothing effect on me before I popped off into a big black void of nothingness! That's what bothers me!'

NOTHINGNESS HAS NO CONSCIOUS TO EXPERIENCE PAIN OR FEAR OR DISTRESS OR SADNESS OR DISCOMFORTS

'I *know!*'

THEN WHAT BOTHER UNIT GREEN QUESTION

'It's just . . .' He paused momentarily, searching for words. 'I loved my life as it is, loved the appeal of thought-provoking information. I loved to keep gathering all new scientific information as it's part of my nature to live for all these things'. He shrugged. 'My life was always devoted to pushing into the unknown, on a quest for that little extra previously unknown scientific information . . . I don't know why, but just because it was unknown, it provided me with an endless stimulus and fascinated me'.

There was no response from the Gorgass. Another long period went by before he realised there would not be any further response from them. He realised that he could do nothing further to change events. Would he see the events being unfolded since it appeared that Emma had been killed in the melee on the UN building? He decided to wait for another orbit of Earth before he could hope to grab a final glimpse of Emma. Maybe?

The hour had proved to be his longest and the most daunting for him. He was starting to resign himself to the idea of his life coming to a full stop in a very short matter of time.

* * *

Brett and Sarah had landed a few hours ago and were in the taxi on their way to the United Nations building when the tumult was unfolding at the rooftop of the building. They heard the news flash on the radio in the car. 'Seems my gut feeling was right!' He nodded to himself. 'But not that soon! Not that *bloody* soon! We gotta be there now before God-knows-what's going to happen next!'

He leaned forward and spoke to the cabbie through the security screen. 'Hey, buddy. Would a couple hundred greenbacks cover your fare plus possibly a speeding ticket? If so, can you please push it and get us there as soon as possible, if not sooner?'

'Holy cows! What is the name of the almighty? Sure thing. Hold on to your hat', the driver muttered after seeing the money, floored the accelerator, and the cab roared forward.

Some 25 minutes later, they could see the majestic building of the United Nations looming up, and they could see some hazy smoke drifting from one of the rooftops.

As the cab skidded to a stop, they leapt out. Brett lobbed the cash in through the driver's window but was dismayed to see several media vans had already beaten them to it by parking in front of the lobby and already spewing out several reporters. However, they were being kept at bay by a ring of police officers who were under orders to prevent anyone from entering the buildings.

There was a group of dignitaries coming out of the lobby to meet the clamour of the assembled press. The central person who was out in front was flanked by a few security men and advisors. With his impressively solid physique and thick neck, it did not take Brett long to recognise him as the one and only Cason Bianchi, the mayor of New York. He strode towards and then paused behind a thin line of police officers that acted like a dam holding back the stormy sea of reporters who were milling around, trying to snatch a hotspot nearest to the mayor.

He had been in radio communication directly with Martinez who had explained to him the full scenario of what had been happening high above on the roof of the building. His face was impassive and unreadable. Several reporters thrust their microphones and communication devices at him. By this time the reporters had already some inkling of the intense and noisy shootout that had unfolded at the top of the UN building, and the arrival of several ambulances at the entrance of the lobby indicated a strong possibility of casualties. Several questions screamed simultaneously at him, all overlapping at one another in the likes of 'Mayor, can you care to brief us all?'

'Has the building been contained securely?'

'Were you expecting the visitation by the alien?'

'How did you know the visitation was about to take place?'

Bianchi threw his hands in the air, a gesture that did the effect of silencing the reporters in their tracks, and quickly, he pointed his finger in the direction of a female reporter who had yelled out a particular question that had grabbed his attention.

He continued, 'Please repeat your question!'

'Thanks, Mr Mayor! Were you advised to expect the visitation by the alien that seems to have taken place right here on this UN building, and if so, how were you tipped off by whom?"

He took a quick breath. 'It was a stroke of luck!'

He went on to explain how he had acted upon receiving a call from an undisclosed source, and it was with a stroke of good fortune that the timing could not be better when he ordered the elite police force on to full situation red status.

'I bet on my mother's grave that the reliable source is obviously none other than Cardinal Marcello himself! Yes, CARDINAL MARCELLO!' a powerful voice roared from one spot, and all the reporters' heads turned sharply in the same direction in anticipation to see who was the person who got the cat out of the bag.

It was Brett. He had opened the door of a stationary media van positioned nearby and stood up on the driver's top step to gain a commanding view of the situation. Bianchi's eyes gave nothing away, even though he was completely wrong-footed and thunderstruck by the totally unexpected interruption. *How on earth did he know that?* he thought.

'SIR! I'M AFRAID TO SAY YOU'VE BEEN SERIOUSLY *MISINFORMED*!' There was no let-up in Brett's full-throated roar. 'ON THE CONTRARY, IT WASN'T MEANT TO BE AS WE EXPECTED IT TO BE!'

The mayor realised he had the people stopped in their tracks in total silence as everyone was listening to him in amazement. How could anyone have the nerve to challenge the mayor so publicly? He quickly lowered his voice and continued, 'For what's it worth, I am letting you all know I've just arrived here from Rome, where Sarah'—pointing admiringly at the woman standing next to him—'and I have had the privilege to hold a full reliable video interview at close encounter with another abductee named Gillian Lee yesterday!' He took another quick breath. 'With thanks to her as being the original abductee aboard the alien spaceship, we've managed to unravel the story in depth and in spades! I'm afraid to say we've been seriously misled by Cardinal Marcello and possibly to a lesser extent by our own ex-president Rachel Wallace!'

'Why on earth should I, or anyone else for that matter, take your word over his?' Bianchi quickly achieved his composure. 'He's a cardinal!' He squinted at his interlocutor and realised who he was. 'Oh, it's you, Brett Fielding, isn't it?'

'Yes, it's me indeed. I may be a journalist, but I do believe in the power and importance of the free press, especially the effect it may have on people's lives worldwide'. He jumped down from the van onto the driveway and started walking towards Bianchi. 'The world deserves untainted and ethical information, or in other words, we owe it to provide them with unvarnished truth, no matter how much it might contradict our personal beliefs'.

The sea of reporters started to swirl aside to pave the way for Brett to walk through with Sarah closely in tow behind him. He stopped next to Bianchi with a police officer standing in between them.

'Believe me, all the mayhem we've endured in the last few months was largely based on ignorance and fear'—turning around to face the reporters—'generated by a comprehensive lack of communication with the extraterrestrials. We based our decision-making on whatever information we had in our hands at that time!'

He looked at Bianchi and pointed his finger at him. 'You, for a start, have been unwittingly made a victim by Cardinal Marcello, who has fed you with false information to get you to ally with him on taking extreme measures against the extraterrestrials!'

'Why should he?!' Bianchi interjected. 'Just how would he benefit? He would have known the consequences to the world are based on credible sources of reliable and accurate information! Why should he think there's much to gain by basing his biased opinion rather than hard facts?'

'That's a good and challenging question I'd love to ask him!' Brett smiled.

'The trouble is, just for the sake of expressing my theory, he's, by nature, a man of the cloth, and that in itself shows us the type of person who he is!'

'What do you mean by that?'

'It's in his very nature to be so devout to his faith, and his very own existence and beliefs are based on blind faith. He is not open to any dialogue that challenges his blind faith'. He took a deep breath. 'That spells out how dangerous it is to have such a narrow mind and not be open to logical reasoning'.

'But to me, he sounds so resolute and genuine with his own reasoning'.

'A classic case of cognitive dissonance, but in a way, it can benefit someone to handle the problems whilst living in collaborative groups. It has evolved into something more counterproductive to rationality. It's the very human thing to have an inherent capacity for collaboration when groups are gathering and mobilising together against any form of rationality, whether it is about evolution, climate change, vaccination or'—Brett pointed his thumb upward to the sky—'in this case, the extraterrestrials'.

Bianchi's stance softened a tad. 'Then what should we do? What steps should we take to install any kind of damage limitation . . . ?' His speech was cut short abruptly when all the reporters noticed new activity ensuing at the lobby entrance.

A small group of four people wearing bright yellow biohazard suits was jostling and pushing a trolley through the lobby and out to a large biohazard service van parked inconspicuously for some time. On the trolley, it could be seen, there was a biohazard blanket fitted closely around a human female form. The rear doors on the van were opened outwardly to receive the trolley.

'Your window of opportunity for damage control is not looking good!' Brett studied the situation and looked at Bianchi whose eyes were still on the van. 'If I am right, that must be Emma! Oh my god, what have you done with her? I believe she's on the mission to deliver some valuable information that could have long-lasting ramifications on our world! Oh no, why did you need to have her cut down so needlessly and downright carelessly?'

'Of course I didn't order her to be gunned down. She happened to be in the wrong place and at the wrong time! She got caught up with a crossfire meted out by the team of SWAT officers!'

'Still, her blood is on your hands!' Brett glared at Bianchi. 'It was you who gave the order to the SWAT team to bring down the drone, didn't you?'

'Yes, but unfortunately, I was acting out in the best of interest to secure the UN compound from a potential threat from the extraterrestrials, so we've got to treat her as collateral damage. Can't be helped anyway!'

All the huge crowd of reporters and TV crews were silent as they were engrossed by the dialogue being slugged out between two men standing face-to-face on the steps.

'Still, I don't buy that. You're as guilty as Marcello!' Brett stared hard at Bianchi. 'Unless you can do something to salvage the whole goddamned mess and get yourself redeemed . . .'

'I know what I'm doing'. He wanted to be the person seen to be in control. 'I'm on top of it'.

'Really?' Brett pointed at the people wearing the biohazard suits. 'If you do, then there's no need for these biohazard suits! It proves one thing about you: the tendency to act out a knee-jerk reaction to the unknown factors generated by the limited information given to you by Marcello!'

Bianchi shook his head. 'Whatever the situation it is, it's just a classical textbook of safety procedures that need to be enforced'.

Brett sighed and took a step closer to the police officers and threw a challenging stare at Bianchi. 'Let me prove to you that I have huge confidence in my source of information that I'm willing to bet my life on it . . .' He pointed at the van again.

'Let me go in that van with Emma not wearing any protective clothing and give me a chance to be with her. Hopefully, I can assess her for something useful information and perhaps be in position to relay that valuable information to you?'

'How the hell did you know her name was Emma?' growled Bianchi. 'You are obviously very well informed. But unfortunately for us, we need to accept she's dead, and you're not able to discuss with her, can you? With a dead body, it's the forensic pathologist's job to do that!'

'Are you confirming she is dead when you mentioned forensics?'

As the rear doors of the van were about to close, suddenly, there was some jerking movement that could be seen on the trolley. Someone in the pool of reporters spotted it and shrieked, 'OH MY GOD! She's alive!'

Brett quickly shouted at Bianchi, 'Then a forensic pathologist is not required at this stage! Please let me get in there with her! It's vital that I can be in a position to glean any important information and compare them with what I have heard from the other abductees in the Vatican'.

Bianchi looked back at the van in question and then stared around the chaotic scene, absolutely dumbfounded at the extraordinary situation in which he found himself. He was unsure of what next step to take. He glanced back at Brett and hesitated. 'What, in god's name, do you mean "another abductee" in the Vatican?'

Brett sensed that he was winning, and the listening reporters were realising that the scene being played out in front of them was of staggering importance.

'Please let me get through', Brett prompted him. 'I promise I will convey any useful information to you, and perhaps you'll be in a better position to relay the vital information to the assembly at the

United Nations. Imagine that'. He was appealing instinctively to the mayor's ego.

'Hey, let him through', Bianchi finally instructed the two police officers to move apart and looked at him. 'You better answer to me!'

But Brett was already dashing towards the van, leaving Sarah behind on her own, and hopped into the rear of the van, much to the surprise of the biohazard team.

At first, they started to try and hustle him out but were quickly distracted by Emma's unintelligible scream.

* * *

The bird's eye view image of the UN compound was seen again on the wall as the Spaceship orbited back into the same position. During these brief windows of time-limited opportunities, Andy had managed to see with horror the mayhem of guns blazing away at the drone on the top of the building. He managed to see several figures in bright yellow clothing moving the trolley into a stationary vehicle. He guessed correctly the figure wrapped fully in yellow clothing on the trolley must be Emma.

He was convinced that she was completely inert. That sort of detail he realised would not be assured under the circumstances. Then he saw a man running towards and bounded up into the vehicle just as the doors were closing. A few minutes later, the vehicle sped off with blue lights flashing. That gave him a glimmer of hope.

But?

* * *

One of the hazard-limitation team unzipped the plastic bag to reveal her face. Emma gasped for air but continued screaming and jouncing about, trying to free herself from the belts that were holding her down securely to the trolley. 'Get it oorff me!' she repeated.

'Calm yourself down!' shouted one of the medical workers. 'You're hurting yourself! Tell me your name!'

But her words had no effect on her, and Emma continued screaming louder and flailing about even more vigorously.

'For god's sake, GET GRIP YOURSELF!' another worker joined in shouting at the patient.

By now, the van was moving at high speed. Brett was sitting next to her and shouted at the medical teams, 'Hey, you guys! It's *your lot, not her,* that needs to get a grip on yourselves! I know why she's noncommunicative with you'. He took out his glasscomm out of his pocket and continued, 'Doesn't it occur to you all that she's totally Deaf, and with these belts strapping her in, she's bound to feel confined and frustrated!'

He quickly typed out a text message on his glasscomm. *YOUR NAME IS EMMA, CORRECT?*

He shoved it to Emma's view, and she focused on it groggily but started to read it slowly and nodded. 'Aye, that's right'. She paused and eyed him questioningly.

'How do you know?'

He ignored her enquiry, and instead of typing, he decided to speak to his device, which translated immediately into readable text. *I WILL TELL THEM TO LOOSEN THE BELTS, BUT PLEASE, CAN YOU BE CALM?*

'Of course, I can', came her response in a slightly toneless voice. 'But just get these bloody belts off me!'

Brett looked at the medical team and beckoned them to start loosening the belts. They hesitated for a moment but started to oblige. Once all the belts came out, Emma groaned loudly and rubbed her chest, whilst the other hand clenched her side of head, where the wound caused by the bullet ricochet was.

One of the medical team grabbed her wrist and said, 'Leave it, don't make it worse. You've got a bad gash on your head'. She pulled her hand away from her head. 'But I think you're lucky. It could have been much worse if it wasn't for your helmet'.

The female team member pulled Emma's damaged helmet from under the trolley into the full view of all people inside the van. 'It has helped absorb the impact of the bullet but not enough to save you from being shot through'. She pointed at a mangled point of impact on the side of the helmet.

Emma looked at her but was at loss to know what she was talking about, and soon she saw her helmet and quickly got the gist of it. She shifted her attention to the only other man who was not wearing the protective overalls of the HL team and who was still speaking to his glasscomm, repeating in a nutshell what had just been said, and shoving the glasscomm in front of Emma again.

She read it quickly and nodded. 'Thank gawd for that! But what about my chest?' She pointed to her sternum. 'It's bloody painful!'

'Aye, let me see . . .' Her clothes were gently opened by one of the team to reveal the bullet wound. With a tweezer, she pulled out the mangled remains of a bullet. 'Gee, you're bloody lucky again, I guessed the bullet has lost its strength when ricocheting off something and hitting you. But we're still taking you to the hospital to have you checked out'.

But by then, Emma had lost interest in her and shifted her attention back to the man with the glasscomm and asked, 'Your name?'

Brett spoke his own name. His device blurted out the message in text, then he shoved his device into her view. *BRETT FIELDING*

'Brett! I can feel the ambulance moving'. She tried to lift herself on her elbow but fell back as the pain in her chest hit her again. 'Where are we going?'

HOSPITAL TO HAVE YOU CHECKED OUT He showed his device to her.

'Bu . . . but . . . how long have I been knocked out?' Her eyes widened. 'What's happening to the drone?'

PROBABLY BADLY DAMAGED AND STILL AT TOP OF THE UN BUILDING

'Brett!' She tried to lift her legs over the trolley but was stopped by one of the team, and she quickly protested, "*STOP HERE! Go back* to the United Nations building!

The sooner I can be there to warn somebody, *anyone* who will listen to me, and it will create a better chance of saving Andy!'

She tried to shove the nearest personnel away and started to grapple with another one before she became overpowered and held down on the trolley.

'You're in no position to demand anything! That can wait! We gotta have you checked out first! If you don't calm down, we've no choice but to get you sedated!'

None of what they had said made any sense to her. She was totally unable to communicate with them. The medical personnel kept shouting at her, struggling to hold her down, and she continued resisting them and looked at Brett. 'You gotta listen to me!'

'Yeah, I'm with you'. Brett waved his hands between him and her to indicate the meaning of togetherness. 'You gotta tell me what I need to know . . .'

'Ouch!' She looked down at her arm and realised that one of the medics had injected her. 'What the *fuck* did you do to me?!'

'We need to sedate you!' came the reply, but she did not hear it but guessed what it was.

'You've got to be joking! There's no need to have me tranquilised *again*!' She could feel that she was going to lose consciousness and desperately pleaded with glazing eyes at Brett, wrestling with several hands holding her down. 'You have gotta help me! There's no time that needs to be wasted!'

'Do you have to do that?' Brett gave a cold look at the medic who was holding the syringe. He was not sure how much sedation they had given her.

'Tell them . . . tell them . . . Andy . . . Gorgass . . .' She slowly drifted off into unconsciousness.

'You gotta wake her up now!' Brett pointed a threatening finger at the nurse.

'The fate of the world rests with her!'

'We will have to disagree with you . . .,' she said defiantly. 'You are in no position to advise or instruct us. Your lack of medical expertise doesn't justify your interference with our patient!'

The ambulance was still weaving along the congested New York roads with its siren howling as the usual traffic congestion did its best to impede its progress.

'For god's sake, what's the matter with you all?' Brett stood up. 'This young lady has vital information!' he said, pointing at Emma. 'She's the vital link to what's happening at the alien starship you have all seen in the recent TV news footage! The sooner we understand their intentions, the better we can know what steps to take to deal with them!'

'Who is in position to instruct us?'

'I'm telling you!' He sighed. 'My sources of information are absolutely unimpeachable, and it is essential that she gets back to the United Nations, even if it eventually costs this young lady her life!'

The argument went on for another 10 minutes, whilst the ambulance continued screaming through the traffic, nearer to the hospital but still miles away, further away from the UN building.

* * *

Andy turned around from the wall and hopped effortlessly, utilising the lower gravity, to another side of the room. He did not want to watch the distressing scenes anymore. He knew his time was up. Since his position of bargaining with Gorgass proved to be untenable, there was nothing more he could do to prolong his life.

A text flashed on the wall.

UNIT GREEN CONFIRM GORGASS OBSERVATION UNIT RED COVERED IN YELLOW QUESTION

UNIT GREEN CONFIRM LIFE OF UNIT RED NOT FUNCTIONING QUESTION

With much reluctance, he looked up and read it.

'Huh, I suppose so', he responded. 'In spite of my efforts to cooperate with you, there's nothing more I can do for you at this stage. Your time is up, and so is mine.

I am not sure now how you can proceed with getting any vital materials you want to take with you to continue your journey. The window of opportunity has truly expired.

'Nevertheless, all I can say to you, even if it sounds strange, it has been a privilege to get know you and work alongside you. I've learnt a lot about you, and believe me . . .' He paused. 'I couldn't have done more for you ensuring your survival'. He could not finish his words.

He realised if what it is worth, it does not sound right to praise them when they were going to put him to death. He sighed.

BASED ON INPUT FROM UNIT GREEN

BASED ON GORGASS OBSERVATION THERE IS NO POINT TO DELAY

GORGASS UNDERTAKE ACTION START FROM NOW

'What action are you talking about?'

ACTION WITH RETRIEVING THE MATERIALS

'Materials? Ah yes, you mean our satellites'. He understood their intention.

'How do you proceed with it?'

There was some vibration made on the floor, but because of the lightness on his feet on the floor, effect of the artificially low gravity, he was not sure if he had detected it noticeably. He looked up at the wall and requested, 'Are you doing something that I need to know?'

Somewhat surprisingly, a large new image of the external shape of the spaceship was projected on the wall. He was rooted to the spot and marvelled at the new movement unfolding before him.

* * *

'Hey, Mr President', Cooper was addressing the newly installed president in the Oval Office who had been sworn in and took over the presidency following the resignation of Rachel Wallace.

Winston Weasley had been a vice president for only halfway through the term before being sworn in as president. Before that, he had been only a mere governor of Rhode Island, the smallest state in America. Not in his wildest dreams did he really expect that he was to become America's first fully blooded African American president. Despite such an awesome achievement made in a relatively short time, in the past week, he had been uncharacteristically subdued. He was only now beginning to understand how hard it would be for him to handle the colossal responsibilities that this office required of him. He would have to maintain the level of security of his country, his beloved America, at a time when there were unprecedented threats, and circumstances also called for international leadership. He would have to win back the trust of people that had been lost so catastrophically by the previous incumbent.

He had been sitting in the room with few other familiar faces he had come to depend for advice.

'Winston, begging your pardon, Mr President, you'd better watch the TV now!' Cooper looked up at him. He had been alerted via glasscomm by the team at the observatory based in Hawaii. 'They're streaming a live video of the alien spaceship! Something's happening to it!'

Everyone in the same room were glued to the large TV monitor. They could see the familiar image of the large umbrella-shaped segment that had always been attached in position in front of the extraordinarily long body of the spacecraft until now. It had started to detach itself from the long slim boom and manoeuvred slowly away from the main body of the spacecraft. Instantly, a new simmering and bluish faint cloud erupted from the tip of the umbrella segment. Soon it started to gather speed and executed a rollover manoeuvre elegantly away from the spacecraft and into a new flight path towards Earth.

'Can anyone tell me what you think it's doing?' Weasley stood up. 'I need advice now!'

'Perhaps an invasion!' Cooper replied. 'As we know, it's an extraordinarily large segment, something over 3 miles wide, so I assume it's got something inside it, like soldiers to dispatch once it landed on Earth!'

'Your opinion?' Winston pointed his finger at Dr George Clark.

'Excuse me, Mr. President, I cannot form any firm opinion based on insufficient data currently available to me!' came his reply. 'However, reckoning it as something for invasion is premature to me, when taking into consideration the apparently large hollow inside of it'.

'You mean it's because it's shaped very much like an umbrella?'

'You got it! Indeed, a thickly skinned umbrella. So we need to sit tight and wait to see what it's doing'.

'No action from us is inviting them to walk over us!' Cooper was clearly alarmed.

'Taking premature action didn't help Rachel Wallace!' Weasley shook his head.

'I don't want to be accused of going on a wild-goose chase and only to be second-guessed by them! I think it's best to have real and tangible information made available to me before I can make the decision!'

He watched the TV for a few minutes before throwing a look at Cooper. 'Are we still at DEFCON level 1?'

'Aye, with all our B-21 stealth bombers up in the air and cruising around Canada and Europe'.

'What about our ageing BUFF?'

'You mean our old big ugly fat fuckers, the famous B-52 Stratofortress?'

'Yep, that too! I know it's about to retire in a few years' time, but it's still formidable." Just throw everything that we have up in the air!"

'But don't you think that's a bit premature?'

'No, maybe you are right, just have them on standby as a precautionary measure!'

'Fair enough . . . Mr President'. Cooper shifts his focus to his communication device. 'I'll inform the Strategic Air Command . . .'

He ignored the rest of others who were all watching the TV closely and wondering what the hell it was doing.

'Whilst we're at it, I want to know what the hell is happening with that Australian girl Emma. I believe our hotshot reporter Brett's holed up with her at that medical centre. Have they debriefed her yet?'

'The report's just transmitted to you now . . .'

'Good! The sooner I get a better picture, the better my decision will be!'

* * *

Brett had already been with Emma for a few hours since she woke up in the special isolation unit located deep inside the medical and military complex located somewhere outside New York City that was relatively unknown to the general public. Both were equally dismayed to see several guards wearing biohazard suits sited outside the special glass doors. They had been under strict orders not to let Emma nor Brett out of the specially sealed room.

Fortunately for Emma, her request for the supply of a freshly charged battery for her CI processor had been granted. And her demand for a backup communication with access to AUSLAN interpreters via the live streaming video relays transmitted from Australia had also been granted. It was widely known to the Deaf community around the world and was called remote-video-relay interpreting.

Both had been debriefed for the last several hours, and despite their initial protests, they were not allowed to make physical contact with anyone outside the building complex.

Brett tried to reason with the doctors to forward the groundbreaking information to anyone who would make a difference to the circumstances with the extraterrestrials.

'It's for your and our safety that you need to be contained in this room until we're wholly convinced it's totally safe for you to go outside. It's part of our protocols that we strictly adhere to!'

'Look, it's really important we need to contact someone higher up in the chain of communication. We've got to alert them that the extraterrestrials are not that threatening as the powers appear to have painted them!' he pleaded with them.

'No worry, someone's already handling it, and it's already captured Pres Winston Weasley's attention. You can be assured he's reading your reports, probably at this very moment. If you said they're not that threatening, then why worry?'

Brett started to relax a little. But he could not help wondering if the timing was anything but up to the mark. On time? Or too late?

* * *

The umbrella segment, which had been gathering speed away from the mother spacecraft, executed another unexpected manoeuvre. It gyrated around gracefully into a new position. This time it was flying backward with its gaping wide-open mouth going into the void and away from the Earth. It kept spiralling erratically without any apparent purpose until it gradually became clearer just what its objectives were: It was harvesting the man-made satellites. In a very short time, it had swallowed 20 satellites all with varied functions, from communication to GPS. It kept cruising around, gobbling up all the metallic debris floating around the Earth. Like a basking shark, systematically, it started to fill up the cavernous mouth.

* * *

'What's happening?' Weasley broke off from reading the report. He's been reading it prudently for the 20 minutes, absorbing all the relevant details. By now, there were few more people added to his team. All their eyes were locked on the various large TV monitors.

'It looks like it's scooping up our satellites!' Clark responded. 'Like a butterfly net!'

'Which type of satellites?'

'The general types, such as communication, GSP, weather monitoring, the whole lot!' Clark sucked a deep breath. 'It looks like they've started with the geostationary satellites!'

'Geostationary satellites?'

'The stationary ones that are located at approximately 22,300 miles, and their orbits take exactly 24 hours, obviously the same length as in tune with Earth's rotation'. Clark looked at Winston with distressing eyes. 'Since they are our major mobile communication satellites, that painted a very bleak picture for us!'

'How bad?'

'If they started to come lower and begin picking off the other lower satellites, such as our several hundred geosynchronous satellites, the GPS types that orbit at around 12,000 miles'—Clark slumping back into the sofa—'then we're totally fucked!'

Weasley looked again at the report and studied it for a moment longer.

'I'm beginning to understand their main objective is in doing what they are doing!'

'Which is?' Cooper asked.

Weasley looked up with an air of resignation. 'They're basically harvesting our satellites!'

'Yes, sir, you got it right!' Clark knuckled his forehead. 'Game, set, and match to them!'

'It could have been avoided in the first place!' Weasley's face darkened when he looked at the report once again. He was seething furious. 'That *bloody* cardinal!'

He shouldn't have manipulated us all with his bloody doctored version of the facts and information! How dare he think he's had the right to hoodwink us when he knew damn well that the fate of the world was so dependent on the credibility of the information that he's supplied us!'

He shot an incensed look at CIA Director Wagner. 'Where's that man?' he spluttered, looking down at the report. 'MARCELLO!'

'My source has informed me he's suddenly vanished into thin air. Since then, I've pooled all my resources into the search for him'. He shook his head. 'I agree with you, he must be caught and be put on trial for deceiving us all!'

'It's gonna be difficult, not with that amount of protection he gets from the church'. President Weasley waved his hand. 'If you try him in the court, then you're trying the whole church! So forget him for now!' He then looked again at Doctor Clark. 'We gotta start doing the damage control now! You said it'll get worse, but how bad is it?'

Clark took a deep breath. 'Couldn't be worse! Let me put you in the picture!

With all our telecommunication satellites swallowed up and rendered useless, then the whole burden of telecommunications would fall upon undersea cables and ground-based communication systems. But whilst many forms of communication would disappear in an instant, I hope there are some others that remain.

'That means millions of Internet connections would vanish. Plus all our mobile phones would become useless. Our dependence on satellites for television, Internet, radio, and so on, virtually all the services will close down . . .'

Unexpectedly, without any warning, one of several TV monitors went blank and filled with static background. Clark pointed at it and exclaimed, 'That's the start!

We're already *seriously fucked*!'

Sure enough, a few minutes later, another TV monitor went blank. They were all staring at the monitors, totally captivated, saying nothing. A total silence ensued in the oval room for a few minutes until Pres Winston Weasley broke it with an instruction aimed at the senior staff. 'Okay, we get the message, so let's start doing damage control!' He stood up. 'How can we overcome it, and what alternative measures can we take to get our infrastructure up and running again? How soon can we do that?'

'You're actually missing my point!' Clark sighed. 'It's not that easy! When I said we're seriously fucked, we must consider the enormous effect it will have on our financial and military infrastructures! A total of transactions where split timing is required and recorded, so that'll be fucked'.

He took out a handkerchief and mopped his perspiration forming on his neck and continued, 'And then with it, a total global financial meltdown is guaranteed!'

Weasley looked at him. 'But why just the military? Everything depends on transmission via satellites, is that right?'

'Yes! Not forgetting with our GPS satellites becoming inoperable, our total military reliance on them for all our intelligence, navigation, communication, and weather prediction would be seriously compromised! In our air and naval battles, it would become like fighting in total darkness where all sides are struggling to even find one another!'

The president said nothing but stared at him in silence.

'It will take decades for us to replace all these satellites, restoring us to our fully digital operational strength as we have created for the past 50 years'.

Another TV monitor went blank.

'Damage control?' Doctor Clark looked at all the staff in this room before homing on President Weasley and pointed at him. 'You'd better start recalling all our military planes and ships back to their bases effectively from now! And not to forget all the commercial planes are utterly relying on GPS networks for charting the most fuel-efficient routes and plotting their destinations, you'd better start issuing red warning alerts to all airports to ground all aeroplanes immediately to prevent any major accidents becoming imminent!'

Pres Winston Weasley stared at him hard and started to nod slowly. 'That's frightfully bad!'

'Aye, I'm afraid that's just for a start!' Clarke said. 'How would you suggest we actually send your instructions out in the first place?'

He sank very subdued into his chair and consciously wished he had not become president under these circumstances.

* * *

For the last 12 hours, Andy said nothing but watched in astonishment the full video display of the drama unfolding before him on the wall, as the relentless umbrella segment kept scooping satellites as it patrolled systematically finding the denser populations. He was fully aware that by the removal of hundreds of satellites, incalculable damage was already inflicted on the infrastructures of the Earth.

'How much longer are you keeping scooping up our satellites?' He finally spoke.

'It looks like you're finally getting materials that you need'.

5.4 EARTH DAYS

'That long!' He looked around the empty room. He realised he had never been so alone in his life until now. He sighed. 'Then what?'

EXECUTING FINAL PLAN IN TWO STAGES

STARTING NOW

'Which are?'

DECIMATION OF HUMAN

FOLLOWED BY DEPARTING TO JOIN OUR CLAN GORGASS

'That is it?' His eyes widened. 'Which races of humans are you going to decimate?'

UNIT GREEN NOT NEED TO KNOW AT THIS STAGE

He was becoming aware of the air in his room becoming slightly sticky and humid. It had been gradual since the day when Emma was gunned down.

'Why not? I thought you're going to dispose of me as I'm no longer of any use to you. At least I deserve to know! What am I going to do in the next five days?'

ALREADY EXECUTING IN PLACE

Sweat beads broke out on his forehead. 'Wh . . . what do you mean?'

DISCONTINUE OF AIR SUPPLY

'Bu . . . but since when?'

EFFECTIVE FROM THE MOMENT UNIT RED DECEASED

He looked around the room and asked, 'So I'm left with whatever the air I have in this room? How much longer have I got to survive on this?'

CALCULATION OF UNIT GREEN RESPIRATION RATE

2.9 EARTH DAYS

'Almost three days!' he wailed. 'So I'm going to be asphyxiated slowly into death! All for the reason of maintaining your energy-efficient philosophy!' He sank slowly to his knees. 'Thank you so much for that! After all I have done, all the cooperation for you! Given a choice, I'd prefer it if you can anaesthetise me and then deposit me in space to conserve your precious energy! It's much less painful that way! I'm pleading with you to grant me my desire for a decent ending!'

GORGASS ACKNOWLEDGED INPUTS FROM UNIT GREEN

'You have a strange way of showing your appreciation!' He sighed.

APPRECIATION IRRELEVANT

EXCHANGE OF FAVOUR UPHELD AND HONOURED

Without any warning, a hole opened in the ceiling. Out of it came a tentacle sliding down towards him. He looked at it and understood what to expect. He did not say anything and resigned to it. No resistance. He knew it was pointless as he was totally trapped in this room. He looked around and focused on the video of the Earth as he did not want to watch what the tentacle was about to do. The sight of Earth itself, with spellbinding blends of blues and greens, had a powerful mesmerising image. A strange, fuzzy, warm sense of peace engulfed him.

Only for a short while, he then became absorbed as a new drama unfolded before him. He could see hundreds of small round satellites burst out in a spray from hundreds of small apertures that had formed along the fuselage of the spacecraft.

They, thousands of them, flew out at a high-speed arcing away towards their target, planet Earth.

He suddenly realised the purpose of their action. 'I supposed they're the carriers of a ghastly virus with the intention of wiping out the people . . . but which races of people? Ouch!' He sensed a stinging pain in his neck.

Up to now, he had failed to see the tentacle had been moving slowly towards him with the intention of anaesthetising him. He rubbed his neck and shot a pleading look at the tentacle. *NO! Not now! Not yet! I want to know what you are going to do to my people on Earth!* He thought he was shouting, but in fact, his voice had become an incoherent murmur. 'I deserved to know . . . kno . . .'

He tried to throw himself spread-eagled at the wall in an explosion of a reactive but predictably futile attempt to protest. The low gravity coupled with the injection meant that he just toppled over in a slow-motion dive towards the floor. By the time he landed on the floor with a soft bump, he was already comatose.

After 10 hours, thousands of balls entered the Earth's atmosphere in searing fireballs.

Brett and Emma were outside the lobby in the premises of the United Nations. Earlier, they have travelled there in the police car from the hospital. They had been released immediately by the order of President Weasley. They were enveloped in a thin ring of security officers, all pushing through the thick masses of reporters trying to get through to the UN lobby.

They stopped abruptly when one of the reporters pointed up at the sky and screamed, 'LOOK!'

They looked up and could see hundreds of fireballs blazing a trail through the atmosphere. Since it was nearly dusk when the sky was basking in a mixture of orange and deep dark blue light, the spectacular effect of the display was spelling out the requiem of much of mankind.

Emma and Brett looked at each other. 'Oh, bloody hell! Isn't this what you are saying that is what they are threatening us? Have they begun to eliminate us with the virus?' Brett asked her, his eyes looking alarmed.

'Probably yes'. She sighed. 'It's looking like it, but the question is, will it be selective and restricted to a particular race? Or all of the population in the whole world?'

A look of absolute horror creased her face. 'Don't know, but it looks like we've made a collective human catastrophe!' She stared at him with tears starting to trickle down on her cheeks.

The decimation of humans had begun.

THE EPILOGUE

As soon as the umbrella segment had repositioned and attached itself back to its original position in front of the long boom, a gigantic portal opened in front of the spacecraft. It had harvested a plethora of satellites, each with diverse material specifications. It had accumulated all the vital materials that the Gorgass so desperately needed.

Soon after this, the whole spacecraft started to increase its speed with the purpose of breaking away from the grip of Earth's gravity. It did not loiter to monitor the destruction of people on Earth affected by the deadly genetically engineered virus, a relatively major incident the Gorgass had decided to disregard with utter contempt.

They resumed their stupendous journey to catch up with their colleagues. By this time, all matters, apart from one, should have been resolved. Just one, namely Andy, alias Unit Green. His lifeless body has been ejected out into deep space.

However, prior to that unfortunate incident, the Gorgass have had an unexpected adjustment to their original decision. They had decided that Unit Green had proved too valuable to be completely discarded. His wealth of expertise and virtuosity had proved to be his salvation but not quite what he would have either wanted or even imagined.

Whilst he was made comatose, they had tapped and mapped deeply into his core of consciousness, all the way to the level of his subconscious, the essence of his id.

His brain waves were read, analysed, and subsequently absorbed into one of their artificial systems and stored whilst in search for a suitable specimen for the contents of consciousness to be offloaded into. In another word, the very essence of Andy's existence had been assimilated into another body, merging and blending two beings into one body, the body of Gorgass.

It was the purplish Gorgass, who had been dealing with Unit Green since the beginning, when he was taken into custody inside their starship, who had offered to donate its body to be unified with Unit Green. It understood the implication and consequence that would be about to inflict on not only itself but also on Andy's level of consciousness. Soon, after several hours of *downloading and remapping the consciousness into the purplish Gorgass, the 'Gorgassised' Andy or the 'humanised' Gorgass or whichever we decided to have it classified felicitously, had started to wake up after being anaesthetised, the new 'Gorgandy' suddenly flew into frenzies of confusion with nightmares raging on. It tried to scream but could not. It realised it could not as there was no voice box in existence within the anatomy of Gorgass.*

No outcry could be heard in any form. Instead, all the bulbous lightings on the chest part of the anatomy were bursting so brightly and consistently.

Andy's usual experience of using biped limbs was not familiar with the movement of four legs, and soon, when it tried to compel itself forward using its four limbs, it found itself falling over with sheer clumsiness. And there were many other aspects of Gorgass characteristic anatomy that got him confused. His usual human senses were there but in phantom dosages. His way of thought was becoming contaminated with Gorgass psyche in a purest 'dissociative identity disorder' or, in a simplistic term, a form of schizophrenia to us.

However, dissociative identity disorder is a severe form of dissociation, a mental process that produces lack of connection in a person's thoughts, memories, experiences, feelings, actions, or sense of identity. Though Gorgass was fully aware of the phenomenal thing about dissociative identity disorder aspect, it had sought to implicit what was thought to be a coping mechanism, where the person literally dissociated himself from a situation or experience that's too violent, traumatic, or painful to assimilate with his conscious self. Andy could sense the previous lifelong vast wealth of knowledge and experience of Gorgass lurking in the background had started to seep into his psyche and consciousness but in a dreamlike state.

The language at first was incomprehensible to him, but Gorgass was aware of it and sought to mould it into pure mental picture. Soon he started to understand it subconsciously.

Still, he was experiencing all the cocktail of emotions in various forms, raging, confusing, bewildering, demoralising living nightmares. He started to intrude himself with a question: 'Where do we come from?'

He was surprised to know the answer was already there as if it was part of his former life, but in fact, it was former experience of Gorgass that had seeped into his thought. The mental image of the answer came to him in a dreamy state. He was cast and floated into the situation of how Gorgass came into existence upon arrival on Earth. He started to dig deep into their history. This was their answer.

What led the extraterrestrials to adopt the extraordinary exodus from their original planet that had similar stimuli to countless, though minor by comparison, migratory treks on Earth, creating threats to the Gorgass existence?

Helios was the hub of their home world. Technically, it was more of a giant moon rather than a planet orbiting another extremely massive rocky planet many times bigger than Jupiter.

Characteristically, as with all large planets, they have proportionally strong gravity. In addition, the interior of Helios contained a high-density iron core that exerted an enormous gravitational force on three small moons orbiting it at high speed. Implicitly and because of its strong gravity, Helios had been bombarded frequently by comets and meteoroids. So frequently and regrettably, it has a major effect on life on Helios, including the pace of evolution, which was severely hampered. Life's progress has become something like a pace of two steps forward and one backwards. It would be much worse if it was not for the three moons orbiting that gave extra 'shield-like' protection to Helios by absorbing most of the comets and meteoroids that were about to slam into it. It was a very convenient 'symbiosis-like' arrangement for a hundred thousand Helios years until an exceptionally larger rogue comet of an unusually hight-density material slammed into one of the moons. The effect of this collision had nudged the moon into a closer orbit with Helios. Eventually, it could be seen that the moon has started to skip across the outermost atmosphere of Helios. The Gorgass has calculated it was a matter of time before the nudged moon would collide with Helios, producing a fallout on an insurmountable scale that would wipe out all living things on the planet, including all the Gorgass themselves. By comparison, the effect of the comet impact that caused the demise of the dinosaurs on Earth some 60 million years ago would be very much on a minor scale. Six Helios years, equivalent to twelve Earth years, is all they would have had left. With this knowledge, it spurred Gorgass into taking drastic action by creating a massive engineering feat on scale never previously achieved in Gorgass history.

Up until then, the success of producing rocket-type machines that could lift them out of Helios had never been seriously attempted. The reason for this was the fact that the high gravity on Helios has impeded their ability to come up with a viable rocket that could produce enough thrust to create a sufficient escape velocity. In comparison to Earth's relatively low escape velocity, which is needed to achieve around 7 miles per second (11 km/s) or 25,000 miles per hour, there was an enormous amount of fuel, never mind a relatively massive payload, just to get anything lifted off Earth. The Earth's gravity did not create such a huge handicap to achieving escape velocity. Therefore, on a massive rocky planet such as Helios, with correspondingly stronger gravity, Gorgass would not have been able to devise projectiles with engines that could produce a tremendous amount of thrust just to leave their planet.

Helios would have been classified as a super-Earth planet, with its mass exceeding ten times that of Earth. The concept of using chemically fuelled rockets would be infeasible. The massive payloads needed solutions never investigated seriously by scientists on Earth.

However, the Gorgass had managed to come up with a farsighted and ingenious solution to the massive impediment of their gravitational hindrance of payload/thrust/weight ratio. They created a multistage construction system on a massive scale.

The first stage saw them swimming a large pilot craft of a type, which could be guided through to the outer part of their thick and dense atmosphere, to get close to the moon. Swimming, rather than flying, was mentioned here because the gravity effect on air within the atmosphere has become something dense and thick just like water. This craft was skimming on the outer atmosphere. Its speed had built up until it was matching that of the moon. The craft had a massive harpoon and cable within it, which it was able to launch and embed it firmly into the moon. The vehicle was then able to winch itself towards the moon to lodge itself on the moon. That was the first stage repeated many times until there were enough materials deposited on the moon to carry out the second stage. The second stage was to move the materials to another side of the moon from where they were able to construct many new rocket engines and would be able to take advantage of the moon's lower gravity to launch their payloads into space. This is to be their third stage.

Once in space, they could start assembling a very large starship. The speed of construction was rapid, and soon they could produce one fully functional starship per two Helios years. Three were successfully constructed before they ran out of time.

Finally, the greatest hurdle to clear was to transport 9,000 Gorgass to the waiting starships orbiting Helios. That was to be the most difficult part of operations and equally the most daunting challenge for them. Why was it to be their biggest obstruction in this operation? To ensure all Gorgass were not at any time exposed to zero gravity as their anatomy had not developed to withstand low gravity; doing so would result in fatal consequences for them. They would suffer from lethal strokes within a very short period of exposure to low gravity. They had to transport the Gorgass inside small cylindrical vehicles, which had to be kept spinning at high speed to create an artificially created high gravity. They were then to be ferried to the moon en route to the waiting starships. Then they had to ensure the speed of the spinning cylinder inside the ferrying vehicle had to be kept synchronised with the larger cylinders located inside the mothership before the transfer could take place successfully.

Once the 9,000 selected Gorgass were successfully placed inside the three starships, the massive engines blasted the three starships away from the grip of Helios. A billion other Gorgass were left to their inevitable ghastly fate.

All Gorgass aboard the three starships, except for an extremely select few on each craft, were put into stasis before the start of the long and hugely dangerous journey to the nearest, most Helios-like planetary system. They had calculated it would take them at least the equivalent Earth time of 45,000 years to reach the destination in question. Fortunately for them, it could have been much longer if the target was speeding towards them, thus reducing their length of the journey. They had observed other systems but discarded them on the ground of relatively lower gravity, they were not favourable amongst other substance for them to establish as their new home world. Though they had detected a watery planet called Earth, it was assumed it did not possess any trace of civilisation with technology capability. It was because light from Earth took a hundred Earth years to reach Helios. From the time seen on Earth, there was no technology in existence that could have been observed.

However, some 20,000 Earth years later, when they were in the position of being deep in space, they realised they had used up more energy on evading so many unforeseen clouds of floating debris. This was much more than they allowed for in their original calculations. They started to sort out alternatives on how to restock their dwindling propulsion fuels plus other recycling materials. Capturing floating comets or meteoroids for their source of materials whilst travelling at high-speed mode had proved to be problematic and not practical for many reasons. Stopping by any planets for the purpose of mining for their materials proved to be a logistically feasible but impractical option when taking into the consideration the astronomical amount of energy required to slow down, never mind stopping, one of the starships into the position next to the planet.

They had pondered and tried to find a solution in their calculation for their best survival rate. They had started cannibalising some parts of the starships in tow.

They had also started taking extreme measures to conserve their materials. They had even considered discarding some of the Gorgass held in stasis.

It was a matter of time when the final drastic action was about to be implemented, until by a stroke of luck, an unexpected and fateful encounter with the Voyager *proved to be a salvation for their need. Or so they thought it to be.*

From that determinative moment made, we have come to understand how the rest of history was made.

Lightning Source UK Ltd.
Milton Keynes UK
UKHW011923270223
417761UK00013B/600/J